PEREGRINE

PIPER SCOTT
VIRGINIA KELLY

To anyone who thinks their story is over.
Darling, don't give up.
It's only just begun.

CONTENT WARNING

Those who are sensitive to topics such as infertility and miscarriage should proceed with caution when reading Peregrine. While a happily ever after is guaranteed, there are scenes involving on-page loss that some readers may find triggering.

PERRY

Present Day

On a Tuesday much like any other, Perry entered the medical office of his brother-in-law, Dr. Everard Drake, and made peace with the idea that, no matter the outcome, he would leave with a broken heart.

"Hello, Silvia," he said to the pretty Attendant seated behind the front desk. She was Everard's secretary, and had been for many years. There were a few more streaks of silver in her hair than there had been the last time their paths had crossed, but the kindness in her eyes remained unchanged. "Could it be that you look even prettier than the last time I saw you? I thought such a feat impossible, yet here you sit, more radiant than ever."

Silvia blushed. "I *am* trying a new lip color."

"Is that it?" Perry dimpled. "It suits you."

"Thank you. I'll let Dr. Drake know you're here."

Perry inclined his head in thanks, then sat in one of the room's comfortable waiting chairs. Everard would not be long. Until he appeared, Perry occupied himself with surveying the offerings left upon the nearby coffee table. At one point, there had only been magazines—*Time*, *Sports Illustrated*, and *Better Homes & Gardens*—but recently, a few well-loved comics, coloring books, and crayons had been added to the mix. With as many children as there were between the Drake brothers, it only made sense. If it weren't for Harrison, who'd offered to look after the boys this morning, Perry's own brood would be clamoring for their favorite titles. The children had much to learn about patience, but they were only eight, the dears. It would come with time.

"Perry," Everard said from a short distance away, stirring Perry from his thoughts. He lifted his gaze from the literature and regarded his brother-in-law, who wore a respectable button-down shirt and a smart pair of gray slacks.

"Everard." Perry rose and offered Everard a tired smile. "You look well."

"As do you. Glowing, as always."

"Which is a problem, isn't it?" The hitch in his voice was embarrassing, so to save face, Perry lifted his chin and fought to maintain his smile. "Are you ready to see me?"

Some of the easy charm slipped from Everard's face. He nodded.

"Then what are we waiting for, darling?" Perry slipped his hand into Everard's and squeezed. "Let's go."

———

Perry did not mind needles. The pain was never unreasonable, and the sight of his own blood didn't bother him. What a world of trouble he would have been in had that been the case. In fact, compared to leeches that pinched, pulsed, slithered, and often-times refused to latch, being stuck with a needle was almost enjoyable.

What he did mind was the uneasy quiet that came after a blood draw while Everard's in-house laboratory processed the results. Modern medicine was a godsend, but it was not instantaneous. As such, after Everard's examination, Perry returned to the waiting room and flipped through a copy of *Better Homes & Gardens*. Then another. And a third. He was on his ninth title when Silvia came to see him. The click of her kitten heels announced her arrival.

"Mr. Drake?" she said. "Dr. Drake will see you now. If you'll follow me, I'll bring you to him."

Perry's throat constricted, but he rewarded Silvia with his prettiest smile all the same. "Thank you, darling."

"Any time." Silvia smiled back. "Are you ready?"

Perry wasn't, but he eased out of his chair and allowed Silvia to direct him into Everard's private office.

Everard was seated at his desk when Perry arrived, his arms folded on the polished oak surface. Its design hearkened back to a simpler time, and seeing Everard positioned behind it reminded Perry of the hundred other times he'd been to visit Everard in offices of yore.

"Mr. Drake, sir," Silvia announced. "Um, Mr. *Peregrine* Drake. I'll be at my desk if you need me."

"Thank you, Silvia," Everard replied. He gestured to one of the chairs in front of his desk, in which Perry didn't hesitate to sit. He folded his hands on his lap and straightened his posture, then made note of the way the sunlight was coming in through the window and tilted his head so the light would best catch in his eyes and dramatize his angles—an old habit from years in the Pedigree, and one that, even half a millennium later, he was unable to shake.

When Silvia was gone and the door was closed, Everard produced a file folder from a drawer in his desk and laid it upon the empty space between them, but left it closed. "The results."

"I would hope, given your request for me to join you." Perry glanced at the folder, then back up at Everard, whose expression was unreadable. It was always the way he looked when the worst had come to pass. At the sight of him like that, Perry's confidence wobbled, and so too did his bottom lip. It was terribly unbecoming, but there was no way he could help it. Not now. Not with the prospect of another loss laid so clinically in ink before him. Perry couldn't bear to look. "What is the verdict?"

Everard pinched his lips as if to speak, then shook his head and glanced out the window, beyond which Aurora bustled with the endlessness of everyday life. "You don't want to look?"

"I want you to tell me." Perry closed one of his hands around the other, squeezing it tight. "Please, Everard."

The unreadable look on Everard's face deteriorated, and at last, he frowned. Sympathy softened his eyes as he slid the folder off the table and slotted it back into the drawer. Silence, punctuated by the ticking of a clock, slid in to fill the space their conversation had left. It seemed to tick forever before Everard met Perry's gaze. "I'm sorry, Perry," he said. "You're pregnant."

Perry closed his eyes to keep the tears from falling and bowed his head in the hopes Everard wouldn't notice. In the quiet that followed, he laid a hand protectively over his flat belly. Deep down, he'd known, but knowing didn't make it any easier to hear that his worst fear had come to pass.

2

PEREGRINE

1508

It was noon or close to it, judging by the length of the shadows cast by the waterfront stalls, and the port at the heart of Ljouwert was bustling. Men and women crowded the streets, some on the hunt for any of the fine spices, grains, or fabrics brought in from lands beyond the Wadden Sea; some simply out and about to enjoy their day; and some simply to gawk at the ships most recently moored, from which imported goods were being unloaded. The clatter of crates being hauled ashore and the smooth sound of rolling barrels undercut the murmur of conversation, and while Peregrine was too far back in the crowd to see any of the goods for himself, he could tell by the design of the ships what had arrived today: wine and grain from France, English woolen cloth, and sugar from Portugal. Farther ahead moored a passenger ship, and farther than that a ventjager from one of the Dutch herring busses currently at sea, the lattermost of which being his destination.

It was a pity he hadn't left the cloister a half hour earlier—if he had, the crowd wouldn't have been as thick, and he wouldn't have had to duck around half as many codpieces.

Codpieces aside, Peregrine was adept at fitting into small and sometimes unusual spaces, being small and somewhat unusual himself, and as such had no problem advancing. The issue came when he arrived outside the passenger ship and found himself face to face with a dragon.

"Good day," said the dragon in English. He blinked his purple eyes at Peregrine, then cocked his head to the side like a dog might when faced with something it couldn't quite comprehend. The dragon's hair, which he wore loose and to his shoulders, flopped over his brow and partially obscured one of his eyes. "And who might you be?"

"I am Peregrine, my lord," Peregrine told him. How lucky he was that he'd been educated in languages. The dragon had no doubt noticed the emblem on his tattered tunic and pieced together that he was of the Pedigree, and it would not have done to ignore him.

"Have you seen my brother?" the dragon asked.

Peregrine had not. It was uncommon enough to see one dragon, let alone two.

"He's quite a bit bigger than me, and taller than me as well," the dragon went on, as if the description would jog Peregrine's memory. "Not one for words, really, or art, or… well… anything, but he is quite strong, so if there were any altercations in the last few minutes, he may have gone to stick his nose in them. Have you seen any?"

"No, my lord."

"Mm." The dragon stuffed his hands into the pockets of his gown, which was made of a fanciful purple silk brocade with golden thread. Beneath he wore a plain doublet and hose of exceptional quality. "I see. Well, this adventure has gotten off to a great start. We weren't supposed to be separated. If you see him, will you tell him his brother Alistair has forged on ahead and is waiting at the inn?"

"Yes, my lord."

"Good boy." The dragon—Alistair—patted him on the shoulder, causing Peregrine to go very still. "Thank you."

"You're welcome, my lord."

When Alistair said nothing more, Peregrine bowed his head and took a small step back with the intention of continuing on his way. Before he could, Alistair narrowed his eyes. "Oh, and by the way—what are you doing out of your cloister?"

Peregrine froze.

"I usually wouldn't ask, seeing as how you're not of my clan, but I must say it is rather unusual to see one of the Pedigree out and about, especially dressed as you are." He gestured at Peregrine's shoddy tunic. His hose was in similarly disastrous state, although the dragon didn't seem to focus on it. "I haven't the foggiest idea how Sapphire cloisters are run. Is this standard wear? It's horrendous."

"No, my lord."

"Are you on the run, then?"

"No, my lord." For every answer he gave, Peregrine's heart beat faster. He had been nothing but truthful with this English dragon, but his scrutiny had begun to make him feel guilty all the same. "I would never run."

"One should hope not. Terrible things happen to omegas who do."

Peregrine was well aware.

"In any case," Alistair continued. "Pray tell, what are you doing out here?"

Peregrine gestured at the ventjager. "I was sent to fetch herring for my cloister. Mistress Fokje always sends me so the others are not deprived their education."

"I beg your pardon." Alistair's eyes went very wide. "Mistress *who?*"

"Mistress Fokje. She is the one who oversees Ljouwert's cloister."

This gave the dragon pause. He rubbed his chin and knit his brow, then shook his head as if chasing off a fly. "Well, flavorful name aside, I suppose there is no issue. You should be on your way, and I should be on mine. That brother of mine has to be around here somewhere. Do remember to tell him where I'll be should you meet him."

"I will, my lord," Peregrine promised. "Good day."

"And good day to you, fair Peregrine."

Peregrine did not feel very fair in his ragged clothing, but he bowed prettily as he'd been taught and hoped he'd been courteous enough not to disgrace the Ljouwert cloister. If Alistair complained to Mistress Fokje about his behavior, she would have his hide.

Happily, the dragon went off in the opposite direction from the cloister, and when Peregrine could no longer see him from his bowed position, he righted himself and continued on his way. If he was out too long, he'd be punished, and he'd rather not go without dinner again.

In the time it took Peregrine to breach the general vicinity of the ventjager, its barrels had been rolled off the ship and set bung-side up on the towpath. The crowd had thinned somewhat, but it still took a significant while before Peregrine was able to approach the seafaring merchant overseeing the sale of offloaded goods.

To his delight, he discovered Lus was the one hawking the ship's wares.

"Good day, Lus." Peregrine smiled at the Attendant, who was nearing his fortieth year, and had started to go silver at the temples. Years at sea had toughened his skin, and fine lines now wrinkled the corners of his eyes. One of his ring fingers was missing—the result of an accident during a catch—but rather than hide the imperfection, he wore colorful woven bracelets on the wrist of his damaged hand that Peregrine was sure were meant to draw the eye. To most, it would seem intimidating to so boldly display an injury, but Peregrine was of the opinion that Lus was one to celebrate differences. He was rough-and-tumble, yes, but beneath his hardened exterior lived a gentle soul Peregrine had come to consider a friend.

"Good day, Peregrine," Lus said with a curt nod. "Harbert came through this time, didn't he?"

"What do you mean?"

Lus slapped the top of one of the barrels of herring several times, drawing Peregrine's attention its way. "He's afforded the cloister an entire barrel. About time, with the king's ransom he's been making from the fishery. Rumor has it there will be fifty new herring busses joining the fleet next season."

Peregrine cared little for the size of his grandsire's fleet. What he did care about was the barrel Lus had declared the dragon had set aside for his cloister. If set upright, it would come squarely to Peregrine's chest and was twice as wide as he was, if not more. And filled to the brim with salted herring, it would weigh twice as much as well.

"You can't be serious." Peregrine flicked his gaze from the barrel to Lus, but there was no trace of humor in his eyes. "All of it?"

"Every last stave."

"How am I supposed to carry this?"

With a grunt, Lus rolled the barrel forward. "You aren't. You're supposed to push."

It seemed impossible for someone as small and slender as Peregrine to be able to push such a massive thing all the way back to his cloister, but he had no other choice in the matter. Lus was busy with his work, and the crew was not responsible for ensuring delivery. Mistress Fokje would punish him if he returned empty-handed, and that would mean no dinner for the foreseeable future. And if he were to request one of the Pedigree omegas abandon their lessons to help him, he might never eat again.

"It isn't that bad," Lus assured him as Peregrine positioned himself behind the barrel and braced his palms against its metal rings. "Once you get it moving, it'll stay in motion. From there, all you need to do is steer."

"Steer?"

"With your body weight," Lus explained. He came behind Peregrine and leaned over him to give the barrel another push. With his help, Peregrine was able to get the barrel pointed in the right direction. "Now, off you go. Come track me down in the next few days if you find yourself in want of a conversation and I'll regale you with tales from my adventures at sea."

"I will," Peregrine promised as he rolled the barrel down the towpath. "Good day, Lus."

"Good day, Peregrine."

With nothing more to say, off went Peregrine and his barrel. While he walked, he dreamed of the stories Lus would share, and hoped someday he might have one to share of his own.

An incline brought the barrel to a slow stop minutes from the cloister. To keep it from rolling backward, Peregrine had to throw his body against it and push with all his might, but he wasn't strong enough to get the thing to budge. The more he pushed, the weaker he became, until the barrel began to slip.

"Please, no," Peregrine begged through gritted teeth. "Don't roll back. You can't. I need you at the cloister."

The barrel, curmudgeonly as it was, did not listen. Worse, it seemed to grow heavier. Peregrine's arms began to tremble, and even as he leaned into it with his shoulder, he was aware that he was being pushed back.

Mistress Fokje would not like this one bit.

Peregrine squeezed his eyes shut, dug in his heels, and fought, but it was a losing battle. The barrel would not go up the hill. He would have to set it somewhere, return to the cloister to ask for help, and pray no one took it while he was gone. When Mistress Fokje found out, he would be denied dinner, and he would go to bed more hungry than he already was.

It all seemed so impossibly cruel.

Tears leaked from Peregrine's closed eyes, and he pushed with everything he had, but it made no difference. The barrel was too heavy. There was nothing he could do. Bit by bit, the barrel slid back until it found level ground and came to a stop. Too exhausted to get it back into motion and too emotionally drained by the prospect of another day without a meal to dream of, Peregrine crumpled down onto the barrel and allowed himself to silently cry. It was unbecoming, but what did it matter? All the standards he was expected to live up to were pointless. He was the son of a Disgrace, and therefore regarded as a Disgrace as well. He would never be chosen by a dragon.

"There he is, Sebastian," came a very familiar, very English voice, sealing Peregrine's fate. A dragon had seen him at his worst, defeated and crying over herring, of all things. Peregrine did not know what happened to Pedigree omegas who disgraced their cloisters to such a severe degree, but whether his suffering was short or prolonged, he was sure he wouldn't live to see his twentieth year. "Do you see him?" Alistair continued. "Tiny thing, isn't he? Little more than skin and bones, if you ask me. Don't you think?"

There was a grunt in reply.

"Do you think they're starving their omegas? I can hardly believe it. We simply must tell Father."

Another grunt. This one sounded closer.

"Sebastian?"

There was no grunt this time.

"Sebastian, what are you doing?"

Arms scooped Peregrine up from his resting place on the barrel and lifted him into the air. Peregrine gasped and opened his eyes, but the world was a blur—he was being turned around. When he came to a stop, he was face to face with a dark-eyed Amethyst dragon who made Peregrine's heart stand still.

"Sebastian!" Alistair chided from a safe distance. "We do not touch the omegas!"

Sebastian stared deep into Peregrine's eyes, and despite all of his training, Peregrine couldn't look away. Sebastian was the most gorgeous creature he'd ever seen.

"*Sebastian!*"

"What is your name?" Sebastian demanded, paying no attention to the dragon behind him.

"Peregrine."

"Who is your master?"

"I answer to Mistress Fokje of the Ljouwert cloister, my lord."

Sebastian grunted, then shifted Peregrine so he was tucked beneath his right arm. With his left, he pushed the barrel up the hill, crouched so his hand was palm-up and flush with the street, then let the massive thing roll onto it. Once it had, he scooped it up like it was nothing and rested it on his shoulder. Peregrine stared up at it with wide eyes and said nothing. He'd known that dragons were strong, but Sebastian had to be the mightiest of them all.

Once the barrel was settled, Sebastian began to make his way up the hill.

"Come," Sebastian demanded.

"*Come?*" Alistair squawked. "God's teeth, Seb! To *where?*"

"The cloister."

"You cannot be serious."

"I am."

"What for?" With the way he was being carried, Peregrine couldn't easily get a good look behind him, but he heard Alistair trailing after them helplessly. "Do not tell me that you're about to start trouble. Father sent you with me for protection, not so you could go making enemies with other clans and throwing me into harm's way!"

"I'm not looking to start trouble."

"Then why are you going to the cloister?"

"Because I've found something that belongs to me," Sebastian rumbled, stirring Peregrine in ways he'd never felt before, "and they need to know I'm taking it."

3

SEBASTIAN

1508

"Where is this cloister of yours located, omega?" Sebastian asked.

The omega under his arm shivered. Possibly with cold, as he had no doublet or jerkin and his hose had worn quite thin. Cloisters were sponsored by the local dragon. In this case, Harbert. Sebastian had never heard he was a parsimonious sort, but dragons could be deceiving. This would all need to be reported to Father. He wanted to make a bid for head of the council in the next century or so, and any bit of information regarding the finances of another dragon would be useful.

"Not much farther, my lord," said the omega. "It's just after the bend in the road."

Sebastian grunted his acknowledgment.

"You cannot go around purloining omegas," his brother, Alistair, bleated in his ear like a troublesome insect. "It isn't done. Especially since you're not sanctioned!"

"Write Geoffrey and have him make arrangements. My finances are not an embarrassment to the family."

"Have you gone utterly mad?" shouted Alistair, ignoring the dig at his paltry hoard. "Since when did you want to try for a clutch? We're on a journey, Sebastian. This is no time to set up your nursery with random omegas."

The young omega he held stiffened and Sebastian tightened his grip so he wouldn't fall.

A clutch had honestly not occurred to Sebastian. He just knew, when he'd seen the omega, a feeling of rightness that he'd never before experienced. This man was not in any way random. He was Sebastian's. He felt it in his scales.

Alistair was not so convinced. "Why don't you express your interest to the cloister and they can hold on to him until we return? That seems like a reasonable option."

Sebastian stopped and Alistair, too busy spouting nonsense to pay attention, walked into his back. Not that Sebastian was in any way discomforted. Alistair, runt of the clutch, was as likely to knock Sebastian over as a goose feather to fell a mighty elm.

"No," Sebastian said, scowling at his brother. "The omega comes with me."

Alistair sighed deeply. "Fine, brother. Don't listen to my advice. I see reasoning with you is quite useless."

Sebastian grunted and began walking toward what had to be the cloister Peregrine had mentioned. The one run by the matron with the strange-sounding name. It was a wattle and daub half-timbered structure comprised of three stories with a large barn behind. The fenced-in pasture contained both cows and horses. All looked to be better cared for than the omega he clutched to him.

Sebastian began to grind his teeth.

A frumpy woman of late middle age flew out of the cloister's front entrance and started screeching in a way that was even more annoying than Alistair. "Peregrine! You lazy, evil omega. What have you done now?"

Sebastian put down the barrel of fish with a thump at the matron's feet, just barely missing the toes of her soft shoes. He then gently put down his omega. He cupped the boy's face in one hand and looked into eyes the same delicate blue of harebells. "Do not move," he admonished. "I've little time today to chase down an omega. Do not run from me."

The pale blue eyes scrutinized him. Coming to some sort of internal conclusion, the omega nodded his head once in assent.

That settled, Sebastian turned to see the matron closing in on his omega.

"Peregrine!" she cawed. "I swear, this time it will be a week with no supper. What have you done, you miserable creature?"

Beside him, the omega quivered but said nothing in his defense.

"I say," Alistair began, sounding like an injured peacock. "There's no need for—"

Speaking in his very halting Frisian, Sebastian interrupted his brother's squawking. "The omega is mine. Have the paperwork drawn up and forwarded to Geoffrey Drake in Richmond."

The beta matron's jaw fell open unattractively, then she dropped into a deep curtsy. "Sir," she said, switching to English. "My lord, I humbly beg your pardon on behalf of the omega. He has long been a thorn in my side. You can't mean you wish to contract with the creature. He is the get of a Disgrace and therefore a Disgrace himself. We have much better omegas with spotless lineages. Why don't I show you them instead?"

Beside him, Peregrine stiffened up like a poker. Sebastian looked down and saw bright scarlet shame color his ears.

It made Sebastian want to destroy something—something like the miserable excuse for a cloister—pulling it down brick by brick and beam by beam until nothing was left but rubble.

He sighed. Alas, there was no time.

"The omega is mine. That is the end of it. My father and

brother will take care of whatever legalities exist. Have the omega's things packed in a trunk and brought down. We are leaving with the morning tide."

Alistair clutched at his long hair. "This is madness, and somehow I will be to blame for it. Mark my words, Sebastian. Father will hold me responsible for you absconding with a Pedigree omega, and a Disgrace at that. What can you be thinking?"

Thinking had no part in the matter. It rarely did. Sebastian trusted his instincts, and they had told him the omega belonged to him. That was the beginning and end of it.

There was a slight tug on the sleeve of his doublet. Sebastian looked down into worried blue eyes. The omega was biting his lip.

"Yes?" he asked, trying to make his voice sound as gentle as possible. It wasn't an easy task.

"I have no trunk, my lord, nor anything to fill it with. My belongings can easily fit into a satchel."

"Will it take you long to collect your things?"

Peregrine shook his head. "No, my lord."

He patted the omega lightly on his far too skinny rump. "Go then, and be as quick as you may."

Once Peregrine was out of earshot, Sebastian said, "My omega needs things to last him through a long sea voyage. He cannot spend the entire journey naked."

The matron gawked at Sebastian, utterly speechless.

Alistair sighed. "What my brother means, madam, is that he expects a packed trunk full of suitable clothing for a claimed omega, and he would like this accomplished posthaste."

"Now," Sebastian growled, letting smoke escape from his nostrils.

"Or there will be hell to pay, madam. I suggest you start now. My brother hasn't demolished anything in a fortnight. Do not tempt his temper."

The matron's eyes flared wide, then she fled. By the time Peregrine returned with his miserably small bag of belongings, a trunk had been brought and laid, with reverence, at Sebastian's feet. Alistair, ever curious, pawed through the contents and pronounced them suitable. That was more than good enough for Sebastian. He hoisted the trunk easily onto his right shoulder, then hoisted his omega onto his left.

"We go," he said.

They went.

After they arrived at the inn where Alistair had arranged for rooms and a private parlor for the night, Sebastian pulled his brother aside. "See to it the omega gets a hot bath and a good meal in him. I'll be back before nightfall."

Alistair goggled at him. "Where the devil are you going?"

"Out." Sebastian wagged an admonishing finger in front of Alistair's nose. "Do. Not. Touch. My. Omega."

"As if I would be that foolhardy." Alistair sniffed, his nose clearly out of joint. Not that Sebastian cared overmuch. Alistair had a history with omegas, and while he was fairly certain his brother valued his life far more than getting his dick wet, it never hurt to remind Alistair that there were things you could look at but not touch.

Sebastian frowned.

Not looking would also be good.

With a final glare at his brother, Sebastian set about on his errands. First he needed to find an apothecary, then a nice, cold pond or river.

The private parlor was empty when Sebastian returned to the inn. He instructed the innkeeper's wife to bring him a suitable meal: cucumber salad, pea soup, stewed onions, roast pork, marinated roast beef, fried shrimp, cheese, and a compote of cherries cooked in wine. After supping, he went to his room where his future waited for him.

For politeness's sake, Sebastian knocked.

"Is that you, my lord?" came a voice that only sounded a little tremulous. His omega had courage, Sebastian was pleased to note.

"It is."

After a moment, there was the sound of a latch being drawn back and the door opened a crack. Sebastian pushed it open, secured the door, then set down his small sack of purchases on a table near the bed. Only then did he turn to fully gaze upon the omega he'd taken for his own.

Since Sebastian had left to attend to his chores, Peregrine had freshened up and changed out of his tattered clothing. His new raiment was far too large for him, but was of better make than the rags he'd worn prior. His hose was of pale rose silk just a shade darker than his own skin, and over that he wore a linen tunic so fine, it was translucent in the light of the fire. Instead of a belt, he had cinched the outfit in at his waist with a wide scarlet ribbon.

The glimpse of his slender body through his tunic aroused Sebastian greatly. He wanted nothing more than to tear the cloth from the omega's body and ravish him right before the fire, but the boy had a somewhat uncertain look about him, so Sebastian made himself stay still.

"Are you still a virgin?" he asked.

Peregrine's jaw went slack with shock, but he was quick to compose himself and lifted his chin prettily. "I am, my lord."

Sebastian grunted his satisfaction with the answer.

"But I have been instructed in ways you will find pleasing," Peregrine assured him. He stood at an angle to the fire that made its light dance in his eyes and catch all of his fairest features. "My station is to please you, and so please you I shall." For the briefest moment, a somewhat wistful look crossed his face. "I am quite adept at it. I enjoy learning, and it is the majority of what I've been taught."

Being desirous of education was a novel concept for Sebastian. "You'll get on well with Alistair, then. He's always got his nose stuck in some tome or another and tries to get me to listen to his blather. He'll appreciate a new audience, no doubt. If you wish it, I'll have him teach you to read. Can't abide it myself, but if it will amuse you on the journey, then I see no harm in it."

For Sebastian, that was quite a speech. He looked at Peregrine expectantly. To his satisfaction, the boy looked pleased. Happy he'd made forward progress, Sebastian began to disrobe.

"You would do that?" Peregrine asked. "For me? The omega child of a Disgrace?" He sounded honestly bewildered. "I might learn to read?"

"If you wish it." Having removed jerkin, doublet, and shirt, Sebastian unfastened his codpiece, then began to remove his hose.

Peregrine didn't squeak, but as his eyes took in Sebastian's more intimate details, he did go quite pale.

"It'll fit," he assured the omega. "I vow it."

Peregrine did not look so sure.

Naked and semi-erect, Sebastian straightened his stance. "Come to bed," he ordered, and slid between the dry, sweet-smelling sheets.

Peregrine did not hesitate, but he did not hurry. "I never thought to use my training," he admitted quietly as he approached the bedside.

"Think nothing of it." Sebastian patted the empty space beside him. "Now, come. You seem chilled. I will warm you."

"Yes, my lord."

Peregrine glanced at the bed, then at Sebastian, then down at his own body. Slowly, he undressed, folding his clothing as he shed it. He was, Sebastian saw as he disrobed, far too thin. It spoke not of nature but of deprivation, and made him want to go back to thrash the matron of the cloister. He'd kept himself from doing so earlier that day, but it had been a very near thing.

Now that events had caught up with him, Sebastian wondered at what he'd done. He never went for omegas, Pedigree or not. Today he'd acted far more like Alistair than himself. Even so, his dragon was sure, completely and utterly, that this skinny, waifish, and shy omega belonged to him. There was no question of leaving him behind. But Sebastian also felt a bit awkward bedding the boy.

Did Peregrine desire him, too?

It had never mattered what an omega wanted, but it occurred now to Sebastian that perhaps that wasn't right or fair.

He shook his head. Clearly Alistair was rubbing off on him, and not in a good way. What did fairness have to do with anything?

Still, though the omega stood naked next to his bed, Sebastian did not immediately mount the boy.

Slow, his dragon cautioned, and that seemed wise.

It would be better that his bedfellow respect him, as they would be spending quite a long time together on this journey. Therefore, he endeavored to seduce Peregrine, so that Peregrine would crave his knot as keenly as Sebastian was eager to give it.

Like the perfect Pedigree omega he was, Peregrine climbed gracefully onto the bed on his hands and knees and presented himself to Sebastian. "I am ready for you, my lord."

No, you're not, Sebastian thought. Carefully, like he was touching an unbroken horse, Sebastian ran his hand down Peregrine's flank. His skin was softer than expensive silk.

Peregrine trembled, so Sebastian stilled his hand. "Are you frightened, little bird?"

"Little bird?" Peregrine lifted his head and looked over his shoulder at Sebastian.

"Peregrine," Sebastian explained. "I'm not certain what the

word is in your language, but in English, a peregrine is a type of falcon."

"Oh." Peregrine stopped trembling and now stretched under Sebastian's hand like a contented cat. "I think I am more a sparrow, my lord dragon, despite my name. You are more the falcon than I."

Sebastian gave Peregrine the very gentlest of pushes so the boy fell first onto his side, then to his back. "No," he said. "I am the hunter. Peregrines are my favorite falcons. They are intelligent, loyal, and easily tamed." Sebastian smoothed a lock of fair hair away from Peregrine's brow, then ran his fingers lightly over his brows, nose, lips, chin, and jaw. "And they are very beautiful."

"I have already been tamed, my lord," Peregrine said earnestly. "I will not fight you."

"Allow me to court, then."

Peregrine shook his head. "I have no need of courting, either. You took me from the cloister. I am yours."

Sebastian's dragon snorted in disbelief. Peregrine wasn't savage, but he wasn't tame, either.

Arguing, however, was not Sebastian's forte, so he held his tongue but kept his hands busy by lightly caressing the boy's skin.

"You must tell me," Sebastian urged, "if I do something you do not like."

"Yes, my lord," Peregrine replied, then bowed his back and moaned when Sebastian bent his head to take one of his nipples into his mouth. "Oh. *Oh!*"

While Sebastian licked and sucked one nipple, he rolled the other between two of his fingers. Peregrine's eyes fluttered shut and he pushed himself as close to Sebastian as he could get. He was, Sebastian was happy to see, responsive to touch.

It was good, but somewhat of a surprise.

Pedigree omegas were not encouraged to express their pleasure. Their priority was, and always would be, their dragon. Whether or not they enjoyed being bred was of no consequence.

But there was something special about Peregrine.

Something that glimmered beneath his polished surface.

Sebastian longed to set it free.

He increased the pressure of his ministrations until Peregrine moaned and sighed and writhed, then worked his way down the boy's body until he came to his very pretty, and thankfully erect, cock. The sensitive tip, exposed when the foreskin pulled back, glistened wetly. It was the color of a deeply pink rose. Sebastian couldn't wait to taste it, so he drew it into his mouth, easily swallowing the entire thing.

Peregrine arched his back, his whole body taut, and strained a noise through his teeth like he was trying his best not to scream. The noise was punctuated by a series of breathy moans that verged on whimpers. They were an indication that Sebastian was —so far—doing a credible job of seducing his omega.

Assured that Peregrine was enjoying himself, the carefully added layers of caution and chivalry he'd thrown over his baser nature began to fall away. Wetting his finger in his mouth, Sebastian brought it down to first circle Peregrine's entrance, then plunged it inside his tight, hot passage. Peregrine cried out in full this time and tightened around Sebastian's finger.

He was small.

So small.

But Sebastian was persistent, and he pushed in until Peregrine took him to the last knuckle.

As soon as he could move no deeper, Peregrine gasped and came into Sebastian's throat. It happened quickly, but Sebastian was able to pull back enough to be able to taste the boy's spend all the same. He'd heard it would be sweet.

It was.

Peregrine tasted like sun-warmed honey sucked right from the comb. He was, quite literally, the sweetest thing Sebastian had ever tasted, and he wanted more. He wanted everything.

Sebastian lifted Peregrine's hips with ease and licked and

lathed at the tight ring of flesh clamped down on his finger. Even without the slick of heat, Peregrine tasted better there than his spend had. Sebastian felt he might never get enough.

He tarried there greedily long enough that Peregrine's cock rose again. The omega bucked against Sebastian's finger and mouth, begging for "more more more," and Sebastian obliged him. He sank two, then three of his fingers into the boy's body, and Peregrine began to keen in such a piteous way that Sebastian pulled back to look at his face.

There it was again.

The wild thing lurking beneath his meek exterior.

The one Sebastian wanted to coax from him.

It was so close to the surface now. How much more would it take to set it free?

"Please, my lord," Peregrine begged. "Please, I need you in me. I need you now."

How fortunate it was that Sebastian needed Peregrine, too.

He took a jar he'd purchased at the apothecary and opened it. Inside was a sweet-smelling substance that would ease the way for both of them. He applied it liberally to first Peregrine, then himself.

"After this," Sebastian vowed, feeling it down to his scales, "you are mine. And I am yours."

Peregrine opened his mouth to say something when he was forestalled by Sebastian's cock breaching his body. His eyes snapped closed, and a look of utter bliss transformed his sharp, pretty face. He moaned loudly, and Sebastian quieted him the only way he knew how.

He kissed Peregrine and took the noise into himself.

The omega's lips and hot, sweetly drugging mouth were nearly enough to make him forget himself, but then Peregrine's body clamped down around Sebastian. That spurred him to move, slowly and carefully at first, but as Peregrine showed no signs of wanting him to stop, Sebastian sped up his pace and increased the power of his thrusts. He knew, in the back of his mind, that he was probably bruising the boy with the tight grip of his fingers, but there was no way to cease. Sebastian's dragon urged him on. *Take. Claim. Breed. Knot. Mate.* They were curious thoughts to have, but they didn't matter. Nothing mattered beyond the boy's slick, tight heat, and his cries of pleasure that were even better than his taste.

"I need... I need..." Peregrine gasped.

"Anything. Speak it, and it will be yours."

"I need... something. Oh, my lord. Please. *Please.*"

Peregrine reached down to latch on to Sebastian's arse and dug his nails in deep. That was all it took for Sebastian to flood Peregrine's body with his seed, then lock the two of them together with his knot. Inside him, his dragon roared in utter satisfaction and triumph.

Slowly, by small degrees, their breathing calmed. Sebastian fell onto his side and took Peregrine with him. Peregrine seemed to doze for a bit, then he roused and stretched his lithe body.

"Is it always like that?" Peregrine asked, breaking the silence between them.

Sebastian stroked his soft hair, now clean and shining from the bath he'd ordered earlier that day. "No," he confessed.

"Oh." Peregrine didn't frown, but Sebastian could still sense his disappointment.

He looked a little sad and lost, so Sebastian truthfully added, "It is often much better. It will be next time, I swear it."

A slow, wide smile spread over Peregrine's face, reminding Sebastian of the other things he'd bought from the apothecary. Sweets for the sweet. He reached for it and presented the small box of candy to Peregrine. Not knowing his taste, Sebastian had bought a bit of everything from marzipan to candied fruit to rose sugar drops to sugared nuts. It seemed a pity now that he saw the glimmer in Peregrine's eyes that he hadn't procured a larger box.

"Truly, my lord dragon?" A mein of hopeful greed spread across Peregrine's features. It made him look almost draconic.

Sebastian's answer was to kiss his omega.

No, growled his dragon. *Our omega. Forever ours.*

And that felt absolutely, completely right. Peregrine was his prized treasure and Sebastian would never let him go. Not ever. No matter what.

4

SEBASTIAN

Present Day

Anyone who saw Sebastian Drake cut through foot traffic on the Brilliant Boulevard, Aurora's premiere shopping district, would see him as an alpha on a mission. Nevertheless, something in a shop window caught his eye and he stopped. Even though he'd become a serious impediment to forward progress, no one bumped into him. Humans could sense a predator in their midst, be he man or otherwise, and wherever he went, they gave him a wide berth.

Which was as it should be.

In another time, Sebastian would have feasted on their flesh and picked his teeth with their bones, but the world was a different place now. One did not eat humans on a whim. They were to be consumed only when necessary, and unfortunately those times were few and far between.

Sebastian spent a moment longer assessing the window display, then entered the store and pointed at the item that had caught his eye.

"Can I help you, sir?" one of the associates asked. She was polite, but she eyed Sebastian warily.

"I'd like that scarf," he rumbled. "The... ah... one the color of harebells."

The associate blinked at him.

"The bluish one," he clarified. "I'll take it. Quickly. I have an appointment."

"Yes, sir. Would you care to know the price of—"

"No." Sebastian handed the girl a black credit card. "It's not necessary."

"Yes, sir." She swiped the card and hurried to wrap up his purchase.

Sebastian did not dawdle in the shop any longer than was necessary. Once the scarf was wrapped and bagged, he left and walked another block, where he came to a stop in front of another business. The door was locked, as it always was, so he pushed the buzzer and assured the disembodied voice who answered that he had an appointment. Only then did the door open.

Sebastian entered the shop.

Unlike other storefronts on the Brilliant Boulevard, this particular business was not open to the public, and private appointments were booked months in advance. Sebastian was amongst their few clients who kept regular appointments—he visited once every three months, which was just long enough to ensure that whenever he visited, there would be new wares to sample.

The inside of this particular establishment was peculiar in that it resembled the lobby of a small, if very grand, hotel more than it did a store. A huge crystal chandelier hung from the domed ceiling, shining light down upon the polished marble floor below. Sebastian strolled forward, steps echoing, until a tall woman in towering high heels glided over. "Mr. Drake. Welcome to Luxe. Won't you please come this way?"

She led Sebastian through a door and into a chair situated by a silk-covered table.

"Would you like refreshment?" she asked. "We have coffee, tea, champagne, port, still water and sparkling water."

"No," he said gruffly, then added a, "thank you," because he could hear Perry admonishing him to be polite in his head.

"Can I get you anything at all, sir?" She sounded a little anxious.

"Just send out Sadie," he said.

The woman blinked. "But—"

At that point a short, plump young woman came bustling through the door holding a large silver tray covered by a white cloth. "It's all right, Grace," she said, putting the tray down on the table. "I'll see to Mr. Drake."

Grace frowned, but at last nodded and glided back to whence she'd come.

"Sadie," Sebastian said cordially when the two were alone. "What do you have for me today?"

Sadie grinned back at him. "I can't wait to show you!" She lifted the cloth away like she was presenting a magic trick, and that wasn't far off the mark. Sadie was a magician, only her potions consisted mostly of sugar, butter, cocoa beans, milk, spices, fruit, and nuts.

On the tray were twenty-four sets of assorted truffles. Each had one whole truffle, and one sliced in half to show its interior. Sadie pointed to the first one. "This is the Valencia. The interior is a burnt butter caramel ganache flavored with house-made orange liqueur and pink peppercorn. It's covered in dark chocolate and decorated with candied orange peel. I'd ask if you wanted to try it, but I already know the answer."

Sebastian nodded gravely.

"Okay, then," Sadie went on, enthusiasm undimmed, "how about this one?" She pointed to the next truffle, which was white and crowned with a sugared rose petal. "It's pistachio marzipan, rose water, dark chocolate ganache, and white cocoa butter chocolate, with, of course, an edible rose petal."

Sebastian nodded again and she went on to describe the next truffle, then the next, then the next. He nodded at them all, but ended up choosing only sixteen.

Happy with his selection, Sadie said, "I'm sure your husband will love them." Her eyes twinkled. "Now. Can I interest you in macarons?"

Sebastian nodded again and Sadie clapped her hands in delight. "Fantastic! Let me go get you a sampling." She scurried away, taking her tray with her.

By the time Sebastian's appointment was over, he had several boxes filled with chocolates, macarons, petit fours, and miniature fruit tarts.

"So," she said as Sebastian readied himself to leave. "Is this for a special occasion?"

Sebastian shook his head.

"Your husband is a very lucky man," Sadie said brightly, but Sebastian shook his head again.

"I am the lucky one," he said as he hefted the bag of sweets from the counter in the main foyer. "Good day, Sadie."

She smiled and curled her fingers in a wave. "Until next time, Mr. Drake."

"Daddy's home!"

It was shouted in a chorus of voices, but one that seemed much smaller than usual. Indeed, when Sebastian counted heads, four of his children were missing and an extra one had been added—Everard's whelp, Darwin. Alarmingly, there was a pair of metallic wings strapped to his back and a little scuff of dirt on his cheek. Julius, his closest friend, stood next to him, grass stains on his knees.

Fearing the missing whelps had been launched into space, Sebastian zeroed in on the most reliable of the clutch. "Cornelius," he barked. "Report."

"Yes, sir," Cornelius piped up enthusiastically. "Hadrian, Octavius, and Elian went over to the Opal Consulate and Maximus went to go play with Chaucer and Olive. Uncle Everard and Uncle Harry came to see Papa and—"

"Brought me!" Darwin finished excitedly. "I've been studying aerodynamics. Aren't my wings neat? They don't work so well just yet, but they will if I keep trying, so Jules and I have been experimenting on them to make them better. We built a ramp. It's fun! I'll have to build one at home so Steve can have fun, too. May we have cookies?"

Sebastian frowned at his youngest child. "What did Papa say?"

Julius looked between Darwin and his father and seemed torn.

"Not until after dinner!" Cornelius pronounced, eliciting groans from the other boys.

"Correct. Now, go play," Sebastian ordered, and off the boys scampered.

How strange it was to think that it had been eight years since they'd hatched. It felt like not much time had passed at all, but here they were, well on their way to becoming respectable young dragons.

Sebastian's heart clenched, but it was a pain he quickly swept aside. There was no point in suffering the inevitable. The whelps would grow up whether he wished it or not. It would be better to cherish the time they had left rather than mourn what was already behind them.

"Oh, hello, Sebastian!" came a familiar voice from across the foyer as Sebastian plotted ways to join the boys in their games. It belonged to Harrison, his brother Everard's mate and Darwin's father. It appeared, owing to the direction he was coming from, that he'd recently left the atrium. It was where Perry had to be. "Perry said you weren't home."

"I was not."

"Oh." Harrison crossed the foyer and came to stand just short of Sebastian. To Sebastian's displeasure, he did not possess the same sense of self-preservation as the average human. Or, unfortunately, the average anything. "I suppose it is getting late, isn't it? Everard sent me to find Darwin so we could head home, too. Have you seen him?"

Sebastian pointed in the direction the boys had gone.

"Over there?" Harrison turned to look. "Thanks. I'll go take a peek and see if I can find him."

"Wait."

Harrison turned to face him. "Yes?"

"Is Everard with Perry?"

Harrison frowned as though puzzling it out. "Well, he was when I left the atrium, but there's a chance he left since then. So as far as I know, yes, but it's not a sure thing. Do you want to talk to him? I can try to find him, too, while I'm off looking for Darwin."

Sebastian shook his head. "No, thank you."

"You're welcome." Harrison beamed at him. "I'd better go find Darwin. If I don't see you again before we leave, it was nice seeing you!"

Sebastian nodded in agreement, so off Harrison went, leaving Sebastian alone with quite the mystery.

What was his brother doing with his mate?

It wasn't unusual for Harrison to visit, but Everard, while nosy, did not tend to be as social. He was not the kind to drop in out of the blue, and certainly not on a whim. There was a reason for him to be here, Sebastian was sure, but what it was would have to wait for later. After Everard was gone. No good would come of investigating while he was still in the house, as Everard was wily and would find a way to keep his secrets hidden. It would be better to find out the truth from Perry directly, so off Sebastian went to bide his time. In a few hours, he would go in search of his mate.

Sebastian found Perry in the atrium. The hour was approaching twilight and shadows filled the room. His mate lay on his side by the pond, his fingers trailing in the water. He was forcibly reminded of a twilight centuries ago when he'd found Peregrine lying melancholy beside the pool in the oasis on the grounds of their palace, southeast of Beirut. Back then he'd been wreathed by a veil of sadness, and while he was much better at hiding his emotions now, Sebastian sensed all was not well.

Deceit, his dragon hissed. *Sorrow. Despair.*

"Perry?" Sebastian asked softly as he approached.

Perry startled, then looked up at his mate and smiled his familiar sweet smile. For a bare few seconds, however, before the smile had come, Perry's face had seemed utterly tragic.

Sebastian came to him and dropped to his knees at Perry's side. "Are you well? Is something wrong?"

Perry's smile wobbled slightly, then strengthened. "I'm fine, darling."

"But—"

Perry put a finger to Sebastian's lips. "No buts. I am fine. We shall leave it at that."

"I brought you a present," Sebastian told him, wanting to bring the smile back into his mate's eyes. "Presents," he amended, remembering the scarf that had caught his eye in the shop window earlier that day. But to his dismay, Perry didn't perk up. Rather, he dipped his fingers back into the water and spun them in slow circles, tempting the koi below.

Whatever was wrong had to be very wrong.

In no way did Sebastian believe he was fine.

"That's very sweet of you, but later, darling," Perry said at length. "I can wait for presents. Right now all I need is you."

Sebastian needed no further instruction. Without another word, he scooped Perry into his arms and carried him into their hoard. It was the one place in the house where no one would disturb them.

He laid Perry on their hoard bed and climbed on after him, stripping them piece by piece until they were bare. Perry, pliant and needy, folded back his legs, and Sebastian took care of the rest, prepping him and pushing him into the perfect position for pleasure.

He started their lovemaking slow and sweet, showing Perry how precious he was, but his mate was having none of it. Perry's fingernails dug into his back, and he fought the pace Sebastian had set, working himself harder than Sebastian was willing to go. It was unusual in the extreme, and Sebastian sought to remedy it by kissing and licking his way down Perry's body, paying particular attention to his most sensitive spots.

Perry tossed his head restlessly on their pillows and couldn't seem to keep his hips still. "More, please. Sebastian, I need more."

Sebastian knew what to do about that. He lifted Perry's hips to his mouth and took Perry's hard and leaking cock into his mouth, then down his throat. It was something he'd done thousands of times before, and something he knew how to do well. Perry always came undone for him so easily like this, but today, no matter how Sebastian licked or sucked or swallowed, Perry would not relax for him.

His mouth would not be good enough.

Something had to be truly wrong.

"Please, Sebastian," Perry begged, tugging at Sebastian's hair. "It's not enough. I need you back inside me."

Sebastian pulled off Perry's cock and went to fold back his legs, but Perry shook his head, and he stopped at once. Once he had, Perry scrambled out from beneath him and pushed hard at Sebastian's shoulders. He was not strong enough to move Sebastian no matter how hard he tried, but Sebastian humored him by falling onto his side and then rolling onto his back as Perry continued to push.

"There," Perry breathed, and stilled Sebastian once he was on his back. He straddled Sebastian's hips, grasped his cock, and sank down onto it until Sebastian had nothing left to give. The pleasure was unimaginable. Just as Sebastian had learned how best to please his mate with his mouth over the last five hundred years, Perry had long ago learned how best to use his body to bring Sebastian pleasure. He tightened and loosened and rode hard, bangles jingling as he went.

"Perry," Sebastian groaned, and grabbed his hips not to hold him in place, but to better support him as he rode. "Oh, Perry."

His mate was too lost in pleasure to reply, his head thrown back and his back arched. A crown of dainty golden chains glittered in his hair, and a single diamond drop earring swayed with every rise and fall of his hips, its inner fire dull compared to the man who wore it.

Perry lurched forward all at once and braced his hands on either side of Sebastian's arms. At this new angle he rode savagely, and Sebastian, as strong as he was, was helpless against the pleasure that followed. He teetered on the edge of orgasm, roused not only by the tightness of his mate's body, but by the sight of him. How even nude, Perry was perfect. How gorgeous he looked drenched in gold.

"Breed me," Perry begged through ragged gasps. "Make me yours."

And so Sebastian did.

He shot deep into Perry, marking him with his seed, then let go and allowed his knot to lock the two of them together. Perry cried out and bore back onto him, taking his knot deeper, and as he did, he came as well, striping Sebastian's chest with his spend.

"Yes," he panted as he rode, coaxing Sebastian's knot to keep thickening. "Yes, *yes*."

It was utter ecstasy.

Sebastian tightened his grip on Perry's hips and pushed him

down, causing Perry to wiggle and moan as the knot stretched him and locked him into place.

When it could grow no more, Sebastian let him go, and Perry slumped onto him bonelessly. Sebastian gathered him in his arms and held him while their bodies rode out the last of their orgasms, and even after that, as his knot would keep them together for quite some time.

"Tell me what's wrong," Sebastian said once Perry had settled, trying not to make it a demand. He rubbed his mate's smooth skin to comfort both himself and Perry. "Tell me what it is and I shall destroy it."

Perry chuckled and laid his cheek on Sebastian's chest. "I'm afraid this isn't something you can bludgeon or threaten into submission, my love."

"But—"

"No. Hush." He placed a silencing finger on Sebastian's lips. "I haven't been feeling well lately, and it occurred to me that it's been two weeks since you rescued me from that rascal, Hugh, and whisked me off to bed to celebrate a job well done. Do you remember it? It was the day of the children's birthday party."

Realization struck, and it felt like a shard of ice had been stabbed through Sebastian's heart. "The day you thought you might go into heat."

Perry hummed sadly. "That's the one. I'd thought maybe my old injuries were flaring up and interrupting my cycle, as they do from time to time, but... the dates lined up too well, so yesterday I went to visit Everard at his office." Tears began to pool on Sebastian's chest, and without Perry having said anything, he knew.

It was happening again.

"Perry..."

"He confirmed it," Perry admitted in a small and broken voice. "The testing he did was conclusive. I'm..."

"Shh." Sebastian tightened his arms as if to shield him from the world. "It is enough. I know."

Perry began to sob, so Sebastian did what he always did and held him until there were no more tears left to cry. Then he stroked Perry's hair, shoulders, and back, until the omega went limp and his breathing slowed and became even.

"It will be different this time," Sebastian whispered in a hollow voice to his sleeping mate. "I don't know how, but it will be."

Perry didn't stir, and Sebastian was grateful for it, because no matter what he said, words were of little comfort after five hundred years of pain.

5

PERRY

Present Day

When Perry woke, he was in the hoard bed at Sebastian's side. He'd hoped, naively, that a nap would ease some of his inner turmoil, but it hadn't. Life was seldom so forgiving, and today in particular, it was relentlessly harsh.

All of this was his fault, of course. He hadn't been careful. He'd known his heat was on the way and he'd let Sebastian ravish him regardless. If he'd been more responsible, none of this would have happened, but it had been such an awfully long time since he'd last been kidnapped, and in the excitement of it all—

"You're blaming yourself again," Sebastian grumbled. "Stop it."

"It's my fault, Sebastian."

"No. It's not."

"I—"

"It's not your fault." Sebastian's voice rumbled like rocks crashing down a ravine. "I was the one who knotted you. Without my seed, there would be no child. You have no part in this. Which is why I will be the one who makes this right."

Before Perry could object, Sebastian collected him in his arms and lifted him out of bed. Perry, long used to being carried, rested his head on Sebastian's shoulder and sighed. There would be no reasoning with his stubborn dragon. Not now, at least. When Sebastian got an idea in his head, it was exceedingly difficult to get it out, and Perry had neither the physical stamina nor the mental wherewithal to set about extracting it. Perhaps tomorrow, once he'd rested. Or later this evening, after a long nap. For now, he'd let Sebastian beat his chest and roar at whoever might listen. It was better this way.

"Where are we going, Sebastian?" Perry asked as Sebastian carried him away from the bed.

Sebastian grunted and carried Perry through the door leading from the main hoard chamber into the adjoining bathroom. Following the Topaz attack several years back, Sebastian had decided it prudent to have proper facilities installed in the event Perry or the children had to take shelter there again. The addition pleased Perry, not so much for its future usefulness, but for how convenient it was in the present. Previously he'd needed to walk all the way upstairs to the master bedroom to shower, and while it had been a simple nuisance while their nest was empty, now that they had whelps again, it was a logistical nightmare. Perry did not relish the days he emerged from the hoard damp with sweat and slick with other, far more unmentionable things only to be beset upon by eight darling children.

His only regret was that they hadn't installed it sooner.

The hoard's bathroom, like everything they owned, was opulent, and was spacious enough to comfortably fit every one of Sebastian's brothers and their mates, although it was perhaps not as big as Perry would have liked. Still, it was quite beautiful, and Perry adored it from the dome of its cathedral ceiling to its glittering inlaid diamond and labradorite floor tiles.

The lights blinked on as they entered, dim at first, but gradually brighter the more time passed. The marvels of the modern age were all so impressive. Even now, Perry could hardly believe that magic like this was theirs to command.

From the central powder room, they traveled through the arched doorway to the right, through which the bath was waiting. It was irregular in shape, more closely resembling a natural pond than a tub, and sunken into the stone quartz flooring. To further the illusion, the room was stylized to look like a cave, its back wall rounded and irregular, and made of the same solid quartz as the flooring. Decorative boulders and other outcrops of rocks took things another step further than that, although for the most part, they were hidden beneath lush, leafy plants that gave the room a much-needed pop of color.

While, like everywhere else in the bathroom, this room had excellent ventilation, a delightful natural humidity seeped into the air from the stone that Perry found soothing.

Sebastian set Perry down near the edge of the tub and ordered him to stay, then dropped to his knees to run the water and activate the tub's interior lights. Soon enough the room was filled with steam and sweet perfumes—Sebastian had added something to the water. Lavender, if Perry's nose was to be believed.

Perry sighed with pleasure. After the atrium, this was his favorite room in the house. He loved green, growing things. He didn't think he'd be happy in any place where he was deprived of them for a lengthy amount of time. He leaned against one of the boulders while he waited for Sebastian. It was smooth and moss-covered. It was also vibrating very softly. Perry laughed, but softly, so as to not wake his "boulder." Pake, the sweetest—and likely oldest—giant tortoise on the planet moved very slowly and liked to sleep. When he wasn't sleeping, he liked to eat. Now that Perry looked closely at the foliage, he saw that some of the leaves had been chewed on a bit.

It was a mystery how Pake kept getting into the bathroom. Like Perry, the tortoise loved the new bathroom and somehow kept finding a way in. No one was entirely sure how. Perry wasn't particularly interested in solving it. He liked to think of Pake as being a silent and deadly ninja tortoise who would defend Perry's life every bit as heroically as Sebastian would, should it ever come down to it. Giving Pake a kiss on his shell, Perry scooted closer to the tub and didn't alert Sebastian to the tortoise's presence. Their pet was soundly asleep and removing him from the vicinity for Sebastian's peace of mind was far more trouble than it would be worth. Sometimes it was best to let sleeping boulders lie.

When the tub was filled, Sebastian turned off the water, stood, and gathered Perry in his arms. Then, with great care, he stepped into the tub and set Perry down, where he proceeded to bathe him. He started with Perry's feet, massaging their pads and arches in turn before running a soapy washcloth with great reverence between each of his toes. He cleaned Perry's ankles and calves with the same attention to detail, then sat and drew Perry onto his lap to wash between his thighs.

His touch was an old, familiar love song, and while Perry felt very poorly indeed, it comforted him to know that there was still goodness in the world. Sebastian truly was the sweetest dragon of all.

With a contented sigh, Perry rested his head on Sebastian's chest and hummed his appreciation, prompting Sebastian to reward him with a kiss to the top of his head. The washcloth inched inward and very gradually, Sebastian's touch became suggestive. It didn't surprise Perry in the least when his thickened shaft pushed between Perry's cheeks.

"I will make things right," Sebastian whispered in Perry's ear. "I will protect you. I vow it. I will find a way to make this time different. We shall not lose another child."

Perry rolled his head back, exposing the long arch of his neck. It was, at times, easy to forget how large and powerful Sebastian really was, but here in his arms, seated on his lap, it was inescapable. Next to him Perry was a doll, dwarfed in height, size, and might. It was easy to trick oneself into believing a creature of such magnitude could right every wrong in the world, but such was not the case. Sebastian was a mighty warrior and a fine hero, but some evils were unvanquishable. Defeat did not mean that he had failed. It simply meant the battle had not been his to win.

No matter what happened, Perry vowed to remember it.

Sebastian was not the reason why his heart was broken. If anything, he was the reason why it hadn't yet fallen apart entirely.

Still slick from their time in bed, Perry lifted his hips and guided Sebastian's cock back where it belonged.

"You are mine, Perry," Sebastian told him as Perry arched his back and rode. "Mine. And what I take, I defend. No matter how many times I fail, I will never give up. I will protect you until my dying breath."

The words were as sweet as the truffles Sebastian fed him later that evening, after the children had been put to bed and their lair was quiet once more. And, like the truffles, Perry delighted in them in small bites, savoring them, afraid that soon he'd eat them all up, and there would be no more.

6

PEREGRINE

1508

"Do you want another?" Sebastian held a piece of colored marzipan to Peregrine's lips. "Eat."

It was the fourth marzipan of the night, and the seventh sweet Sebastian had asked Peregrine to consume. The first had been a piece of candied orange with a flavor as bright as the southern lands it came from. Next, a curious creation Sebastian had called a "rose sugar drop" that, upon entering Peregrine's mouth, had dissolved into sweetness on his tongue. Then had come a candied pecan, and finally, the first piece of marzipan. Peregrine had never tasted anything so good. He'd had honey before, yes, but sugar— sugar was a rarity, reserved exclusively for the rich. It was not the kind of food meant for a Disgrace.

Sebastian, however, seemed to care little about that, because he kept selecting sweets and staring Peregrine down until he accepted them. It was uncommonly frightening. Peregrine had been taught that dragons were fearsome creatures, but truly, Sebastian was menacing to the extreme. It seemed to him that if he were to disobey, Sebastian would split him open where he lay and see to it that the sweets made it to his stomach whether he wanted them there or not. So he took the candies when offered and didn't dare remind his lord that offerings like this were above him.

It was no hardship.

They truly were divine.

The issue was, Peregrine had made the mistake of humming in pleasure upon tasting the marzipan, and now it seemed to be the only treat Sebastian would give him.

"Eat, omega," Sebastian repeated with some force when Peregrine did not immediately take it from his fingers. "Do you not like it?"

"I like it very much, my lord," Peregrine assured him, then took the marzipan delicately between his teeth, making sure to brush Sebastian's fingers with his lips in as alluring a manner as he could. It was important that he be pleased.

"Good," Sebastian grumbled, then proffered Peregrine yet another sweet that he dared not refuse.

When the latest piece of marzipan had been eaten, Sebastian retrieved a goblet of wine from the table closest to the bedside and tipped it to Peregrine's lips. It mixed with the sugar left on his tongue and produced a wine better than Peregrine had ever known. He hummed in appreciation again, prompting a grunt from Sebastian that was entirely too empty of emotion to decipher.

"Are you sated?" Sebastian asked when Peregrine stopped drinking.

Peregrine nodded.

"Good." Sebastian set the wine aside. "Come here."

Both of them were on the bed, having sat up but not otherwise moved since Sebastian's knot had loosened and their bodies had come apart. Peregrine took a moment to consider Sebastian's invitation, then crawled his way across the scant space between them, ever careful that he held his belly in and his head at such an angle that the light from the room's window would best play across his features. Mistress Fokje had often bemoaned the fact that his beauty had been wasted on a Disgrace such as himself, so Peregrine knew he was attractive, but he also knew that even the prettiest face could be made ugly if one was not mindful of the eye of the beholder. It was why all Pedigree omegas were trained in the art of their own bodies. Even Peregrine. After all, treasure kept alongside garbage eventually became tainted by its filth. In order to keep the other Pedigree omegas pristine, Peregrine was expected to shine.

And shine he did.

Channeling all he'd learned, he straddled Sebastian's lap and loosely looped his arms around the dragon's neck. Sebastian's gaze, which had been cold and intimidating, thawed. It seemed, for a short moment, that he knew not what to do, but then a lascivious look flashed through his eyes and he took Peregrine by the hips. "Mine," he growled, dipping his head to speak the word against Peregrine's jawline. A hot kiss followed, then another, until Sebastian arrived at Peregrine's lips. "All. Mine."

"Yours, my lord," Peregrine vowed in a breathless whisper. "All of me."

A sound like storms sweeping in from the sea rumbled in Sebastian's throat, then, without further warning, his lips crashed into Peregrine's like a wave breaking on a craggy cliffside. Peregrine's spine went rigid, then relaxed as the kiss continued. Like the sea, Sebastian was fearsome and deadly, but he did not intend to be destructive—it was simply his nature. All Peregrine had to learn to do was ride his currents and tides and all would be fine.

"Mine," Sebastian repeated into Peregrine's mouth as he lifted him up and positioned him over his hardened cock. "*Mine.*"

"Yours," Peregrine affirmed as Sebastian pushed his way inside. Like he'd been taught, he arched his back and moved his hips, but it didn't feel like it was enough. With a cry, he rested his head on Sebastian's chest and rode until his legs were shaking and his arms were so tight around Sebastian's neck, he was sure he had to be hurting him. "Yours. Yours. *Yours.*"

The lubricant from before eased the friction between them, but Sebastian was large, and the intrusion stung. Still, he persisted. It was his duty. Sebastian was to be his lord until he returned Peregrine to his cloister. Peregrine would not fail him so soon.

"Please, my lord," he uttered against Sebastian's collarbone, as he'd been taught it was a proper thing to say when mating with a dragon. "Please, I need more."

"Do not toy with me, omega," Sebastian growled in reply. "Tell me what you really want, not what they've told you to say."

Peregrine was so startled by the command, he pushed hastily back from Sebastian's chest and looked him in the eyes. They were dark and determined, and in them, there was no sign of deceit or trickery to be found.

"I want…" Peregrine's mouth fell open as he came down on Sebastian's cock at a new angle, causing pleasure to arrow through him in ways it never had before. "I want this. I want you. And I don't want to ever have to go back."

The last part fell out of him, unprompted and unplanned. Peregrine gasped, but was silenced when Sebastian kissed him hard. It was savage, but then, so was Sebastian. Perfect and primal and raw. The force of their kiss ripped through Peregrine like fire through pine tar and left him burning, and as Sebastian pushed him onto the bed, Peregrine ignited. Like a wild thing, he bucked and squirmed and *took*. And while Sebastian gave with every thrust of his hips, he took from Peregrine in return.

"Yes. Be free," Sebastian urged. His voice was dark with pleasure. The underlying satisfaction in it resonated in Peregrine's heart. "Take. Own. Possess. And allow me to do the same in return."

Peregrine could barely make sense of the words, but it didn't matter—his body knew what to do. Nothing would stop him from it. He moved as Sebastian did, wild and unashamed, with no mind for his angles or his lighting, or even the expression on his face. Sebastian growled as if in appreciation, then bucked into him savagely, but as cruel as he could be, Peregrine did not suffer. Rather, he learned how to ride the waves.

Before long, Sebastian wrapped a hand around his cock, and from there, Peregrine gave in to pleasure. The light of the day ceded its place to shadow, and darkness crept across the room. When it had consumed them entirely, Peregrine jerked a final time into his lord's hand, cried out from a place so deep his stomach curled, and came. Sebastian joined him, roaring, and as his hot cum spilled into Peregrine's body and his knot stretched Peregrine to his limits, Peregrine began to cry.

"Hush," Sebastian ordered, and while Peregrine obeyed, he could not stop the tears from falling.

He did not want to be sent back to his cloister or have to part from the dragon who'd plucked him off the streets, but he knew that, at some point, it would happen. Even were he to do the impossible and bear Sebastian a clutch, it would be taken from him before he could so much as touch the eggs and, duty performed, he would be sent back home and would never see Sebastian again.

"Omega," Sebastian said. "Why are you leaking?"

Peregrine brushed an arm as prettily as he could over his eyes and smiled his very best smile. The hard look on Sebastian's face crumpled, and without another word, he kissed Peregrine softly and sweetly.

"Mine," Sebastian uttered as they kissed. "Mine."

It was the truth, but there was a part Sebastian had omitted, and it was the most important of all. So for every "Mine" Sebastian gave him, Peregrine reminded himself of what his lord had neglected to say: *for now.*

Day had yet to break when Sebastian roused Peregrine from his sleep. A beeswax candle burned in a holder by the bedside, offering modest light by which Peregrine glimpsed Sebastian's face. His expression was guarded but not overtly hostile, and the way he shook Peregrine by the shoulder was gentle, especially considering his size.

"Peregrine," Sebastian said when he noticed Peregrine was awake. "Get up."

The dragon was already dressed. Peregrine couldn't tell the color of his doublet in such dim light, but it was plain to see by the stitchwork that the garment was expensive—worth more, perhaps, than the box of sweets Sebastian had plied him with the previous night.

"Is there something the matter, my lord?" Peregrine asked as he sat up in bed. He blinked the sleep from his eyes and squinted through the darkness in an attempt to make sense of what was happening, but came up short. The inn was quiet, as were the streets outside.

"No. Today we travel, and I must prepare you for the voyage." Sebastian ripped the sheets from Peregrine's lap and lifted him out of bed. "You are filthy. It will not do. I have ordered you a bath."

Shame burned Peregrine's cheeks. "I bathed yesterday, my lord."

"And you will bathe again." Sebastian set Peregrine on the floor next to the bed and ran a hand apologetically through his hair. Like magic, the touch lit Peregrine up from the inside and invoked memories of the night before, and all the passion they'd shared. Greedy for more, he leaned into Sebastian's hand, hoping Sebastian might remember as well and come back to bed. To his delight, Sebastian squatted down, bringing them practically to eye level with one another. Certainly close enough to kiss. Peregrine's heart pounded a wicked beat, and he began to close his eyes in anticipation of Sebastian's lips on his.

Sebastian leaned forward, closing even more distance between them, and passed by Peregrine's lips to withdraw the chamber pot from beneath the bed. "Use it," he demanded.

Peregrine accepted the chamber pot with as much poise as he could muster. He did not want to let on that he'd much rather have something put in him than... well, the opposite. "Yes, my lord."

"By the time you're done, the bath will be cool enough to use."

Peregrine blinked. "Has it already arrived?"

Sebastian gestured into the darkness in the direction of the door. "Yes."

"I see. Why didn't you wake me? I could have seen to it that it was drawn and—"

"No."

Sebastian did not elaborate, and Peregrine knew better than to question a dragon, so he bowed his head and stepped aside to do as he'd been instructed. Once he'd finished and done away with his mess, he returned the chamber pot to its place beneath the bed and ventured into the darkness to find the basin. Sebastian followed, carrying the candle to light his way.

Sure enough, by the door was a wooden basin inlaid with several fresh linen sheets meant to prevent splinters. Steam rose from within. The innkeeper's wife must have filled it with pots of boiling water. Peregrine could think of no other way the bath could stay so hot for so long.

He tested the water with a finger and found it tolerable, so in he stepped. The basin wasn't terribly large, but it would fit him provided he tented his legs. There would be no room for Sebastian, though, a conclusion Sebastian seemed to come to as he stepped to the edge of the tub and watched Peregrine fold delicately into it.

"It's small," Sebastian said in a tone so sinister and serious, a smile wobbled into being on Peregrine's face.

"Yes, my lord. Did you not see it when it was brought in?"

"No." Sebastian paused, then added, "My eyes were interested in other things."

It was unclear what those other things were, but Peregrine thought he might know, and the notion made him blush.

"It is of no matter." Sebastian set the candle down nearby and crouched by the tub. He fished a folded linen rag and a glass bottle from somewhere on the floor, then wetted the rag in the bathwater before applying whatever it was that was inside the bottle. "It will do all the same."

Peregrine watched, chin on his knees, as Sebastian rolled up the sleeves of his doublet then reached into the basin. He took one of Peregrine's ankles in hand, then lifted his leg out of the water and ran the washcloth over his feet, paying great attention to the gaps between his toes and all the little places oft overlooked. The smell of something floral and sweet perfumed the air as he worked.

For all Peregrine's training, he hadn't a clue what to say. Dragons were not supposed to act like this.

"It's too dark," Sebastian grumbled after a time. Upon issuing the statement, he dropped the washcloth on Peregrine's leg and swatted his hand through the air as if chasing away a fly. Quite suddenly, fire burst into existence in the air above them—dozens of flickering flames no bigger than the one burning down the nearby candle's wick. They hung unevenly in the air like living jewels and cast reflections of themselves upon the surface of the water. Peregrine stared at them, awestruck. So this was dragon magic? He'd heard whispers that dragons were capable of wonders the likes of which no mortal man could ever duplicate, but to see it in person was something else entirely.

He sat in silence, too stunned to react, as Sebastian grabbed the washcloth and resumed diligently washing his leg. How was it the fire wasn't tumbling down to burn them? Sebastian had to be extraordinarily powerful, even more so than Peregrine had originally believed. A creature who could control fire to such an extent was a dangerous creature indeed.

With a grunt, Sebastian tucked Peregrine's leg back into the basin and pulled out the other. He cleaned it and returned it, too, then plunged his arm into the water to run the washcloth between Peregrine's thighs. Peregrine noticed, but only peripherally. His attention was held rapt by the flames flickering overhead.

"The fire," Peregrine managed in a small voice as Sebastian worked the washcloth over the more intimate parts of his anatomy. "If one were to touch it, would it burn?"

"Yes."

"And if you were to touch it?"

"No. Only if I were to let it."

How fascinating. Peregrine grinned. "So you control it, then? Every aspect of it? Whether it burns or not, and where it appears?"

"Yes."

"And you can summon it at will?"

Rather than respond, Sebastian held his unoccupied palm over the surface of the water, which promptly caught fire. Peregrine gasped and scrambled back, tripping over the linen beneath his feet in an attempt to escape the flames surrounding him. With a loud splash and an ungraceful flailing of his arms, he tumbled straight through the flame, which yielded to his body and didn't so much as singe the fair hair on his arms.

"It yields to me," Sebastian stated as Peregrine struggled to catch his breath while fire harmlessly licked up his arms and swirled around his legs. "One day, you will yield to me, too, omega."

"I do yield to you, my lord."

Sebastian shook his head. "You do not yield to me any more than the water in this basin, meekly pushed aside when introduced to any kind of resistance. No. One day, you will yield to me like the fire does—shaped by my hand, but still vibrant and alive.

It burns of its own volition, Peregrine. I may control its size and shape, but not even the mightiest dragon can control the way it flickers. I want you to yield to me like it does. Do you understand?"

Peregrine wasn't sure that he did, but he bowed his head regardless. One day he thought he might, and for now, that seemed like enough.

The fire on the surface of the bath vanished, and with it gone, Sebastian washed Peregrine from head to toe until he was pristine. Once he was dried and dressed, they broke their fast with Sebastian's brother, Alistair, who enthused endlessly about their upcoming journey and revealed to Peregrine their final destination—Persia—with their next stop on the tour being Beirut.

7

SEBASTIAN

1508

As it transpired, the omega did not take easily to life at sea. Due to his good breeding, he didn't complain in any way, though, so Sebastian was slow to realize his distress. All had seemed so perfectly normal. During the day, Peregrine kept their cabin spotless and tidy, and was attentive in his daily tutoring with Alistair; and at night, he opened both arms and legs to Sebastian.

It took Alistair, in fact, to alert Sebastian that there was even a problem.

"You need to do something with your omega," Alistair told him several days into their voyage.

"Do you insinuate that I cannot please him?" Sebastian growled.

Alistair held up his hands in mock surrender. "Lord, no. The entire ship knows how well you please the boy. The problem is when he's not in your bunk. Peregrine is peaky, brother. Have you not seen it?"

Sebastian frowned. "Nonsense. What do you know of omegas? Other than how to sniff them out and seduce them, that is."

Alistair colored, but persisted. "Mark my words. Your omega is not well."

To Sebastian's chagrin, he found that Alistair had been right. There was something amiss with his omega. When he thought himself unobserved, his face would fall into fretful lines and he'd hurry to one of two places: either the ship's rail, which he'd retch over while clinging to it so tightly his knuckles turned white; or their cabin, where he'd curl up and fall into a fitful sleep. Unless he knew himself to be watched, he did not smile.

"You were right," Sebastian was forced to admit to his brother three days later. "There is something amiss with the boy." His gut churned with worry and his dragon was remarkably unhelpful. "What should I do?"

Alistair's face brightened. "I know just the thing. His humors are imbalanced. I think Everard should agree with me that what ails him is an excess of black bile. Until we can find him herbs to remedy the situation, you should feed him moist foods and see if you can't do something to lift his melancholy. Maybe you could woo him."

Sebastian glared at his brother. "Woo him? Tis a bit late for that."

"Hardly. You've taken his innocence and snatched him from his home—"

"A bloody horrible home," Sebastian grumbled.

"And you only interact with him with your cock and knot," Alistair continued. "Of course he's not happy. What omega would be in those circumstances?"

"And what do you suggest to remedy this, brother?"

"I know just the thing to bring a sparkle to any omega's eye." Alistair gave Sebastian a dragony grin.

Sebastian stared at his brother blank-faced, waiting for him to explain.

"Poetry," Alistair revealed, grin unwavering. "It never fails. Your omega's spirits will be much improved in no time at all and his excess of black bile should lessen if only you share with him your appreciation for the arts. I swear it. It's worked a thousand times before. Science agrees with me—the answer is poetry."

The answer was not poetry.

The evening started out as normal. Sebastian and Peregrine ate in their cabin. As usual, Sebastian ate heartily while the omega picked at his food, saying that he'd eaten a large meal earlier and wasn't hungry. After the dishes were cleared and removed to the galley, however, Sebastian didn't take Peregrine to bed. Instead, he bade the omega to lie down and be comfortable while Sebastian read to him from a book of poems Alistair had brought with him. The author was Stephen Hawes, and Sebastian had never heard of him, but Alistair assured him that he was a much-admired poet and his verses very romantic.

In a halting rumble, Sebastian started to recite. The poem was silly, to his point of view, but there were two stanzas that did seem appropriate for the occasion. Sebastian hoped Peregrine would like them. Otherwise, he was afraid the entire endeavor was a lost cause.

"The lord and knight deluteth for to here

Chronicles and stories of noble chivalry

The gentle man's gentleness for his pastime dare

The man of law to hear law truly

The yeoman delighteth to talk of yeomanry

The plowman his land for to air and sow

Thus nature worketh in high degree and low

For if there were one of the gentle blood

Consigned to yeomanry for nourishment

Discretion comen he should change his mode

Though he knew not his parents verament

Yet nature would work, so by entendyment

That he should follow the conditions doubtless

Of his true blood, by outward gentleness"

Two-thirds of the way through the poem's recitation, Peregrine had gone a noticeable green shade. That boded ill. Sure enough, Peregrine frantically began to seek for something by the cabin's bunk. Sebastian's words faltered as he watched the omega struggle. At last, he found what he sought: the chamber pot. For a bare second, Sebastian thought Peregrine might have grabbed it to dash its contents at him, as sometimes happened to public orators, but instead, Peregrine vomited into the vessel, which wasn't, when you got down to it, much better.

Sebastian knew he was no elocutionist, but he hadn't thought his efforts sick-inducing. He threw down Alistair's precious book and was at the bunk's side in an instant, stroking Peregrine's fine, silky hair.

"The poetry was Alistair's idea," he told Peregrine as he voided into the chamber pot. "Not mine. He holds the blame." That was petty, but if the omega had to despise someone, Sebastian would rather it be his harebrained brother.

Peregrine let out a wheeze of laughter, then groaned. "It wasn't the poem, my lord. It was lovely, and I thank you for trying to entertain me. I apologize for ruining your efforts. That was not well done of me, but my body was not being cooperative."

Sebastian considered that. "So the poetry did not cause you to vomit?"

The omega wheezed out another short laugh. "No, my lord."

Sebastian stiffened. "Then whatever is the matter? Have you the plague? I can send Alistair to fly with a message to bring Everard. They could be here in a day or two." Humans were so very fragile, and omegas even more so. Sebastian didn't know what he'd do if the young man he'd taken into his care grew ill and died while he was forced to watch.

Peregrine shook his head. "I'm fine, my lord. Nothing is amiss."

"The very full pot by my foot tells a different tale, omega. Either you hate poetry or you're ill. Either way, I will fix this."

"There is nothing to fix, my lord. Not unless you can stop the tide. I've never been sailing before, and my head and stomach do not like it, it seems."

That was puzzling. Sebastian frowned. "You've never sickened in my presence before."

Peregrine colored. "Ah, as to that. For some reason, the tossing of the ship ceases to bother me when you touch me, and it's rare indeed that we're together without being in contact."

Sebastian frowned harder. "Is this why you've been eating precious little?"

Shyly, the omega ducked his head. "Yes, a bit. Also, the portions are very large. I'm not used to so much in the way of provisions at each meal. Even without my affliction, I'm afraid I could never eat a quarter of what you serve me."

"Hm." Sebastian, still frowning, thought about the situation. "But you're fine if I touch you?"

The blush sprang back to Peregrine's cheeks. "Even holding my hand helps, but the more you—"

Sebastian ripped off his shirt.

"*My lord dragon,*" Peregrine squeaked. "It is the middle of the day!"

"I need to make you better," Sebastian said with a shrug. "This must be some form of draconic magic. I've not studied it much. In truth, I'm not much for studying." Carefully, he plucked off the loose shirt that was Peregrine's only clothing. "I prefer bashing my foes about the head to using diplomacy. That's my brother Geoffrey's concern. But from what little I do know of dragon magic, if me touching you helps relieve your illness, more skin contact will only improve your situation." Sebastian crawled into the bunk and pulled Peregrine onto his lap so the boy's back was against his wide chest.

"You can't spend the entire voyage in here with me," Peregrine said gently and, Sebastian thought, somewhat wistfully.

"I can," Sebastian rumbled, wrapping Peregrine up in a tight embrace meant to maximize their skin-on-skin contact, "and I will."

Sebastian was true to his word. He rarely ventured from Peregrine's side, and when he did, he hurried back as soon as he might. They ate their meals cozied up together, with Peregrine nude on Sebastian's bare lap. Not only did that settle Peregrine's stomach, but it allowed Sebastian to ensure he ate a proper amount of food.

Slowly, over the course of the voyage, Peregrine began to put on weight, doing away with his near-skeletal thinness. He'd been lovely before, but now he was breathtaking. Sebastian didn't have to remind himself to touch Peregrine, for it was all he wanted to do. They made love over and over, in as many positions as the cabin's bunk would allow, until Sebastian knew every inch of Peregrine's body intimately. The same, of course, could be said for the omega, who quickly learned what pleased Sebastian best.

"If I didn't know better," Sebastian said into Peregrine's hair, which was getting quite long, "I'd say you were a witch, little one."

Peregrine squirmed in Sebastian's arms to face him. "Why would you say such a horrid thing?"

"Because you've enchanted me as surely as any sorceress or wizard. I cannot get enough of you."

Peregrine smiled, but the expression slowly fell off his face and was replaced by a look of worry. He bit his lip. The sight of him like that made Sebastian want to smash things and howl and set the entire world on fire, but violence would not solve the problem, so he refrained.

"Peregrine," he uttered. "Tell me what's wrong."

Peregrine shook his head. "It's nothing, I swear. Here, let me show you."

He pushed Sebastian onto his back and mounted an assault worthy of a great general on his body. Slender limbs twined with his much larger ones. Soft lips traced endless patterns over his wide, scarred chest, and clever fingers brought him to the brink of release again and again and again. Sebastian usually enjoyed being in charge of his lovers, but for the sake of that sadness he'd earlier seen in Peregrine's eyes, he let the omega do as he would. It was torture, but of the absolute sweetest kind.

"You slay me, Perry," Sebastian gasped as Peregrine yet again lifted his mouth from Sebastian's cock right before he spilled his seed. "I am vanquished. I concede. Please, please put me out of my misery."

A strange look flitted over Peregrine's face, then he said, "Perry. You've never called me that before." His hand toyed lightly with Sebastian's aching bollocks.

Sebastian groaned in utter surrender. "I'll never call you that again, I swear it. Just please… please…"

"No. I like it, I think. Perry. Yes. I think I like it very much." He then bent his head and added his hot mouth to the delicious torture being wrought by his hand.

"Anything," Sebastian promised. "I will give you anything. Everything."

"Hm." Peregrine licked up the underside of Sebastian's cock, and he thought he might go utterly mad.

"I swear it," Sebastian said. "I swear it on my blood and bone and scale." That was a serious oath indeed, and the omega knew it, because he let out a small gasp of surprise.

"What if it's not yours to give?" Peregrine asked. Then he set his lips once more upon Sebastian's member and sucked it down into his throat.

All thoughts and vows flew out of Sebastian's head as finally Peregrine brought him to orgasm. It was full of so much pleasure it was part pain as well. He roared loud enough for the entire ship to hear, but they were used to such bellows and would let the two of them be. Peregrine's mouth milked him dry, then his eager tongue cleaned away all the seed that had escaped down Sebastian's knot. Peregrine himself had some on his mouth and chin. Sebastian hauled him upward and kissed and licked it all away.

Mine, his dragon said. It was, prior to meeting Peregrine, the only thing it ever had to say, and it only spoke when there was something it desperately wanted.

The omega is ours, Sebastian promised. *Forever. I vow it.*

With a sigh, Peregrine tumbled off Sebastian's chest to lie beside him. He cuddled close, touching as much of his body to Sebastian's as was possible. To Sebastian, it felt very much indeed like he would burst from happiness. Touching Peregrine was a high more intense than even the poppy juice Alistair had shared with him once. The boy was addictive. Sebastian could not get enough.

I would ruin myself for him, Sebastian thought. The implications of that should have been terrifying, but Sebastian was not easy to scare. It was due, his sire had often said, to lack of a proper imagination. Case in point, Sebastian could not, no matter how hard he tried, imagine his life once Peregrine was no longer in it. He'd ask

Alistair for advice, but he'd likely just give Sebastian more poetry to read. Instead, Sebastian held Peregrine a bit tighter and listened to his dragon say, over and over, *mine,* until, at last, he fell asleep.

8

SEBASTIAN

Present Day

It was just the three of them in Everard's office. Harrison had been banished, Sebastian knew not where, nor did he care. A calm and quiet environment was best for Perry, and with Harrison around, the office would be neither, no matter how well-meaning the omega-beta tried to be. Sebastian had more cause than most to know that under Perry's beautiful shell was a core of unbreakable iron, but even iron could become brittle and start to fracture under too much stress and pressure.

Sebastian held Perry's hand and they both looked toward Everard, who cleared his throat to speak. "Congratulations are in order. So far, all seems well with fetal development."

"You can't fool me, Everard. I can hear that 'but' in your voice." Perry's sweet trill of a voice held a telling note of uncertainty.

Everard smiled, and it was one of his rare genuine ones. "I think you might be the last person I could ever fool, Perry, so here it is: I'm a little worried about your blood pressure. It's higher than I'd like."

Perry clutched Sebastian's hand tighter. His heart beat hard and fast, like that of a captured bird. Sebastian closed his eyes and thought of cool, still, silent things, pushing them through their mate bond. A clear pool of water with a surface like glass. An immovable boulder in a misty field. A vast forest untouched by time. It did the trick. Perry's heartbeat began to slow and his breathing evened out.

"Good." Everard nodded at Perry. "That's exactly what I'd like you to do. We need to keep you calm, well-rested, properly nourished, and hydrated."

"I am very calm, I assure you," Perry said primly.

Both Drake brothers harumphed in unison.

"I'm not ordering bed rest," Everard continued. "At least not yet. But if your blood pressure doesn't stabilize, that will happen. So take care of yourself. That is an order."

"I will see to it," Sebastian vowed. "Now tell us about the babe."

Next to him, Perry tensed, but Everard did not notice and advanced the conversation. "Do you wish to know the sex?"

Sebastian opened his mouth, but Perry jumped in before he had a chance to speak. "No."

"That sounded very... ah... decisive," observed Everard.

"It is. I don't wish to know." Perry dipped his chin. "It's too soon."

He was thinking, Sebastian knew, of the heartbreak they'd suffered over the babes they'd lost, each one conceived in love, each one dearly wanted by both fathers, and each one never having survived long enough to draw a breath on his or her own. Most were lost quickly, but some had lingered long enough for Everard to tell their sex, and their passing was all the more painful for it.

"Things are different now," Everard said gently. "It's been a good century since your last dragonet pregnancy. Not only has modern medicine come quite a long way since then, but I am a more skilled doctor as well. Just because things have always been a certain way doesn't mean that they can't change."

Perry bit his lip and nodded, his right hand cupped protectively over his nonexistent bump.

"However, until you decide you'd like to know, I'll respect your wishes." Everard folded his hands on top of his desk. "At two months since conception, it's too early to determine the sex, anyway, but I'll keep my future findings to myself. In any case, male and female markers are inconsequential. What I have yet to share is far more important."

Perry's shoulders tensed, causing Sebastian to bristle. "Well, brother?" he barked. "What is it?"

Everard rolled his eyes. "Really? Put your hackles down, Sebastian. I wouldn't dream of announcing bad news so casually. I am a man of integrity, you know."

"And a dragon of chaos."

That brought a sparkle to Everard's eyes. "How very fortunate it is that my dragon does not have a doctorate. Now, allow me to share my findings from today's examination. So far the baby is healthy, if a bit small for their gestational age, and there are no abnormalities I can detect. For the moment, all is well." Everard tapped his hands on his desk. "If this was a normal pregnancy, I'd expect to see you back here in three weeks, but I'm going to shorten that to two. We'll have to be careful as to when we schedule our appointments, as per our longstanding agreement, my delightful butternut squash remains unaware of Perry's pregnancy, as do the rest of the family. In any case, it will be a slight inconvenience at best, and I will do my utmost to maintain confidentiality," Everard shot Sebastian a pointed look, "despite my... what did you call it the night of Reynard's little disaster, brother? 'Enormous mouth'?"

Sebastian met his gaze with narrowed eyes but did not deign to give him a reply.

Everard was being modest.

"Enormous" did not begin to encompass how large his mouth really was.

"But that said," Everard continued when Sebastian did not reply, "I will do everything I can to see that this pregnancy goes as smoothly and as secretly as possible, and when it comes time for you to deliver, I will make sure both father and child are safe."

Perry sat very straight in his chair and folded his hands anxiously on his lap. "Do not give me false hope, Everard. My heart simply cannot take it. How can you be so certain we'll reach that point when I've never been able to keep a pregnancy beyond six months?"

At that, Everard smiled, although it was tired and strained. "Much has changed over the last decade, Perry. Dragons are finding their mates and clutches are being laid. What was once thought impossible has been achieved. In comparison, seeing you through a pregnancy should be quite simple. As long as you heed my word, I will take care of the rest, and we will put this impossibility behind us together."

On the drive home in the back of their limo, Perry lay cuddled in Sebastian's arms. "Everard is worried," he said. "He puts on a brave face and plays up his confidence, but I can tell. He was entirely too nice. He only gets that way when he's afraid of something he can't control."

"We will do everything we can to save this one," Sebastian promised. "You've borne two clutches. There is no reason you can't bear a babe as well."

Perry laughed. "You can't just growl and expect the universe to bend to your will, Sebastian. Life doesn't work like that. Not even our lives, which are magical, I will admit." The humor faded from his face, and a sad little frown took its place. "There is something wrong with me," Perry admitted in a small voice. "There has been since the beginning, perhaps stemming from my injury all those years ago. Magic can only go so far. I don't believe this is something even Everard can fix."

Perry's plaintive voice, trying its best to be strong, tore Sebastian in two. "You are perfect," Sebastian said into his mate's silken hair. "From the very first time I ever saw you, you were perfect."

"In my rags?" Perry asked, amusement back in his tone that Sebastian was relieved to hear.

"In your rags. In anything. Or in nothing at all." Sebastian slid a hand down Perry's hip and around to cup his ass.

"Impossible dragon."

"You wouldn't love me any other way."

A sweet, musical chuckle burst from Perry. "What you mean to say is that you couldn't be any other way, and that's exactly why I love you, darling." Perry caressed Sebastian's cheek with cool fingers. "Just know that as hard as it is, and as much as I mourn, I have you and the boys, and it is enough."

Emotions churned within Perry. Hope and resignation and anger and despair and love. So much love, always. But for all his grace, there was sorrow, too. Sebastian felt it through their bond, which told the truth even when Perry did not.

"But I promised you everything," Sebastian said after a time.

"And you have given it to me. By your side I have raised a clutch, seen the world, and learned so much. I can weave tapestry and brew beer, both paint and sculpt, cut and polish gems then set them into precious metals, and grow a mighty tree from a tiny acorn. I have learned to ride a horse, to swim, to fence, and to defend myself. I have managed to read nearly as many books as Alistair. Truly, my love, you have given me everything any omega could ever want."

"Not entirely." Sebastian's hand wandered back up Perry's body, stroking along his side. "You can try to hide the truth from me, but you will never succeed. You are my mate, Perry, and through our bond, I know what you feel. You long for this child. You don't have to pretend otherwise."

Perry made a delicate noise of irritation in his throat, then rolled onto his back so his head was on Sebastian's lap and his body was stretched across the limo's bench. In his new position, his curls fell away from his face, showing off the golden ear cuffs he wore and the pearl-studded posts in his lobes. "It's not right of me to want more when you've already given me so much," he admitted quietly.

But Sebastian would not have it. "It is right, Perry, because you are a dragon. Wanting more is in our very bones."

"Gold, perhaps," Perry argued, but his heart wasn't in it. "Or jewels, or art, or coin, but this? It's not the same, Sebastian."

"It is."

"How?"

Sebastian swept a stray curl off Perry's brow and afforded him a smile. "We hoard the things we consider treasure, Perry. Be they art or gold or the ones we love. This is the way of the dragon. And I promise you, I will do everything in my power to make sure you never lose another treasured thing again."

Perry took a sip from the goblet Sebastian proffered and then turned green. He bolted out of their bed and fled for the bathroom. There, he was noisily ill.

Sebastian sighed. Perry was not being a cooperative patient. He wanted to be up and doing, not stuck in a bed, forced to eat and drink the things Everard recommended.

What could be so bad about beet juice?

Sebastian looked into the goblet at the villainous juice that had made his mate ill. It was a deep red color and had a rich smell that reminded him of autumn, after the leaves had fallen from the trees and become crisp.

Perhaps it was morning sickness. What else could it be?

Sebastian tilted the goblet back and forth, watching the liquid swirl and pool. Perry had been feeling so poorly lately that he'd been forced to stop venturing out, lest any of the more observant members of their family notice that something was wrong. For the sake of Perry's heart, not one of them knew of the struggles he'd been through, save Everard, and the three of them endeavored to keep it that way. Once it had been because Sebastian had doubted any of them would understand why they'd mourn the loss of a Disgrace, but now that hearts were changing, it was simply for Perry's sake.

It hurt badly enough to suffer a loss like that in private, but to have to relive it time and time again when well-meaning family inquired after the health of the babe who'd passed? It was too much.

Sebastian absentmindedly took a sip from the goblet and reeled back like he'd been struck. Only his strong constitution kept him from spitting it out. No wonder Perry couldn't keep it down. Beet juice tasted like liquid dirt. How did humans drink this? It was, in a word, disgusting.

When Perry came back to their bed, he pointed at the offending glass of dark red liquid. "That's it," he said. "I don't care how healthy Everard purports it to be—I'm not drinking it. I refuse."

"I cannot blame you." Sebastian set the goblet aside and held out another, this one filled with a clear and colorless liquid. "It's quite vile."

"Quite," Perry agreed, and regarded the new goblet with suspicion. "I don't suppose this will prove any better?"

"It's water."

"Good." Perry cuddled up to his side and took the goblet from him, sipping the water slowly.

"To be fair," Sebastian said after a while, "the beet juice may taste terrible, but it is good for you."

"I don't care. At this point, anything that doesn't make me want to vomit is good for me. The morning sickness is very bad this time. I would say I wish that it would end, but..." Perry fell silent and shook his head, and a single note of despair rang through their bond. Sebastian's heart ached from it. He wished he had the words to tell Perry how much he was loved and needed, but he lacked the language. That was Alistair's domain, or Geoffrey's. They were good with words. Sebastian was not.

A bit of doggerel song sidled into Sebastian's head. It had been a very popular song once, and it seemed he'd heard it everywhere. Every line reminded him of Perry, and how devastated he'd be without him.

He started singing, softly at first, but then growing in volume.

"You are my sunshine, my only sunshine

You make me happy when skies are gray

You'll never know dear, how much I love you

Please don't take my sunshine away."

Perry chuckled wetly. "I love you, but not even that excellent rendition can convince me to drink beet juice."

"Will you at least eat some breakfast?"

"Yes, my tyrant. For you, I'll try."

"And for the babe."

Perry's lip trembled. "Yes. I'll try."

"Good." Sebastian left the bed and gathered Perry in his arms. "Then allow me to carry you to the safety of the dining room table. There is an army of small dragons waiting for us beyond the door, you see. You'll need your strength to withstand them."

Perry laughed and the sound warmed Sebastian through and through. "How lucky I am to have such a valiant knight to defend me."

Sebastian snorted, and off they went.

At the door to their bedroom, Perry signaled for Sebastian to stop. "No matter what," he said, "I want you to know that you are enough. That they are enough. I have more love in my life than I ever thought possible." He gave Sebastian a slow, soft kiss that gave Sebastian half a mind to bear him back to their bed. "And I can see that look in your eyes, naughty dragon. There will be time enough for that later."

Sebastian didn't think there would ever be enough time, but he didn't argue with his mate. Rather, he bellowed, "'Ware the door," then flung it open. Behind it stood eight young boys, all of them looking for attention.

"Good morning, my darlings," Perry chirped as though nothing was wrong. "Are you ready for breakfast? Hands clean? Show me. Ah, very good. You're such very good boys."

"I love you, omega," Sebastian rumbled low enough for only Perry to hear. "No matter what."

Perry smiled brilliantly then gave Sebastian a quick kiss to a chorus of moans from their disgusted progeny.

"They're at it again," groaned Atticus.

"That's what the hoard is for," Cornelius added sternly.

"So gross," decried Hadrian. He covered his eyes with his hands.

"That's quite enough, darlings," Perry trilled. "Now, time for breakfast. If you're very lucky, Cook will have made chocolate chip pancakes."

The boys whooped and ran toward the breakfast room. When they were all gone, Perry reached up and cradled Sebastian's cheek. "And I love you," he said. "Always. No matter what."

9

PERRY

Present Day

Once the boys were fed and their syrup-sticky hands were cleaned, Perry kissed them each on the top of the head and left home to visit a certain Harrison Lessardi-Drake. In the week since his appointment with Everard, he'd come to the conclusion that while his brother-in-law was a very fine doctor, there were some matters an alpha simply could not understand. How fortunate it was that his mate was just as capable a physician. With his sharp mind, unending curiosity, and love of all things reptile—human-shaped or otherwise—Harrison was bound to know something that would help Perry's condition beyond simple bed rest and beet juice, and if not, Perry had no doubt he'd bury his nose in a book and plumb the scientific depths of his mind until he did.

It was a quick trip from Sebastian's lair to Everard's estate. Perry's personal chauffeur, Williams, slowed the Lexus to a stop before its impressive front staircase, shifted into park, and turned in her seat to make eye contact. "We're here, sir. Are you sure you'll be fine on your own?"

"Of course. Why wouldn't I be?" Perry offered her a smile that did nothing to ease the concern on her face. "Harrison is a dear friend and I'm here to pay him a visit. There's nothing more to it than that."

Williams did not look convinced.

"Despite that, I'd appreciate your discretion." Perry chewed on his bottom lip. "Sebastian is not entirely aware of where I am, you see, and for simplicity's sake it should remain that way."

Williams looked less convinced than ever, but she was nothing if not trustworthy, and offered him a curt, professional nod. "You have my word."

"I shan't be long," Perry promised. He smiled a little more brightly, but no amount of love nor joy could do away with the knot lodged in his throat. It reflected in his smile. It had to. "Your sister lives near here, doesn't she? Why not stop in to see her? I'll be in touch when I'm ready to leave."

"That's very generous of you, sir."

"Think nothing of it." Perry moved forward in his seat and laid a hand delicately on her shoulder. "After I'm done here, there will be nowhere else I have to be. You're welcome to take the day off once my business has concluded."

Williams paused, then sighed and tucked a strand of gray-streaked hair behind her ear. "I understand that you're nervous for your friendly visit with Harrison, sir, but you don't have to buy my silence. You and Master Sebastian have been nothing but kind, and there is no reason in the world why I'd treat you with anything other than my utmost respect. I will keep your secrets. I will keep them all. And you have my word that the rest of the staff will do the same."

She knew, then. Perry's hand trembled, then fell from her shoulder. He laid his head there instead. "Thank you."

"Silly boy," Williams whispered. She ran her fingers through his hair. "We hate to see you so out of sorts. Don't let us—any of us—worry you. You already have so much weight on your shoulders."

"I'm so afraid, Alana," Perry whispered as he closed his eyes. "I can't have this happen again. I can't. My heart can't stand it, and Sebastian..." Despite his best efforts, the knot lodged in his throat tightened, and he let out a shuddering sob. "Sebastian always acts so strong, but I know—I *know*—he grieves. I see it in his eyes and I can't stand it. I cannot."

Williams laid her head against his. She said nothing, but the heaviness in the air spoke for her. In it, Perry knew her heart.

"He tries to keep me safe," he whispered after a long while. "He does his very best, I know, but there are some matters that simply cannot be helped. Not by traditional means."

Williams nodded, nuzzling Perry's hair in the process.

"So I will see Harrison." Hope trilled in Perry's voice, but even then, it was uncertain. "I will see if I can protect myself and in doing so, shield Sebastian as well. So much has changed since we were first mated. Surely there must be something that can be done."

Williams hummed reassuringly. "Of course, sir. You are very brave."

"I am very foolish," Perry admitted with a sad laugh. "To think this could end differently than it has for the last five hundred years is insanity, but what other choice do I have?" He laid a hand over his belly. "I have to try."

Williams kissed his hair. "And try you will. Go to Harrison. See what he has to say. I will be here for you when it's over, and no matter what happens, all will be well."

With time Perry knew it would be, but knowing didn't stop it from hurting any less.

"Good day, Master Peregrine," said Cleaver, the very prim and proper butler of the Drake-Lessardi household, upon opening the front door. "What an unexpected but delightful surprise."

"You flatter me." Perry smiled for him. "It's a delight to see you, too, Cleaver. Are you well? How is your ankle?"

A hint of a smile perked Cleaver's stern lips. "I'm well, and as for these old bones?" He lifted a foot and shook it illustratively from side to side. "They feel younger than ever, no doubt in large part to Master Everard, who personally sees to my arthritis."

"He is a gem, isn't he?" Perry laid a tender hand on Cleaver's arm. "And your daughter?"

Cleaver's face lit up. "She is exceptionally well, Master Peregrine. Little Elijah will be celebrating his first birthday next month—can you believe it? I'll be making a trip out of the occasion and staying with her and her husband for the week."

"One year already? How time flies."

"Indeed, indeed." Cleaver, in a much livelier mood than before, stepped away from the door and gestured inside. "Please, come in. Shall I bring you to see Master Everard?"

"No, thank you. I'm here to visit with Harrison today."

Cleaver blinked, which was about as close as he ever got to looking surprised. "Master Harrison?"

"Yes, darling." Perry stepped into the house and took Cleaver by the arm. Cleaver blushed—a rare treat. "Harrison is a delight and I am very eager to see him, but between you and me..." Perry leaned in and stood on his toes to speak quietly into Cleaver's ear. "If you wouldn't mind, would you keep word of my arrival a secret? Some conversations are simply too sensational for reptilian ears. I'm sure you understand."

"Of course, of course." Cleaver patted his hand and off they went, stopping only to check in on Andre, who was in the middle of making sandwiches and brewing tea.

Harrison's office was empty when Perry arrived, so he settled in one of its armchairs and passed the time in quiet introspection. There was much to think about. Part of him still wasn't sure that telling Harrison the truth was a good idea, since Harrison, as earnest as he could be, was sometimes careless about the things he said, and there was a chance he might let slip to the rest of the family that Perry was expecting. But it was a risk Perry had to take.

There was something wrong with him, he knew it, and if Everard was only willing to treat him with bed rest and beet juice, a second opinion was necessary.

Several minutes later the door opened, but it was Hugh Drake's dark-haired secretary, Finch—not Harrison—who stepped into the room.

"Finch." Perry suppressed his surprise with a smile. "How good to see you. How are you? Are you well?"

A dull look saddened Finch's eyes. It was nothing like how Perry had last seen him when they'd gathered for the boys' birthday party several months back, and it was alarming enough of a change that Perry sat at attention.

Something was certainly wrong.

"Did Harrison tell you, then?" Finch asked in a dreary tone.

Harrison had certainly not, but the dots were beginning to connect all the same.

"I would never do that," Harrison said as he stepped into the room. "I may not have my M.D. yet, but I do know a thing or two about doctor-patient confidentiality, and I would never break it. I promise."

Finch reddened with embarrassment. "I do beg your pardon."

"Oh, it's all right." Harrison offered him an easy smile. "I'm not mad. It's a very easy mistake to make, and I'm glad we were able to sort it out before any feelings got hurt."

Perry's attention drifted from Finch to Harrison, then back again. The last time he'd seen Finch, poor clueless Hugh had been courting him without realizing it. It seemed matters had progressed since then. Omega secretaries did not make a habit out of paying Harrison Lessardi-Drake house calls. Not unless they were consorting with dragons.

Whatever the case, the distress on Finch's face was plain to see, and it felt terribly rude to be witnessing him uninvited during such a trying time.

"Would you like me to leave, darling?" Perry asked. "I had no idea you were visiting, and I didn't mean to intrude. I can wait in another room until your business has been concluded."

"No. No, it's fine." Finch looked miserably at Harrison, then even more miserably at Perry. "I suppose I should get used to talking about it, as word will spread soon enough, and everyone will know. Hugh took my heat and I didn't catch. I've failed to give him a clutch."

So that was it, then. What a miserable turn of events. Perry's heart ached for him, for it was a pain he knew all too well.

"That's not entirely true," Harrison interjected. "Finch could be pregnant with a dragonet." He gestured at Finch's midsection. "I couldn't detect eggs during his ultrasound, but a fetus would be almost undetectable at this stage. We need to do blood work to accurately conclude what's happening. Or a pregnancy test, but blood work is way more accurate, and I'd rather do the tests myself than rely on something that's been mass manufactured."

The bottom dropped out of Perry's stomach.

A dragonet.

Finch could be pregnant with a dragonet.

The conversation continued, but Perry heard very little of it. Awful, poisonous thoughts distracted him. In his mind's eye, he imagined a babe harbored in Finch and saw the life she might one day have. The love, the laughter, and the joy. She would experience all the things his own dragonet children had never been able to experience, would make her mark on the world and be marked by it in turn.

What color would her eyes be?

Her hair?

Would she grow up to be timid and shy, or as bold and colorful as Hugh's beloved Funfetti?

White-hot jealousy seared Perry from the inside.

If Finch were pregnant, he would get to know all those things that right now, he seemed so ungrateful for. When it came to Perry's own child—so badly wanted, yet so much at risk—he might never know.

It was a hideous, yet unshakable thought. Hating Finch for being able to have what he couldn't wasn't right, but it was easy, and after hundreds of years of heartbreak, it was a hard emotion to shake. But nothing productive would come of being bitter. Thinking ill of someone else would not give Perry the baby he wanted. So he reframed his thoughts.

Finch, much like himself, had been raised to believe that no dragon wanted a human child, and that they were a source of shame. It didn't matter if none of it was true—it hurt all the same. What Finch needed was support and, more than that, someone to listen. Not to judge.

No matter how bitter the taste in his mouth, it was the right thing to do.

Perry tuned back in to the conversation in time to hear Harrison ask if Finch would like Cleaver to show him to the door.

"No need," Perry said, cutting seamlessly into the conversation. With a tinkle of the bangles on his wrist, he rose and placed a gentle hand on the small of Finch's back. "I'll show our friend out. I'll be back shortly."

Perry steered Finch from the room. Once there was a door separating him from Harrison, he leaned in close and said, "Loving a dragon isn't always easy, especially when one isn't marked."

Finch flinched. "That really isn't any of your—"

"It's also hard to dream of children when you know, when you are *certain* in the deepest part of your heart, that you will never have them. That you will never have anything."

A shiver ran through Finch, whose posture tightened. There was silence for a moment, disrupted only by the sound of their footsteps. Out of the corner of his eye, Perry thought he saw a door farther down the hallway close, but it may have been just a trick of the light.

At last, with a tiny shake of his head, Finch said, "But you're mated to Sebastian and have been for half a millennium. You have everything."

If only he knew.

Perry smiled, but there was little joy in it. "Perhaps not everything. But my situation is neither here nor there."

"I don't think I can bear it," Finch admitted in despair. They reached the staircase and began their descent.

"Bear what, darling?"

"Seeing his disappointment. Seeing it reflected in his eyes every day that he sees me. I... I just can't."

Pain arrowed through Perry anew. "I think you sell yourself short," he said as they crossed the marble floor of the grand foyer. "And Hugh. You sell him short as well."

"My best-case scenario," Finch said bitterly, "is to be carrying a human Disgrace."

Perry took a moment to compose himself so he wouldn't lash out. Finch was only repeating what draconian society had believed for so long to be true, and lessons so deeply ingrained were difficult to shake. "Hugh can only father dragons and dragonets. There's no such thing as a Disgrace. A dragon's offspring, no matter what form they take, are never human. A dragon can only sire more dragons."

"It doesn't matter. None of it matters. Hugh doesn't want a Disgrace or a dragonet. He wants a clutch. All he's ever wanted was a clutch."

It was, perhaps, the truth as Finch knew it, but it wouldn't be the truth forever. Hugh's heart was larger than that.

He brought them to a stop by the mansion's large front door and smiled at the footman, Gerald, a Topaz transplant who'd yet to warm to life in Amethyst territory. "Gerald, please get Finch's coat and hat. He wishes to go home."

"Yes, sir."

Gerald bowed his head and went to fetch Finch's belongings.

When he was out of earshot, Finch shook his head. "I can't believe you know the names of servants that aren't even your own."

It seemed that Gerald was not the only one in need of warming to life as an Amethyst. Perry smiled. "I wasn't always the mate of a dragon. But never mind that. I think that you'll find Hugh doesn't really want a clutch."

Finch snorted. "I can assure you he does."

Perry squeezed Finch's hand. "I think that what Hugh wants is to be a father." Gerald reappeared, carrying with him what Perry could only assume was Finch's outerwear. "Oh, and look. Here's the very efficient Gerald now with your hat and coat. Think about what I said, Finch."

Finch nodded but said nothing and was gone shortly after, but in his absence, Perry's pain only grew. He wished he could reach out to Finch and tell him that he wasn't alone, that his pain was valid, and that there was a brilliant future ahead of him, but he couldn't. His was a suffering he shouldered alone, as it had been since the very first time he'd fallen pregnant all those years ago.

But maybe…

Perry slid a hand over what could—*would*—one day be a baby bump.

Maybe one day soon, that would change. He would see what Harrison had to say. The only way forward was to speak the truth and do away with the pretty lies he always told about his past. Hopefully it would be enough to save the babe.

It did not take Perry long to return to Harrison's office. When he arrived, the omega-beta was tapping the tip of a pen thoughtfully on the margin of an agenda, but he stopped and looked up when Perry entered, awarding him a beaming smile. "Hello, Perry! Thank you for helping Finch. He did seem awfully out of sorts."

"He did, the poor dear."

"Are you feeling out of sorts, too?" Harrison gestured invitingly at one of the armchairs in front of his desk. "Come have a seat and tell me what's been going on. Just remember that while I'm a doctor, I'm not a medical doctor yet, so if it's something serious, you're probably better off making an appointment with Ev. I wouldn't want my lack of practical experience to make things worse."

"That is very sweet of you." Perry came to sit in the armchair Harrison had gestured at, crossing one leg over the other and laying his hands daintily on his lap. "But you see, the reason I'm here today is because I have already been to see Everard, and I am left in want of a second opinion. One from an individual such as yourself, who I hope is more likely to understand."

"An individual such as me?" Harrison pushed his glasses up his nose and crossed his arms on the desk, leaning forward on his elbows. "Do you mean as a descendant of the Opal clan, Perry?"

"No, darling." Perry smiled thinly. "I mean as a dragonet."

"Oh." Harrison paused for a few seconds, seemingly to puzzle out his meaning. "Is there something the matter with your estrus cycle? The boys are eight now, so your heat is bound to start again at any time. Are you worried about being caught unaware? Because I sure was. Iggy says that as long as I can still feel the whelp bond I shouldn't worry about it, but it's so faint now that I'm sure it won't be long before it goes away completely. I've got some heat dampeners on standby, just in case, but I'm not even sure if I'll need them since I was born a beta. I can't wait to find out!"

"My heat resumed after the boys' seventh birthday," Perry confided in him once he was sure Harrison had finished speaking. "My latest heat began on the day of the children's birthday party. You remember the one?"

"Of course! Steve got to eat a strawberry. He's been talking about it ever since."

Perry paused. "I... suppose he did, yes. But all that aside, the reason I'm here has nothing to do with the regularity of my heats. They have, over the centuries, become more and more infrequent. I think it's because I'm getting older. I could be wrong, certainly, but that feels right. I have discussed it with Ingrid, the oldest dragonet I know, and she says the same is true for her, but seems to be less the case for Yinju." Perry shrugged. "But that has nothing to do with my motivation for coming here today. The trouble is..." He frowned. "I must confess, I haven't been entirely truthful with you, darling. I have not been truthful at all."

Harrison blinked. "What do you mean?"

"Many moons ago, I told you a fairy tale," Perry admitted. He chose his words with care, not only for Harrison's sake, but his own. "I did not do it for any nefarious purpose, I assure you. It's just that there are some things that are too painful to talk about, no matter how many years go by. You see..." Perry's lips wobbled, and he held back a sob. "I think there is something wrong with me. I do not know if it is some genetic defect, or if it is the result of an old injury, but there has to be something. It can't be a matter of unending bad luck. Not after five hundred years."

"I'm afraid I'm not sure what you're talking about." Harrison smiled hesitantly. "I'm happy to help you, but I need to know exactly what it is you think is wrong."

"I have been pregnant many dozens of times," Perry confessed in a hushed voice as centuries of old pain roiled inside of him.

"But I have only been able to carry two pregnancies to term, and both of them clutches, never dragonets."

Harrison, the dear, sat up quite straight. His eyes went very wide. "How many dozens?"

Perry closed his eyes and thought about something he usually tried not to dwell on. "The lost babes have become less common over the last three centuries or so, but added together, I think the number might be close to a hundred."

"A hundred. I can't believe it. It never even occurred to me that a mated dragonet could have so many children, but it makes sense. With two heats a year and without effective contraceptives or heat dampeners until relatively recently, there would be nothing stopping so many births from happening. Perhaps that's why some dragonets have fewer heats over time. I need to study that. I might have a hypothesis that—"

"Harry, darling, please focus. I do need you to help me. If you can."

"Oh. I do tend to go off onto tangents, don't I?"

Perry smiled, even though anxiety chewed through his heart. "Science is a hard taskmaster."

"Indeed it is." Harrison blinked at Perry. "Where was I? Oh! I meant to say I am so sorry. I can't imagine how terrible all of that must have been. What can I do to help?"

Perry dabbed his eyes with the sleeve of his blouse. "I'm pregnant again," he admitted. "Everard has told me the best course of action is to rest and stay hydrated, but I know something more is wrong. I suspect it has to do with this..." Perry unbuttoned his blouse to show Harrison his most shameful imperfection—four long pink scars spanning from his pectoral to his hip. Marks left by a dragon's claws. "This is an injury I sustained before I was Sebastian's mate, and while it was healed by magic, none of the Drakes were as skilled then as they are now, and medicine has come quite a long way. The original injuries did sink quite deep

83

and were longer than my scars. I fear there was internal damage done that has long gone unaddressed."

Harrison hummed thoughtfully and came out from behind his desk to look at the scars up close. "Would it be okay if I touched them, Perry?"

"Please do."

Harrison rubbed his hands together to warm them, then gently laid one of them over Perry's scars. "I'm not very good at magic," he admitted. "I've been learning it from Ev, but I'm still a beginner. If it hurts, tell me, and I'll stop."

Perry, who was well aware of how magic could be painful—even the kind meant to heal—nodded.

"Okay," Harrison said, taking a deep breath. "Here I go."

For a moment, nothing happened, then a rush of exploratory magic flowed through Perry. It was uncomfortably warm, but didn't burn, so he said nothing and allowed Harrison to work.

"Oh, wow. This is interesting." Harrison slid his hand from Perry's chest to his abdomen, below his scars. "You're right. At one time, these wounds were much larger. The tissue here is different than the tissue that surrounds it—a little tougher. It's recovered from the trauma, but signs of it have never really gone away. And..." The magic lurched. It was rather like being on a ship, if Perry's rising nausea was to be believed. He sank into the armchair and closed his eyes, hoping it would end before he retched all over Harrison's carpet. "Oh," Harrison breathed. "Oh, Perry. You are pregnant, aren't you? I can feel it. How neat."

"I'm sure you're having a marvelous time, darling," Perry said as cheerfully as he could, "but I am feeling a tad bit queasy. Would it be possible to wrap things up?"

"Oh, yes. Of course."

The pool of magic inside of Perry, once free-flowing, collected in a very small and centralized place low in his body. Perry breathed out a sigh of relief. While the heat of Harrison's magic was still somewhat uncomfortable, at least now he didn't feel at risk of losing his lunch.

The magic remained stationary for a few minutes before Harrison spoke again. "Like I said before, I'm not a doctor, and I'm certainly not a reproductive specialist, but I think you do have some scar tissue. The problem is, magic can't do much after an injury has already been healed, and it can't fix any natural defects. It's why Pavel needs his mechanical wing and leg brace, and why I still need glasses."

Perry's spirits sank. "So there's nothing that can be done?"

"Well…" Harrison pushed his lips to the side. "I can try to use a little magic, just to see what it will do. It can't hurt. The best-case scenario is that it changes something inside you that fixes the problem. The worst case is that it does nothing. Would you like me to try?"

"Please."

"Okay. Get ready. Here I go."

Perry had been healed with magic before, and even brought back from the brink of death thanks to its power. He had suffered through clumsy and painful attempts to knit wounds shut and, conversely, experienced how pleasant magic could be in the hands of an experienced user, but he had never felt any magic quite like this. It was a little clumsy, yes, but it was tentative and thoughtful instead of headstrong. Perhaps such was the difference between the power of a dragon and a dragonet.

In any case, the magic coalesced inside of him, shrinking down until it barely felt any larger than a pearl; burned hot and pulsed for a brief moment; then disappeared.

"There," Harrison said cheerfully as he took his hand away. "I hope it helps."

"As do I."

Perry buttoned his blouse and, once Harrison had stepped out of the way, stood. Physically he didn't feel any different than he had before, but there was hope in his heart now, and if nothing else, it alone was worth the risk.

"Do you promise to keep my secret?" Perry asked as Harrison saw him to the door. "The family doesn't know—not even Grimbold—and I'd prefer to keep it that way."

Harrison nodded. "Of course. It's a matter of doctor-patient confidentiality. Your secret is safe with me."

Perry kissed his cheek, which turned a pretty shade of pink. "You are a true friend, Harry."

Harrison lifted his hand to his cheek and smiled the same cheerful smile he always did. "Thank you. I really do try my best. But it's not all that hard when I have friends like you."

PEREGRINE

1508

It was not a second too soon when the ship moored and Sebastian carried Peregrine bridal-style onto dry land. From over Sebastian's shoulder, Peregrine watched a perturbed Alistair trail behind them, doing his very best to look anywhere but at them. In his efforts to avert his eyes, he failed to notice a raised board on the gangplank, tripped, and toppled with a shout into the Mediterranean.

"Brother," Sebastian grumbled.

Alistair splashed wildly in response. One or two of them sounded somewhat like, "Fuck!"

Sebastian set Peregrine down with a sigh, dropped to his knees, and gazed down at his brother. "Cease this at once. We must secure my omega."

"I'm *drowning*, Sebastian. Your omega can wait."

Sebastian grumbled again, this time with increased irritation, and hopped off the pier into the water.

While the two splashed around, Peregrine turned his back to

the ocean to take in the sights. Beirut was every bit as impressive as he had heard. Peregrine hadn't seen very much of the world, but he had never imagined a place could be so busy. A sea of heads crowded the port and, from what he could tell, the streets beyond. Stately buildings blotted out the skyline, sunlight sparkling off the veins of quartz streaked through their stone facades. Here the smell of the ocean mingled with spices and perfumes and smoke, and the babble of conversation he was used to in the streets back home sounded far more like a roar.

It was chaos, but it was fascinating.

So this was the world of dragons.

Peregrine vowed to remember it for the rest of his life.

"Out, you cumberground," Sebastian growled. There was a wet plop, which Peregrine turned to investigate.

There, on the pier, was a waterlogged Alistair. A tangle of seaweed crowned his head.

"I am no cumberground, brother." Alistair tore the seaweed off his head. "Nor am I a frog, which is why intervention was necessary. I am a creature of the sky, not the sea."

Sebastian pulled himself onto the pier. "And what, exactly, do you think I am?"

"Well, I don't take you for a frog, but you are by far a better swimmer than I am, and I'm not ashamed to ask for help when help is needed. Should you ever find yourself in need of a scholar, you know on whom to call."

Sebastian wrung water from his shirt, but it was of little help— he was well and truly soaked. It seemed to occur to him that he was fighting a losing battle, as he gave up the cause and left his brother to approach Peregrine.

Peregrine smiled sweetly at him, which did seem to improve Sebastian's mood, if only by the barest margin. He took Peregrine by the hand and, once he was secured, forged a path through the crowd.

"Sebastian, wait!" Alistair squawked. "There's water to shake out of my boot!"

"Shake it on the way." Sebastian's hand tightened around Peregrine's. "My omega has been sickly and needs his rest. We will not delay."

Peregrine looked over his shoulder at Alistair, who was hopping along behind them. It wasn't his place to meddle in the affairs of dragons, but to him, it didn't seem right.

"Please wait, my lord," Peregrine pleaded. "We're in no rush. I'm well."

Sebastian stopped immediately.

"We can wait for your brother to be ready," Peregrine said earnestly. "It won't take long."

Sebastian looked him over with wild eyes, their pupils huge and dark. It was the same look he gave Peregrine before he brought him to bed, and seeing it sent a shiver down Peregrine's spine.

Sebastian desired him.

What a strange, impossible, powerful thing.

"Thank you," said a hopping Alistair as he struggled to return his soaked boot to his foot. "I shan't be long. All it takes is a shake or two."

"Fine." Sebastian spoke in low tones, but his voice was loud in Peregrine's chest, where it made his heart pound. "We will wait."

"Some sense from you at last. You know, perhaps gallivanting about with this omega isn't as terrible as it seems if he's able to reason with you. Maybe next he can convince you to let me sun myself. The pier is radiantly warm."

Sebastian growled, and Alistair, surprised, gasped and fell straight on his ass with a squishy plop.

"Please, my lord," Peregrine murmured. "He means you no harm."

Sebastian's dark eyes turned on Peregrine. "You're right,

Perry," he said, then ran his fingers through Peregrine's curls. "I will be more gentle."

Pinpricks of pleasure shot through him. "Thank you, my lord."

Sebastian drew close and kissed him on the forehead. "Anything for you."

Sebastian obtained a room at an inn and made love to Peregrine through much of the night. When Peregrine was no longer able to come, the dragon gathered him in his arms and held him until they both fell asleep.

The following morning, they met a much-improved Alistair in the central room in anticipation of travel. Alistair was destined for Persia, where he planned to tour its largest and most culturally important cities to view and procure art. However, Persia was quite far, and would require them to shelter in several cities along the way. From Beirut, they would travel to Damascus, and then from there to more cities than Peregrine could recall. He knew very little about any of them, which turned out to be fine, as it seemed Sebastian knew equally little, if not less.

"Where are we to procure horses?" Sebastian demanded after they had broken their fast. "Did you happen to notice a stable?"

Alistair shook his head. "There are no horses. Only camels."

"Camels?"

"Yes, brother. Like horses, only sandier."

"I do not care for sandy horses."

"And you will care even less for walking." Alistair flapped a hand. "Leave it to me. Omega, can you ride?"

Peregrine blinked owlishly at Alistair. "Yes, my lord. I've been told I ride quite well, but you'll have to take my word for it. It would not be proper to show you."

"Proper?" Alistair narrowed his eyes. He spent a moment in thought, then clapped a hand over his mouth, aghast. "Lord, no!

No. I didn't mean it like that. What I meant to say is, can you ride a *camel?*"

"Oh." Peregrine thought about it. "I've never seen a camel before, so I suppose I'd have to try."

"It's much like riding a horse," Sebastian said, leaning in so his lips brushed Peregrine's temple while he spoke. "Or at least, so I assume. You will be fine. And if not, you will ride with me and I will make sure you are fine."

Peregrine's cheeks heated. "Yes, my lord. I would like that."

"Good." Sebastian kissed him. "Alistair, procure the camels. We will ride."

While Alistair went to arrange for their transportation, Peregrine lingered with Sebastian at the inn. There were fewer people present than there had been yesterday, and as a consequence, the room was quiet enough that Peregrine was able to hear an ongoing argument between a young man and the innkeeper.

"I have never heard a more ridiculous thing in my life," seethed the young man. He was dressed for travel and seemed to have come far, judging by his accent and the threadbare state of his clothing. It was impolite to eavesdrop, but his tone of voice was so aggressive that Peregrine couldn't help it. "You will let me stay."

"I will not," said the innkeeper. "You must go."

"All I need is—"

"You must go."

The young man balled his fists and tightened his shoulders. Peregrine was half convinced he was about to throw a punch, but instead he slammed a fist against the counter. It struck with enough force that Peregrine flinched.

"You will let me stay where I wish," the young man uttered, "or I will be forced to—"

"Forced to what?" interjected the innkeeper with a snort. "Do you think I'm afraid of a tiny omega like you? No. Now leave."

It seemed to Peregrine that the young man wasn't the kind who'd give up so easily, but to his surprise, he said nothing more and turned away from the counter. Doing so allowed Peregrine to get a look at his face.

The omega was exceptionally beautiful with large dark eyes and inky black hair. The sun had coaxed out color from his skin and darkened a spattering of freckles that stretched from cheek to cheek over the bridge of his nose. Peregrine thought there was a rather cunning look to him. It manifested as a sharpness in his eyes and a tightness in the way he pinched his full, lovely lips.

In the second or two Peregrine took to study him, the omega noticed him and came to a stop. He met and held Peregrine's gaze. It was unsettling. Peregrine had never had reason to be afraid of another omega before, and had no sensible reason to be afraid of this one, but goose bumps rose up his arms all the same.

It felt like the omega was peering straight into his very soul.

Only a second or two passed before the omega broke eye contact and went on his way, but it felt like much longer. It was fortunate Sebastian was there, as without him, Peregrine wasn't sure what he would do. It was ridiculous to think a stranger would cause him any kind of trouble, but something about him triggered an instinctual response in Peregrine that warned him to take heed. To ward it off, Peregrine took Sebastian's hand. The dragon perked right up and focused on him, and Peregrine rewarded his attention with a smile.

"Will it be long before the camels arrive?" he asked.

Sebastian shook his head. "No. Not long at all."

"Good. I'm very excited to meet them."

Sebastian smiled at him as though he were a very precious thing, and while he didn't pursue the conversation, he never let go of Peregrine's hand. It was a tremendous reassurance and a rare treat. Moments like these, quiet as they may be, were the ones he would remember when he was sent back to his cloister. A dragon's affection was a hoard-worthy treasure, and Peregrine was lucky to have it, even if only for a time.

The camels were not all that difficult to ride, although they did sway an awful lot. At first Peregrine fought against it, but when Alistair noticed, he informed them that it was best to move with the animal instead of against it.

Still, it was a hard thing to do when it felt like every swaying step would be the one to finally knock him off.

Thank goodness for Sebastian, who shared a camel with him. With his arms around Peregrine, an uncomely encounter with the ground was far less likely.

Unfortunately, the constant swaying wasn't the only issue. Camels, Peregrine discovered, were uncomfortable, and that wasn't a thing a dragon could fix. Within several hours, Peregrine was sore. It was a relief when they stopped to shake out their legs.

"We're making quiet excellent progress," said Alistair as he stretched his arms high over his head. "If we push onward at the same rate, we'll arrive in Damascus within two days. How are you holding up?"

Sebastian grunted in response. When Peregrine turned to see what he was doing, he found that Sebastian had come up on him from behind, and no sooner did they make eye contact than Sebastian whisked Peregrine into his arms. With seemingly little effort, the dragon cradled him to his chest. Peregrine, unsure of what to say, looked up at him with wide eyes. Sebastian looked down at him in turn, and although he seemingly did his best to keep his expression stoic, a hint of affection perked his lips.

"My omega is sore," Sebastian declared.

Peregrine colored. "It's no issue, my lord. I—"

"He is too delicate to ride by camelback," Sebastian continued, addressing Alistair even as he kept his attention focused on Peregrine. "I will carry him the rest of the way."

"We've a full twenty-four hours still to travel."

"I am aware."

"You can't tell me you intend to carry him for all that time."

Sebastian looked up and his eyes flashed a challenge. "I can and I will."

Alistair sighed in resignation and flapped a hand. "As you will. I know better than to try to convince you otherwise. But I will warn you, brother, that there is a long road ahead of us, and you may come to regret your choice after your thighs are made to work doubly hard for your indiscretion."

"My thighs will be fine." Sebastian carried Peregrine to the shade of a nearby tree, where he set him down in a seated position. In a quieter voice, he said, "And you will be fine, too, Perry. I vow it."

Peregrine knew not what to say, so he craned his neck to press a sweet kiss to Sebastian's jaw. It seemed an appropriate response, as Sebastian immediately sank to his knees and crowded Peregrine until his back was to the tree. Once he was in place, Sebastian kissed him deeply, and it was perfect. Simply perfect. Peregrine sighed into his mouth and, even if only for a moment, felt his pain melt away.

"Control yourself, brother," Alistair grumbled, but only half-heartedly. Peregrine heard the shuffle of his feet as he went elsewhere, likely to give them some privacy. It mattered not. Sebastian would not be intimate with him now—the kiss was only a precursor of what was to come later that night when Sebastian bred him, as he always did.

"How did you know I was sore?" Peregrine asked when the kiss concluded.

Sebastian touched their noses together. "I saw how you limped when you walked."

It seemed like such a small detail to notice, but Sebastian had noticed it all the same. Peregrine's heart beat wildly upon realizing it. All his life he'd been told that he didn't deserve even the smallest luxuries, as Disgraces were shameful and unwanted creatures, but the way Sebastian treated him proved those teachings wrong.

Maybe he did deserve the devotion of this handsome dragon.

And maybe, against all odds, he would bear him a clutch.

Wrapped up in the idea of such an impossible happily ever after, Peregrine tilted his head and brought their lips together again, kissing Sebastian with the same hesitant but excited passion that was bubbling up inside of him. Sebastian returned what Peregrine gave and doubled it, stripping all doubt and hesitancy away. A growl sounded in the back of his throat, and as it did, he threaded his fingers through Peregrine's curls and held him in place. It was a frightening sound, but it made Peregrine shiver not out of fear, but desire. In those low, rumbling tones he heard Sebastian's truth—that Peregrine was *his*. His for now. Maybe even his forever.

What a pretty dream.

If only it could be real.

When the kiss ended, Peregrine was short of breath and eager, despite Alistair's presence, to serve his dragon as only an omega could. He tilted his chin upward and angled his face to best feature its attractiveness, but his efforts were for naught. Sebastian pressed a chaste kiss to his lips and stood.

"Rest now," he said. "I will see to Alistair and make sure we are on track."

Peregrine nodded, and so off Sebastian went.

In his absence, Peregrine settled properly against the tree. Mistress Fokje had always said that sex was a duty, but with Sebastian, it didn't feel much like work at all.

While Peregrine thought on it, a blur of movement entered, then exited his peripheral vision. Startled, he turned his head to see what it was, but by then it was already gone.

Strange.

It must have been a bird—maybe one of the ones who made

their nests in the ground. If not that, then some other burrowing animal. It seemed the only reasonable explanation.

In any case, it wasn't worth fretting over. Peregrine pushed the thought from his mind, closed his eyes, and got comfortable. It wouldn't be long before they were back on the road, and before that happened, he needed all the rest he could get.

Sebastian kept his word and carried Peregrine for the rest of the day. It was a trifle awkward, but also lovely in unexpected ways. Peregrine spent the majority of his time in Sebastian's arms with his head rested against his chest and his eyes closed, committing the feel of his body and the subtle, clean notes of his scent to memory. When he bored of that, he used those new memories to daydream of what it would be like to carry Sebastian's clutch.

They stopped after it became too dark to safely continue. While Alistair and Sebastian set about establishing a campsite, Peregrine sat by the camels and watched them work. Alistair flitted this way and that, gesturing at one thing, then another while Sebastian tagged along behind him and did what Alistair instructed he do. By the looks of it, not only would they have a small fire to gather around tonight, but they'd have tents to shelter in as well.

How handy Sebastian was to be able to fashion something like that so quickly and with such ease.

What a wonderful provider he would be.

Smiling, Peregrine tucked his knees to his chest and rested his chin atop them. Tonight, he'd thank Sebastian for all his kindness with his body. He'd hold nothing back. He would ride Sebastian until—

A hand clamped over Peregrine's mouth and yanked him back-ward. Before he had time to yell, the cool kiss of a blade's edge cozied up to his neck.

"Don't make a sound," a familiar voice whispered. "I don't want to hurt you, but I will if you don't do what I say. I'll tell you everything you want to know later, but right now we need to go. Get up. Move quickly. And so help me, if you scream, it'll be the last sound you ever make."

11

SEBASTIAN

1508

It took every bit of self-control Sebastian possessed to keep from immolating his younger clutch-mate. Not that it would slow him down all that much. Alistair was the fastest healer in the family, bar Everard. The source of tonight's contention? Besides ordering Sebastian around as if he were a mere servant, Alistair wouldn't cease nattering on about the things he longed to see in Damascus. There were the ruins of Jupiter's temple, Trajan's Forum, the grand palace of the Caliphate, as well as the more mundane—but to Alistair, equally exciting—artisan market, where Alistair would no doubt squander his meager hoard on useless junk. The only time Sebastian was at all interested was when his brother spoke of the legendary steel of Damascus and their recently built, and very sturdy, city wall.

If Alistair was his typical flighty self, they might be in the city for weeks. Dawdling typically irritated Sebastian to no end, but perhaps in that time, he could have something fashioned for Peregrine out of the city's famous steel. A chain, perhaps, or a set of them. While not as coveted as gold, steel would be more durable, and the dark silver marbleized color would be gorgeous against Peregrine's pale skin.

He imagined the inky strands wound around the omega's wrists and ankles, draped over his slender waist, and encircling his hard and weeping cock.

Sebastian shivered in pleasure.

A few weeks in Damascus would not be intolerable should it result in that.

"Ho, there, brother," Alistair called out, sounding distressed. "I think you've erected enough tent poles for the night."

"What?" Sebastian was still distracted by his thoughts of flexible steel wrapped around Peregrine's lithe frame.

Alistair pointed down to Sebastian's groin with a grimace.

Sebastian looked down and saw he was sporting a sizable erection. "Oh, that. Since when are you put off by a cockstand?"

"Since it belongs to my oldest brother, who I know is about to use it on a sweet omega he doesn't deserve."

In seconds, Sebastian had his brother's frock grasped in his fist. He lifted Alistair into the air until his feet dangled. "Watch your tongue, brother," he hissed in a low tone that Alistair would hear, but Peregrine would not.

"It was merely a jest, brother! A simple jest!" Alistair struggled futilely in Sebastian's grasp. "Oh, do put me down. I meant no offense."

Sebastian gave his brother another shake for form's sake, then let go of his clothing. Alistair crumpled to the ground in an awkward heap.

"I say—" he began.

Sebastian, who was beginning to suspect something was wrong, scented the air. "Where's Peregrine?"

Alistair gave Sebastian a bewildered look. "Here. He's got to be here. Where else would he be? Do be sensible."

"Quiet, runt." Sebastian stalked about the camp, using all his senses, but Peregrine was nowhere to be found. He let out a mighty bellow of rage so loud, Alistair had to cover his ears.

"We'll find him, I swear." Alistair patted Sebastian's arm. "He can't have gone far."

The idea that he was gone at all terrified Sebastian down to his marrow. Peregrine was his and now, without him, Sebastian felt as lost as a babe in the woods. He let out another bellow.

"You sound like a badly wounded beast, brother."

Sebastian turned around to snarl at Alistair, who held up his hands in surrender.

"We'll find your omega, Sebastian. Never fear. It's not like he has any particularly good hiding places out here." He began to walk about the campsite, looking in spaces too small for even Peregrine to fit, and calling out the omega's name as if he were a lost kitten.

Sebastian moved away from their camp, shed his clothes, and transformed. Doing so was always a risk, but Sebastian was prepared to immolate anyone he came into contact with. And perhaps eat them. He was in that kind of mood.

No matter what, he would find Peregrine if it was the last thing he did.

Mine, his dragon roared. *Find, take, keep.*

Sebastian agreed, but deep down, he worried. It was unlike him, but he couldn't help the emotion any more than he could the beating of his heart.

Why had Peregrine run away?

Was it something he had done? Or perhaps not done?

Did the omega truly despise him that much?

When he found Peregrine, what could he do or say to make him stay?

What if he couldn't find him at all?

Heedless of Sebastian's morass of doubt, his dragon searched for Peregrine's scent and found it leaving the campsite. He had not left alone. There was the scent of another omega with him, and the scent was not wholly unfamiliar, but neither Sebastian nor his dragon could place it.

"Sebastian! What on God's earth do you think you're doing?"

Sebastian turned back to find Alistair standing there, hands on his hips, like a nursemaid scolding a naughty whelp.

Alistair glared at him. "Don't give me that look, sirrah."

That made Sebastian blow fire at Alistair, although he nimbly dodged it.

"Stop that at once!" Alistair huffed as he stomped out a bit of flame that had caught on a patch of desert grass. "You nearly set the tents on fire! And you can't just go rampaging about in that form. What if someone sees you? It'll be disastrous. You cannot be serious. He's only an omega!"

Sebastian lowered his great head until he could look his brother in the eye. In this form he couldn't speak, but he was quite adept at glaring. He growled and smoke poured from his nostrils and throat.

"Fine!" Alistair shouted, throwing his hands into the air with agitation. "Just don't say I didn't warn you when the natives go hunting for you and try to take your stupid, scaly head. It's not like anyone ever listens to me, anyway. Go hunt down your omega. Never mind that there's an Onyx cloister just on the other side of Constantinople."

Sebastian growled at Alistair again, then turned his back on his brother to follow the scent trail.

"My lord," his brother exclaimed. "You really do care for the omega, don't you? That is... well... it's... all right, then. I will come as well, if this is to be a noble quest."

With another huff, Sebastian set off, not waiting for Alistair to transform and uncaring of any human who might see him. The only thing of consequence was finding Peregrine, and after that, never letting the omega out of his sight again.

He roamed over the sand dunes, following in Peregrine's wake, nose skimming the ground like he was a large, scaly scent hound. Peripherally he was aware that Alistair had joined him, but he was a much smaller dragon, and he wisely kept a few steps behind. They traveled for quite some time until, suddenly, the scent trail mingled with a new smell.

Something sharp and unmistakable.

Blood.

Speckles of it darkened the sand.

It belonged to Peregrine.

Sebastian's heart tore, and he roared into the night sky.

Whoever had taken his omega would pay for every precious drop of blood they'd caused to spill. His teeth and talons would make sure of it.

The sun had dipped below the horizon before Sebastian spotted a small light ahead. A fire. He scented the air and smelled smoke. It obfuscated the other scents around them, but both Sebastian and his dragon knew that if Peregrine wasn't here, he was close. It wouldn't be long now before he was within reach.

The fire seemed to be coming from a pile of rocks that could've been a natural formation or the ruin of an ancient building. Sebastian signaled to Alistair, then crouched down in the lee of a nearby hillock. This close, the scent of blood was nearly overpowering, making his dragon crazed.

Kill, rend, maim, take, now now now.

No, Sebastian insisted, and transformed back into a man. His dragon continued to grumble about death and destruction, but he did it more quietly in the back of Sebastian's head.

Alistair cocked his head at his brother, clearly asking for instructions.

"Stay here and keep watch," Sebastian whispered. "I'll bring back Peregrine. If I call out to you, come to my aid. Otherwise, stay put."

Alistair gave Sebastian an incredulous look.

"'Tis naught but Peregrine and another omega that I scent. Does your nose tell you any different?"

With a slow shake of his head, Alistair agreed.

"Good." Sebastian patted the side of Alistair's jaw, then moved soundlessly on his bare human feet toward the flickering light. As he neared, he heard two voices speaking in a language he didn't know. Which was curious, as he'd only picked up on one scent. Alistair no doubt would recognize which language they were speaking, but that was neither here nor there. He could worry about an interrogation of the thieves once he'd reclaimed Peregrine.

Sneaking up on the bandits was child's play, as the two seemed far more intent on bickering than they did in paying attention to their surroundings. Sebastian hid himself behind a fat crumbling column and assessed the situation.

In the glow of the campfire stood a lean, wiry omega with dark hair. He held Peregrine close and pressed a knife to his throat. His partner in crime stood across from him, his face in shadow. He was a man, by the looks of him—far too tall and boxy to be any woman Sebastian had ever seen. This man could be a beta, but Sebastian sensed he was an alpha.

At first, Sebastian supposed the alpha was in charge, but despite not understanding the argument, it quickly became clear that the men were not working together. What Sebastian didn't know, however, was if that made the alpha an ally or a different sort of antagonist.

If not for the knife to Peregrine's throat, Sebastian would've already charged and gutted the omega, but he could see a thin trickle of blood run down Peregrine's neck from where the knife cut shallowly into his skin. If he were startled, the omega would likely cut Peregrine out of reflex and he'd die before Sebastian could even reach his body.

The best course of action, therefore, was to wait for an opportunity to strike.

While he waited, the dynamic of the tableau changed. The voice of the alpha grew deeper and darker. Almost, Sebastian thought, seductive. All the words did, however, was cause the dark-haired omega to startle. His hand jumped and more blood appeared on Peregrine's neck. Peregrine made a soft, keening noise of pain but otherwise held utterly still.

Then the omega did something unexpected.

Urging Peregrine along, he approached the alpha.

It was almost as if he couldn't resist the sound of his voice.

This was the chance Sebastian had been waiting for. He inched forward, ready to take a closer position to the ongoing events, when the omega stopped and looked up at the sky, and the man in the shadows stopped speaking.

Sebastian looked up as well. There, in the sky, was his hare-brained brother. He circled around them a few times, then dove down toward the kidnappers at breakneck speed. Knowing that his only chance of surprise was coming to an end, Sebastian leaped out from behind the pillar and ran toward the offending omega, praying to any god that would listen that he would be faster than the knife.

The omega wasn't looking at him, however. He was distracted by Alistair. Sebastian easily wrenched the knife from his hand and brandished it against the villain's neck instead. "Let my omega go," he snarled.

It seemed, for a second, like the omega would listen, but then there came a snarl from the shadows and out stepped the alpha. He was mid-transformation, but it mattered not. Sebastian recognized him at once.

It was Bertram.

Or Frederich.

Whatever name he was going by now, the family hadn't seen him in decades. Him being here, of all places, paralyzed Sebastian's brain. Much like Sebastian had feared would happen to Peregrine, Sebastian's knife cut clumsily into the dark-haired omega's neck as he fumbled it in surprise.

Blood bloomed on the blade.

The second the scent of it hit the air, Sebastian realized what he was doing and stopped, but Bertram's nostrils flared, and he rushed toward Sebastian with murder in his eyes.

"No!" Peregrine cried, and just as Bertram got within striking distance, he wriggled out of the other omega's loosened grasp and stood with his arms outstretched in front of Sebastian.

Bertram didn't stop. He tore into Peregrine, rending him down the chest with his wickedly sharp claws.

Peregrine shrieked in agony, but he did not back down.

He took all of Bertram's wrath into himself.

Sebastian let loose with a strangled cry and released the strange omega. Quick transformations were painful, but nothing could compare to the anguish he felt upon having failed Peregrine, and so he rushed into his dragon form. Scales and teeth and creaking bones changed him while his inner dragon roared as though it had been slain.

He would kill his brother for doing this.

He would tear him limb from worthless limb.

But before he had a chance to strike, Alistair thumped to the ground. His tail knocked out the fire, snuffing the only source of illumination.

Everything was plunged into inky darkness. Sebastian tore forth, intending to rip Bertram apart, but his brother was already gone, and without a scent to track him by, there was nothing Sebastian could do.

He snarled his rage into the emptiness, then pulled back his transformation and rushed through the dark to find Peregrine.

The villainous omega was gone now, and Peregrine was a crumpled heap on the ground.

"My love," Sebastian uttered as he dropped to his knees and pulled Peregrine's still body into his arms. Tears streamed down his cheeks and would not stop, no matter how he tried. "Oh, my love. Do not die. You cannot. Hold on just a little longer and I will find a way to make this right."

12

SEBASTIAN

Present Day

"Is the omega dead?" Sebastian pinched his cell phone to his ear with his shoulder as he held the metal post in place with one hand and twisted the wrench in his other. He'd been in the middle of assembling a new jungle gym for the boys when his brother Hugh had called to share troubling news. Apparently, an omega had drugged Hugh's beloved secretary, Finch, who he'd been unwittingly courting since forever. Commissioning Perry to smith that impractical dragon pipe now made sense. It had to have been a courting gift for the omega. Now, several weeks later, after Hugh had come to his senses and taken Finch's heat, the secretary was missing.

And while Hugh did not correlate his disappearance with the incident of weeks past, Sebastian was more discerning. Omegas were no threat to dragons, but toward other omegas, they could do quite a lot of damage.

Hugh's situation reminded Sebastian all too much of a time five hundred years ago that he would prefer to forget.

"Oh, no, not in the least," Hugh said. "I believe he remains very much alive. Bertram took off after him, but if he was smart, he evaded capture through the cellar door. But the strange omega is beside the point! Have you not been listening to the rest of what I've had to say? Sebastian, you must accompany me. Geoffrey says I must not leave Amethyst territory, but how does he expect me to stay in one place when Finch has been matenapped!"

"Kidnapped, you mean."

"Yes, but for mates."

"Is he your mate, then?"

"Well, no, not quite. But that is also beside the point! He will be. He is carrying my clutch, after all. It's simply a matter of time."

Sebastian grunted, but his impartiality did not derail Hugh, who continued his panicked monologue. "I found his cufflink, Sebastian," he said. "It was hidden under a piece of furniture, no doubt tossed there by Finch himself as he was forcibly removed from his room. Why else would he part with it? He loved those cufflinks so. They were a gift to him from me, you know. It was a rare sight to see him without them. He would never leave them behind, and especially not just one of them. What in the blazes is a man supposed to do with a solitary cufflink? The writing is on the wall! Or, in this case, under the armchair. Finch was kidnapped, and this was his way of crying out for my help. However, I am but one dragon, and I fear if the worst has come to pass and a group of unsavory secretary snatchers has set their sights on Finch, I won't be able to fend them all off. I need you to help me. You're very strong, you know. And large. And your teeth are very sharp. Come with me on my travels and help me recover my secretary. There's a very good chance that if you do, you'll be able to eat some very bad men along the way."

Sebastian's dragon perked up at the thought, but Sebastian ignored it. "But the omega has not been killed?"

"No. Why are you so hung up on this omega? I'm sure Bertram has dealt with him. There's no need to—"

"Bertram," Sebastian growled, "does not have an excellent track record when it comes to omegas."

"And I will not have an excellent track record when it comes to them, either, if you don't come at once and join me on my noble quest to recover my mate!"

Sebastian frowned. He truly did feel for Hugh, but if there was a rogue omega on the loose, Sebastian's hands were tied. Especially now. With Perry in such a delicate state, he could not leave. Not even for his brother. Should it come to it, and the council determined this omega a threat, he would go reluctantly on their command, but to traipse around the world while his brother searched for a secretary that could be anywhere? No. He would not risk it.

"I'm sorry, Hugh," Sebastian said. "I cannot."

"What?" Hugh sounded positively affronted. "But you adore eating horrible people."

"I do, but I cannot."

"Why?"

Sebastian set the wrench down and looked across the lawn at the skeleton of the jungle gym, then beyond it at the house, in which the ones he loved went about their day unaware that anything was amiss. "There are things I must tend to at home."

"Then you must pledge to keep my secret," Hugh huffed. "I will go after Finch with or without you, Sebastian, but you mustn't tell anyone."

"I shall not."

"Good, then. Thank you for listening, and if you'd like to change your mind, I will be glad to accept your help at any time. Goodbye, brother."

"Goodbye."

Sebastian hung up, tossed the phone to the side, and got back to work on the jungle gym. It was imperative he finish it soon, as there was another Drake he needed to speak with… and if the conversation went the way he thought it might, everything left undone would stay that way for quite some time.

"I need to see you, brother," Sebastian barked into his phone.

He sat in his study, his second-favorite room in the house. Even more than his hoard, it was his sanctuary, a leather and wood barrier between himself and the chaos outside. Not that Sebastian didn't enjoy a bit of chaos here and there, but the boys were often a bit much. Their sire's study was the one part of the house they were completely forbidden from entering unless they were to be punished. Thus, to the boys, his study was a realm of staring into corners, forfeited desserts, writing lines, and a general lack of fun.

They avoided it like the plague.

Sebastian, therefore, retreated into it whenever he had important calls to make, whether it be with the council, his father, or in this case, the thorn in his side.

"I'm busy," Bertram replied, sounding distracted. "Later would be better. I've got my hands full at the moment."

Sebastian growled low in his throat. "I need to see you *now.*"

"Now isn't convenient," Bertram growled back.

It was time for the big guns. "I need to see you now, Frederich."

Bertram was quiet for several seconds. "Will tomorrow suit?"

"I suppose." Sebastian didn't appreciate the delay, but he was willing to give his brother a bit of time to clean up whatever mess he'd gotten himself into.

"How generous of you. I can come by tomorrow afternoon."

"No. You here at the moment would not be good for Perry. He's delicate."

Bertram snorted. "Your mate is about as delicate as an anvil."

"I will call on you tomorrow, at your residence. I would advise you to be home." With that, Sebastian disconnected the call. He often missed actual telephones. Not that he'd enjoyed talking on them, but they'd been extremely satisfying to slam down after a heated conversation.

No sooner had the call concluded than Perry stuck his head through the doorway. "Dear. Are you well? You look growly."

"I was talking with my brother."

"Ah. That narrows the field. Which one, darling?"

"Bertram."

"Oh."

The color fled Perry's rosy cheeks, and seeing it constricted Sebastian's heart. He got up from behind his desk, went over to his mate, and gathered him in his arms. "All will be well," he promised.

Perry trembled. "That's what I always say."

"And are you not always right?"

"I am, but there's something you're not telling me. I can feel it."

If that was the case, it was up to Sebastian to ease his mate's worry. He pulled away from Perry and began to unbutton his shirt.

"Sebastian Drake." Perry arched an eyebrow. "What are you doing?"

"The opposite of hiding something from you." Sebastian shrugged off the shirt and unbuckled his belt.

"Darling, if this is your way of distracting me away from your deception, you're..."

Sebastian pushed his trousers down. Underneath he wore tight pink boxer briefs with hearts on them. A present from Perry.

"...possibly right."

"And just to show I've got nothing at all to hide—" Sebastian pulled his underwear down.

"Sebastian... are you trying to distract me with your manhood?" Perry eyed Sebastian's body appreciatively. "I will remember this later, I'll have you know."

Later could take care of itself. Right now Sebastian wanted a distraction and Perry needed one, so he took his cock in hand and stroked it, watching the avid expression on his mate's face and his corresponding arousal.

"You, sir," Perry chided, "are very naughty."

Sebastian put his hands on his hips and raised an eyebrow. "Are you going to punish me for it, love?"

Perry let out a trilling laugh that Sebastian treasured hearing. "Maybe later. For now, I think I'll have to reward you for your… transparency. Come closer, darling, and prove to me just how sure you are that all will be well."

Bertram's home was close to their father's and nearly identical on the outside. It was meticulously, if impersonally, landscaped and looked utterly unlived in. Even at his sire's imposing mansion there were signs of occupation. A holiday wreath on the door. Smoke rising from the many chimneys. Lights shining through windows. Paw prints marring a smooth blanket of snow. Here, nothing spoiled the appearance of perfection, but it was also sterile and unwelcoming.

Just as Bertram liked it.

Sebastian's driver pulled up to the front entrance and hurried to open the door of the Bentley for Sebastian. Once he had, Sebastian got out and stared up at the imposing edifice. It seemed calculated to repel visitors, but he had business with the master of the house, who had better be home if he knew what was good for him.

The door was answered with alacrity by Drummond, Bertram's butler. "Sir?" he intoned.

Sebastian nodded at him. "Show me to my brother."

"Just a wee moment, sir," Drummond said, then shut the large front door in Sebastian's face.

For a moment, Sebastian stood and stared the door down with

such irritation, it nearly ignited. How long would it take for him to burn it down, he wondered. It was wood, and it would certainly catch, but it was also quite thick and would require a fair amount of magic to entirely incinerate. The math told Sebastian it would take at least half of his magic, perhaps more, and he decided barging in through one of the windows would be much more efficient. The windows were alarmed, of course, but Sebastian only wanted in. He had no need to be stealthy about it.

Sebastian started to disrobe in preparation for shifting into dragon form. He'd be damned if he'd ruin his charcoal Vanquish suit over silliness from his sibling. Before he could remove his jacket, however, Drummond opened up the door anew.

"If sir will follow me," he said as though he hadn't done Sebastian the ultimate discourtesy by having him wait outside.

Sebastian was no stickler for etiquette, but really, this was too much.

Rather than follow Drummond, Sebastian passed the butler and followed his nose to Bertram's office. He opened the door without ceremony, then closed it behind him.

"Brother," he growled.

Bertram looked up from his computer monitor. "Where's Drummond?"

"Patrolling your corridors, no doubt."

Sebastian surveyed the room. It was paneled in cherry, the walls hung with wine-colored silk, and was furnished with elegant yet sturdy furniture. For all the room's richness, however, it, like the exterior of the house, was entirely sterile. The only notes of discord in the preternatural harmony were his brother's disheveled hair and something adhered to the case of his laptop.

"I do wish you wouldn't abuse my staff," Bertram said mildly, but there was steel under his pleasant tone.

"He shouldn't have left me cooling my heels, quite literally, on your front stoop. And I didn't abuse him. I didn't lay a finger on him."

"Nevertheless—"

Sebastian sat in a leather chair opposite his brother's desk. "Brother, I've come to discuss the rogue omega who has been terrorizing our family."

Bertram winced. "I don't suppose you're referring to Everard's mate."

Sebastian glared at his brother.

Bertram sighed. "I suppose you aren't, then. Ask your questions."

"Hugh," Sebastian began, "has recently related a very fantastical story to me. It appears a certain omega infiltrated his staff, abducted his secretary, and drugged him."

"That's not a question."

Sebastian ignored Bertram's interjection. "Then, too, we have the abduction of Reynard's clutch. It was six years ago, yes, but it was also by an omega. One you called Raven during the melee, who you prevented me from killing." Sebastian cracked his knuckles pointedly.

Bertram smiled blandly. "Still not a question."

"Five centuries ago, there was an omega who abducted Peregrine. I was prevented from killing that omega as well. By you. And your actions. My mate still bears the scars."

Again, Bertram winced. He also seemed to look, for him, uncharacteristically uneasy.

"The name of that omega was Raven, if I remember correctly. You confided to me that you'd take care of him."

Bertram's face went stony and he said nothing.

"Knowing all that, brother, why is there a sticker of a raven on your laptop?"

Bertram's eyes opened wide with surprise. "What the..." He pulled the laptop closed and saw the bird Sebastian referred to. "Fuck."

"That does seem to be the issue, doesn't it, brother?"

Bertram glowered at him. "What do you want to keep this information from our sire? Or have you already told him?"

"I have not tattled."

"Then why are you here?"

"This Raven. Have you captured him? Is he in your custody?"

Bertram paused, grimaced, and shook his head.

"Then I expect your help in protecting my mate. He is expecting and I won't have him harmed in any way by rogue omegas. Is that understood?"

Bertram wrinkled his brow. "Isn't it too soon for another clutch?"

"He is expecting a dragonet."

Bertram's face went dead pale and his features froze. "But—"

"Silence." Sebastian planted his palms on Bertram's desk and leaned forward until they were nose to nose. "Nothing," he uttered, "will endanger my child's safety or well-being. Absolutely nothing. That includes your wayward Raven. I will kill him if he gets near my mate. I vow it. Even if he does smell like family." Sebastian drew back and fixed his jacket. "I'm sure you understand."

Bertram said nothing, but he didn't need to. The wounded look in his eyes told Sebastian the message had been received.

So Sebastian left his brother's lair, passing a wandering Drummond on the way. He'd done well, he thought, and would sleep well tonight knowing that his most dangerous brother would now do anything to keep Perry safe.

13

PERRY

Present Day

"Uncle Bertram is here!"

The cry sounded down the hall, prompting a great commotion. One moment the lair was still and silent, the next it had erupted into a stampede of feet and a symphony of discordant shouts. A small army of eight-year-old boys skidded around the corner of the west wing, and in a mad dash of bare feet, flailing arms, flapping wings, and a few other less-than-human appendages, they rushed across the upper foyer and down the grand staircase.

Perry was delighted to see none of them topple over the railing.

Oh, how they'd grown.

"Uncle Bertram! Uncle Bertram!" piped the children as they arrived in the main foyer, their voices layering one atop another until it was almost impossible to discern who was speaking. "Hello, Uncle Bertram! What did you bring us this time?"

"Ah, a fine question, indeed, but what would be the fun in telling you when you can discover it for yourself instead? I've hidden a series of clues around the house, boys. Find them and they'll lead you to your prize. The first clue is waiting for you in the atrium. Last one there is a rotten egg."

The boys whooped and bellowed and proceeded to stampede away.

While they went, Perry came to lean on the upstairs railing and looked down upon the foyer below. The delicate body chains he wore, attached to the solid platinum collar shackled to his neck, twinkled as they made contact with the railing. The sound of them drew Bertram's attention. He looked up.

"Hello, Perry." Bertram tucked his hands in his back pockets and offered a dazzling smile. "Pardon the intrusion. You wouldn't happen to know the whereabouts of my brother, would you? He and I have some matters to discuss."

"I do indeed. Sebastian is in our hoard. Would you like for me to fetch him?"

"No need. I'll show myself in."

The fine hair on the back of Perry's neck stood on end. "You most certainly will not. The hoard is secured."

"Is that so?" Bertram's smile grew. "If that's the case, today's visit won't take nearly as long as I originally anticipated."

"What are you saying?" Perry pursed his lips. "What are you here to do, Bertram? There's always a purpose behind your visits —I know that well enough by now. You'd be wise to tell me. I very much do like to keep track of what's going on inside my own lair."

"You injure me, Perry." Bertram's smile persisted. "Is it wrong to want to pay my brother a visit?"

To engage in argument with Bertram was akin to howling at the moon in the hopes it would change its shape—futile, useless, and ultimately depleting. There was no sense in it. For Perry's own sanity, it was better not to engage.

Which wasn't to say that Perry was helpless.

Bertram could not be reasoned with, but like any Drake, he

could be influenced. All that was required was an act, and Perry was nothing if not an excellent actor.

"Of course not," Perry said, sweet as can be. "Why, I can't imagine what it would be like to live in a world where it wasn't proper to visit one's siblings. My boys would be so lonely, I'm sure. I'm thrilled for Sebastian that you'd visit... but darling, you really mustn't venture into our hoard. It's been left in an embarrassingly improper state, you see, and I doubt Sebastian has done anything since I've left to rectify it. I'm afraid that until it's been tidied, it's best you not enter lest you see all kinds of things no brother-in-law should ever see."

Bertram raised an eyebrow. "Is that so?"

"Quite." Perry stopped leaning on the railing and glided along it to the stairs, one hand dusting the surface of its cool gold plating. He descended a step at a time, never rushing, graceful as always. "To spare your eyes, I'll fetch Sebastian. It really is the least I can do."

Upon arriving at the bottom step, Perry came to a stop. When he was sure Bertram's eyes were on him, he lifted his chin and laid his hand reverently on the barely noticeable swell of his stomach. The child was a secret, of course, just as every human child of his had been, but there were few reasons why Bertram would arrive unannounced, and Perry did not think it was a coincidence he had done so in the midst of his pregnancy.

Bertram knew.

Perry wasn't sure how—although he had his suspicions—but he did know that now was no time to play his cards close to his chest. Something unusual was afoot, and if he wanted to be involved with it, it was in his best interest to prove he saw through Bertram's ruse.

A tense moment of silence passed. Bertram, hands still in his pockets, looked Perry up and down with great appreciation, then met his gaze. "Radiant as always, Perry. My brother has exquisite taste. I do so appreciate a good work of art."

Perry maintained a pleasant, somewhat neutral expression. "Thank you."

"It would be criminal of me to let a creature as fair as yourself fetch my lug of a brother. Your beauty ranks you leagues above such menial tasks. Go sit. Relax. Enjoy the sunshine. The day is bright and clear, perfect for basking. While you indulge, I'll show myself to my brother."

"Nonsense." Perry flashed him the prettiest smile he could muster and swept forward in a flutter of sheer chiffon and a tinkling of bangles. "Living art is not maintained by relaxation, you know. When you've had as many children as I have, you have to watch your figure. A little walking will do me some good. Besides, I shan't be long. I'll bring Sebastian back with me shortly and all three of us can chat. Wouldn't that be nice? Think of what kind of tea you'd like served while I'm gone. Oh, and do stay put, Bertram." Perry dimpled. "I would hate to have to send the children in search of you."

Bertram clicked his tongue and took his hands from his pockets to spread them, palms up, in concession. "I see I can't stop you. Very well. I'll wait here for you to return."

It was a small victory, but it was a victory nevertheless. Perry bowed his head in acknowledgment, grinned to himself, and spun on his heel to fetch Sebastian.

Sebastian was lounging, naked, on the hoard bed when Perry entered. Their sheets, rarely pristine but typically tidy, were crumpled about him, and the blanket was in a heap at the foot of the bed where Sebastian had kicked it when they'd made love half an hour ago. Coins and other precious things were scattered about the mattress and tucked into their bedding, some of which were spread across Sebastian's chest, down his stomach, and onto his groin. From amongst them, he'd selected a fat, round-cut ruby and held it aloft, passing the time by twisting it this way and that.

It was a short distance to the bed, but not one Perry was able to make with any kind of stealth. The *clink!* his anklets made as he moved prevented him from moving silently. Upon hearing his approach, Sebastian lifted his head. A moment later, a different, more southern part of his body did the same.

"Perry," Sebastian growled in the dark, seductive way that Perry favored. "Come. Be with me. I lust for you."

"And I lust for you, too, darling, but there is a dragon in our lair who wouldn't much appreciate it were we to ignore him for each other."

Sebastian sat up in a rush of arms and legs. "Who?"

"Your brother."

"Which one?"

"Bertram."

Sebastian swore and hurried out of bed. Gold coins tumbled to the floor, knocked from his body. He brushed a few off from the backs of his thighs and stomped through the treasure littering the area to grab yesterday's pants.

"Why is he here, Sebastian?" Perry asked while Sebastian dressed. "He won't say, but I know him—he wouldn't visit for hospitality's sake."

"It's no concern of yours, sweet." Sebastian tugged on the zipper of his fly, sending it clacking up its track. "Bertram is here to help fortify our lair."

"Fortify?"

"Yes."

"From what? We already restructured our security system following the Topaz attack all those years ago. Surely the measures we took to keep out hostile dragons should be enough to keep us safe?"

Sebastian shook his head.

"I love you with all my heart, Sebastian," Perry told him flatly, "but there are times I do so wish to strangle you."

"Tonight, after Bertram's left." Sebastian thumbed the button of his pants into place and lumbered, shirtless, toward the door. "I've heard it said one of my brothers enjoys such treatment. If that's the case, it can't be all that bad."

Perry blinked after him. "I beg your pardon?"

"Forget it." Sebastian paused in front of the door. "Try not to worry yourself, Perry. Nothing is wrong."

"Then why won't you tell me what's going on? I know that it's related to..." Perry's lower lip trembled, but he strengthened himself. Now more than ever he had to be strong. Sebastian and Bertram would not share their secrets with a man one wrong word away from breaking down. "To my pregnancy, but I can't figure out how. Thicker windows won't help keep the babe inside me. You know that."

A fearsome sound like old bones snapping came from Sebastian's direction. Scales the color of eggplant by midnight plunged down his spine and tumbled over his shoulders. There was a look to him that wasn't quite right—an unusual bulge in his muscle here and a troubling elongation of bone there—that made it seem like he'd been sketched by an artist from another planet who'd only ever heard a man described, but had never actually seen one.

Perry had seen Sebastian like this before, usually when he was moments away from slashing through something with his claws. That wasn't the case this time, but it spooked goose bumps out of him regardless.

It was, at times, easy to forget that Sebastian was dangerous.

Perry would not forget it again.

"True," Sebastian allowed after a time, his voice made raspy by the emergence of his dragon. "Windows won't help us keep the babe, but staying cool and collected might. Do not meddle in the affairs of dragons, Perry. I am simply trying to protect you."

"I am a dragon, Sebastian. Harrison—"

"I don't care what Harrison has to say," Sebastian snarled. "Until you have teeth and claws with which to defend yourself, I will not have you involved with ongoing events. All it would do is make you worry. Let me protect you like I always have. It's my duty as your lover and as your mate."

Sebastian's partial transformation began to recede, but while he could hide his dragon, there was no hiding the truth. Perry had seen him act this way before, and he knew by experience that Sebastian hadn't lashed out because he was angry—he'd done it because he was afraid.

"Sebastian..."

"Please, Perry," Sebastian said in a thin voice. "Please don't take this from me. I'm only trying to do what's best."

There was heartbreak in Sebastian's voice—Perry heard it as clear as anything—and it broke his heart as well.

"I love you, Sebastian." He took a small step toward the door, but didn't come any closer. There was a time and a place for physical affection, and now wasn't one of them. Sebastian did not need his touch, but his support. "I trust you."

Those three words undid the tension in Sebastian's shoulders and loosened his posture by a visible degree. The barest hint of a smile crept onto his face. "And I love you more than anything. I will see to it that no harm befalls you or the babe. I vow it."

Upon giving the oath, Sebastian left the hoard and with it, Perry, who stood in its midst. It wasn't the outcome Perry had wanted, but it was, he supposed, a small step in the right direction. Wars were rarely won from a single battle. In time he would discover the entirety of the truth, but for now he'd arm himself with the fragments he'd discovered from this morning's events.

One, that Bertram was somehow involved.

Two, that there was an outside threat related to his pregnancy fierce enough to scare even Sebastian.

And three, that the threat was not draconic in nature.

Or, if it was, not of the sort they'd faced before.

"Stubborn dragon," Perry murmured to himself as he exited the hoard and headed for the atrium, where he heard the children shouting. With some luck it was over Bertram's silly scavenger hunt and not because they were bothering Pake. Still, it warranted investigation. It would not do to let the boys believe there was no consequence to such rowdy behavior.

Before he could get far, a presence made itself known beside him. A hand slipped into his, soft and approximately the same size as his own. Visions of a time long past, when another delicate creature had blindsided him while he was alone and vulnerable, flashed through his mind—the kiss of sharpened steel as it bit into his neck and the frantic, whispered command he'd had no choice but to obey.

Out of instinct, Perry kept walking like nothing was wrong. The stranger beside him did the same, making sure to stay on the outskirts of his peripheral vision. All Perry could see of him was a black blur—his unwelcome visitor was wearing a hood, which prevented Perry from recognizing him by face. All was revealed, however, when the young man at Perry's side spoke. "I don't know why the *drakons* are keeping you in the dark, but I'm here to put an end to it."

Relief flooded through Perry. "Misha."

"*Da.* My apologies for having startled you, but you'll see that it was necessary. The *drakons* do not know I'm here, and I wish to keep it that way."

"Come." Perry tightened his grip on Misha's hand and led him into the nearest room—a large linen closet in which the staff kept fresh bedding and other cleaning supplies for use in the hoard. Compared to many of the rooms within their lair, it was small, but there was still plenty of space for two omegas to stand without feeling overly crowded.

Perry turned on the light and closed the door. "We can speak here. Neither Sebastian, Bertram, nor the children will think to check a linen closet should they come in search of me."

"Good, good." Misha elbowed a fitted sheet that had begun to slip off a nearby shelf back into place, then turned to face Perry. "It should come as no surprise to you that I actively monitor the Drake family's cybersecurity. Reynard... he's good... but he could be better. Two technological geniuses are always better than one. But I digress." Misha hurried a glance at his phone, which he took from his pocket and returned just as quickly. "Do you remember, before my clutch was hatched, that it was stolen?"

A chill burrowed into Perry's spine. "Yes. It was quite tragic, and nothing short of a miracle all of the eggs survived. I recall quite a few of the guilty parties were eaten that night."

"Yes, but not all." Misha tucked his hands into his pockets. "The mastermind behind the eggnapping escaped and has gone back to sticking his nose where it doesn't belong—in the Drake's digital domain. I wouldn't have noticed if it weren't for my interest in Bertram's accounts."

Not for the first time that day, discomfort prickled in the back of Perry's mind. "I'm not sure I'm following, darling. Why are Bertram's accounts interesting?"

"Because for the longest time, I had no idea they existed."

Perry bit his lip and crossed his arms nervously over his chest. "How could that be?"

"They were hidden in a way not even I could see, tucked behind layers of discreet security that took me two years to break through. Finding them at all was a fluke—I'd been tracking the digital signature of the scum who took my eggs and, to my surprise, it led me straight to them. It turns out the account Reynard tends to on Bertram's behalf is for appearances only. Bertram's real accounts are hidden so well, not even my mate knows they exist."

"Why would that be? It makes no sense. Bertram works for his father, and while he's not forthcoming about the exact details of his employment, it's no secret he does the council's bidding. Why would he need to hide his finances from Reynard?"

"Allow me to explain." Misha fished his phone from his pocket and tapped at it a few times, then turned its screen to face Perry. On it was a collection of things—financial figures, file names, and other digital offerings Perry did not understand. "Bertram receives regular deposits to the dummy account Reynard tends to. By all appearances it seems normal, albeit lacking in funds for a *drakon* of his age and reputation. But there are other funds he receives. They are deposited into his secret accounts and come from faceless entities. Shell accounts, most likely. I have not been able to determine who is sending these amounts, but I am determined to find out. It will take some time. My attention, you see, was diverted by something even more suspicious. Every month, a sizable figure—small for a *drakon*, but large for a mortal man— was being withdrawn from the secret account and being funneled into another. Upon closer investigation, I discovered that this secondary account has ties to the man who kidnapped my eggs. This, I assume, is why Bertram keeps it all hidden."

"That makes no sense," Perry said in a hushed voice. He checked over his shoulder to make sure the door was still firmly shut, then took a timid step toward Misha. "Bertram is a good dragon, Misha. The things he does, he does for the good of us all. He wouldn't have a criminal like the man who stole your clutch on his payroll... and if he does, then surely it has to be for a reason. Perhaps under guidance from the council."

"Ah, payroll. Yes. I understand your confusion. You see, the criminal is not on his payroll. The funds are being deducted from his personal accounts."

Perry widened his eyes. "I beg your pardon?"

"I was surprised, too. So I kept digging. I could not find the identity of the kidnapper, but I did find other suspicious things in Bertram's files. Documents, all of them individually encrypted. I have been working on a cypher, but there is no quick and easy way to recover the data. I have to do each one at a time, and I'm here today because I've finally cracked the code on the first file."

Misha clicked something on his screen, which loaded a document branded in the top right corner with a nameless seal that felt familiar, but that Perry couldn't place. There was no sender listed or any kind of return address, as there often were on such official-looking forms, but there was a file number and a subject line: Request for Immediate Detention and/or Neutralization.

The text below it was short and to the point.

Pursuant to activities reported on 01/11/2020, the threat posed to draconic society by the target has been escalated to level four. Detention is hereby requested with neutralization to follow should the target not be eliminated on sight.

Extreme caution is advised.

Perry scanned his memory for the date mentioned and gasped. "January eleventh is—"

"The date my eggs were stolen." Misha extinguished the screen of his phone and tucked it back into his pocket. "It confirms the 'target' mentioned in this briefing and the mastermind behind the kidnapping are one and the same."

A jolt of understanding struck Perry like lightning, but surely, it couldn't be the case. There had to be something he was missing —a detail he'd overlooked or a fact obfuscated by the astonishing coincidence of it all. What he was seeing couldn't be the entire truth, because that would mean...

No.

No, he wouldn't believe it.

He wouldn't so much as entertain the thought.

There had to be more. There had to be something he was missing. Misha would know. He was ever so clever with his devices. Surely there'd be another document he'd reveal that would shed new light on the situation, because right now, it was looking an awful lot like...

"What are you saying, Misha?" Perry asked, voice trembling despite his best efforts to stay strong. "Say it plainly. My head is spinning and I can't figure it out on my own. I need you to tell me exactly what it is you believe."

"I will, but I have a question for you before I can do that. Do you swear to tell me the truth?"

Perry's panicked heartbeat throbbed in his ears. If what he feared was true, he already knew what Misha would ask, and it terrified him. "Yes."

"Are you with child?"

The question struck like a slap across the face. Perry winced and squeezed his eyes shut, then dropped his chin and laid a worried hand over the swell of his stomach. "I am."

"I thought so. Based on what I know, it makes perfect sense."

It didn't.

It couldn't.

But it was, and while Perry wasn't savvy enough to confirm the validity of Misha's findings, he didn't doubt them. Misha had no reason to lie.

"What I believe," Misha said with a finality that chilled Perry to the very core, "is that Bertram Drake is working with the enemy, and now that he has come to your home, you and the child you carry are in danger."

14

PEREGRINE

1508

Pain like fire ate through Peregrine, worse than any he'd felt before. It tore through his skin and severed his muscle until it reached so deep, he was sure it would impale him entirely.

It didn't.

It did something worse.

It ripped downward and split him open.

As a child of the Pedigree, Peregrine had been taught the value of silence. Dragons who mated omegas for the purpose of fathering a clutch did not want mouthy partners who drew attention to themselves. No matter how painful or pleasurable the stimuli, moaning and screaming was discouraged, and while Peregrine had never expected to be chosen as a breeding partner, he'd learned to control himself all the same. With Sebastian, who was passionate and interested in breeding him even outside of his heat, keeping quiet had never been a consideration. Peregrine vocalized when he wanted to, never having to hold back out of fear of being reprimanded.

But now wasn't like those times.

Now Peregrine actively wanted to scream, only he couldn't. The sound wouldn't come.

His mouth fell open, but not so much as a gasp came out.

Was this what it felt like to die?

There came a great hiss of extinguished flame and with it, darkness, then a shuffling of scales dragged through sand.

Shouting. Men, shouting. Sebastian and others.

Footsteps.

Peregrine's understanding of the world warped and curved, and when it snapped back into place, he became aware that his clothes were saturated with fluid as warm as bathwater, but perfumed not with rose petals, but copper.

Blood.

"My love," came Sebastian's voice from nearby. It was barely more than a choked whisper, and it wavered with uncertainty and fear. "Oh, my love. Do not die. You cannot. Hold on just a little longer and I will find a way to make this right."

If only death could be wished away.

"Bertram," Sebastian roared. "I know you are here. *Fix this.*"

"With what?" came a voice from nearby. "We're in the middle of nowhere, Sebastian, and I'm on the job. You weren't supposed to interfere. None of this would have happened if it weren't for your intrusion. Raven is dangerous, but what was I supposed to do? The council wants him alive."

"A pox on the council!"

"You'd best watch your tongue. You are in no position to—"

"I can heal him!" came Alistair's voice. "I've been practicing. Surely I—" He stopped abruptly. "Good lord, he's nearly been carved in half. I'm not sure that even magic can—"

"Magic *will*," Sebastian growled. "Save him, Alistair."

Peregrine tried to open his eyes, but his eyelids would not budge. The world warped again and only snapped back into place when a burning feeling lit him up from the inside. It crackled through his veins and seared his muscles.

This time when he tried to scream, it echoed through the encampment.

"You're hurting him!" snarled Sebastian.

"I'm healing him! You have to be alive to scream! If I'd done nothing, he'd be silent, but dead."

The bickering went on, but so did the fire that was devouring Peregrine from the inside out. He screamed again, but this time it was hoarse and barely registered as a noise at all.

"You've punctured his squishy bits, Bertram," Alistair complained. "Look at this mess. I have no idea what any of this is, other than broken. I'll put him back together the best I can, but I'm no doctor. Someone must send for Everard."

A piercing pain deep inside Peregrine knocked the wind out of his lungs and the world off its axis. Darkness pushed in on him from all sides, heavier than it'd been before, and Peregrine knew that if he succumbed to it, it would mean death.

"Stay with me, Peregrine," Sebastian uttered. There were arms around him, and while the change in position brought with it a great deal of pain, it brought him comfort, too. If he were to die, at least he'd do so in the embrace of someone who cared.

His dragon. His lord. His Sebastian.

"Don't move him," Alistair snapped.

It was the last thing Peregrine heard before the darkness became too much and crushed him beneath its heel.

Death did not come easily. Between bouts of nothingness, Peregrine caught glimpses of the living world.

Sebastian's voice.

The dull thud of camel feet.

The sway of riding on camelback.

The feeling of Sebastian's strong arms around him.

Sometimes, when reality flooded back to him, it brought pain along with it. Sometimes it did not. Either way, it never lasted long. The darkness was always quick to rise up and drag him back into its depths.

After a time, perhaps hours or perhaps years later, the sway Peregrine associated with riding camelback ceased. Sebastian's arms went away. Even the sounds of conversation abandoned him. The next time the darkness let him escape, Peregrine woke swaddled in sheets and with a pillow tucked under his head. He still couldn't open his eyes, but the darkness was tinged with red, like sunlight bright enough to shine through his eyelids had fallen over his face.

All was silent for a while, then Sebastian spoke from some faraway place. "Where is Everard?"

"Delayed, I suppose. He said he was planning to fly. Perhaps there is bad weather."

"Bad weather won't stop a determined dragon from flying, Alistair."

"And a dead doctor won't stop what's wrong with your omega."

Sebastian grunted.

"I'll continue to treat him until Everard arrives," Alistair said. "It's kept him alive so far."

"But it hasn't managed to wake him up. He's not getting any better. The wounds—"

"Will heal when Everard arrives, I'm sure."

"They seep that awful, unnatural color."

"I don't know what to tell you. I'm a scholar, not a medical professional. The fact that he's yet to perish is a miracle."

This time Sebastian growled, but if the conversation continued, Peregrine didn't hear it. Searing pain throbbed inside of him and the darkness rose up and swallowed him again.

"He's full of rot," came a new voice the next time Peregrine awoke, this one barely masking its disgust. "The skin around his wounds has decayed and fever has all but eaten him up. Really, brother, you'd be better off finding a new omega. This one is fit for the grave."

"*Everard,*" Sebastian seethed. "You will heal him."

"Fine. If you insist. I suppose I did come all this way—it would be a shame to leave without making at least a little effort."

"*You will make more than a little effort.*"

"I always do. There's no need to bring out the scary voice, brother. You really must better learn to control your emotions."

Peregrine wished he could open his eyes, but he hadn't enough strength. All of his energy was being stolen away by a throbbing pain inside of him that pricked him like needles with every new beat of his heart.

"How long has he been like this?" The new voice—Everard—asked as a strange warmth rushed through Peregrine. It had the same feel to it as the fire that'd torn through him right after the attack, only this one was far easier to tolerate. It barely hurt at all.

"Close to a fortnight."

"How is it you managed to keep him alive? The boy's wounds are severe, and the rot has tunneled into him. By all accounts, he should be dead."

"Alistair used his magic to heal him."

"Alistair? Well, I'll be damned."

The warmth flowing through his veins pulled tightly on something painful inside of him, causing him to cry out and thrash. Both men by his bedside gasped and a large pair of hands grabbed him by the shoulders, anchoring him to the bed.

"Peregrine?" It was Sebastian. "Can you hear me?"

Peregrine could, but speaking was impossible. He was too lost to his pain and too exhausted to try to overcome it.

"Keep him still," Everard demanded. "We need to work the rot out or he'll never get any better. The pain will be intense, as the old wounds have to be opened to give it clear passage."

"You're hurting him, Everard!"

"I must, or he will die."

The pain increased. Not only was the warmth pulling on something, but it was splitting him open as well. Peregrine screamed, and screamed, and screamed, and it only ended when he fell back into the darkness.

———

The first time Peregrine opened his eyes following the attack, he found himself surrounded by the comforts of a quiet bedroom. Late-day sunlight streamed through a nearby window, its sheer curtains dancing in a gentle breeze that mitigated the worst of the afternoon heat. On the other side of the window, a fair distance from the wall, was a date palm heavy with fruit. Its sweet aroma drifted into the room.

Peregrine's stomach rumbled.

He was hungry.

From the window, he followed the room's intricately decorated arabesque walls to a large, ornate doorway with a pointed domed top. One of its extravagantly carved double doors had been left ajar.

"My lord?" Peregrine tried to call out, but his voice broke and it came out as a croak. How long had he been asleep? If his dry throat was any indication, it must have been years.

There came a rush of footsteps, then the door swung open and in stepped Alistair. There was a crazed look about him, as though he'd seen a ghost.

"Peregrine?" he asked as he hurried to the bedside. "You're awake?"

"I am."

"Lord, and you speak, too. Sebastian will be thrilled. We feared you might never awake."

"If that is true, I must have been unwell a long time indeed."

"It's been weeks," Alistair revealed. "Sebastian has procured for us this palace. It's south of Beirut, and quite lovely for being a smaller sort of town. There is a fascinating market filled with art and jewelry you might enjoy when you are well enough to stand. It—" Alistair stopped abruptly as one of the large pockets on the front of his gown wiggled. A moment later, a curious creature emerged from inside and tumbled clumsily onto the bedding. "Bother."

"What is that?" Peregrine asked.

"This," Alistair scooped the creature up, "is a tortoise. It was given to me by one of the local artists in appreciation for my patronage."

"Is it meant to be so small?"

"Yes. It is but a hatchling." Alistair approached the bedside and held the tortoise out on his open palm for Peregrine to inspect. It was quite small indeed. The creature barely took up a quarter of the dragon's hand. "It feeds on greens and other things. I was on my way to put it in the central garden when I thought I heard you, and rushed over to investigate."

The tortoise stretched its neck and blinked at Peregrine. It wore a shell like one might a tunic, covering its body so that only its neck, head, and limbs were exposed. Its skin was a dusty yellow-brown and its shell bore honeycomb-like patterns in the same color accented with dark brown. Each of its stumpy legs ended in four tiny claws. If not for its shell and its diminutive size, Peregrine thought it bore somewhat of a resemblance to a dragon.

"Here." Alistair set the creature on Peregrine's chest, where it began to wander across the sheets. "It can keep you company while I go fetch Sebastian. You may have it, if you wish. No doubt you'll take better care of it than I ever could."

Peregrine did not object, so off Alistair went. Once he'd left the room, Peregrine cautiously tested to see if he was strong enough to lift his arm, and when he discovered that he was, he extended a finger and used it to stroke the tortoise's head. It was very smooth and pleasing to the touch, and better yet, the tortoise seemed to enjoy it, too. It lifted its head to nuzzle Peregrine's finger and ambled across his chest in pursuit of it when Peregrine lowered his hand.

"Lus would adore you," Peregrine whispered to the tortoise as it climbed up and onto the back of his hand. "So I shall give you a Frisian name. You will be Pake."

Pake butted his face against the curve of Peregrine's knuckle as if to nuzzle it.

It seemed he had no objections.

A moment later, Sebastian appeared at the bedside. He'd grown whiskers. Peregrine quite fancied them.

"Peregrine?" he asked breathlessly.

"My lord, I—"

"Don't speak." Sebastian climbed into bed as nimbly as a man of his stature could and collected Peregrine in his arms, pressing kiss after kiss to the top of his head. While he did, Peregrine carefully collected Pake in his hand and set him aside, where he would be safe. "I will care for and protect you forever," Sebastian said. "I swear it."

There was no sense in arguing with a dragon, and even less in arguing with one as mighty and headstrong as Sebastian, who made his wants and needs perfectly clear. So rather than defy his lord and ask for food and drink, Peregrine nuzzled against Sebastian's chest and breathed him in.

He smelled not of the cloister, but he did smell of home.

"You are not allowed to die," Sebastian told him in a whisper after planting one last kiss on Peregrine's head. "I will not have it. Not now. Not ever. Do you understand?"

Peregrine nodded.

"You will not leave me again."

Sebastian held him closer and for a while, they sat with each other in silence, Peregrine on Sebastian's lap and Sebastian's nose in Peregrine's hair. The dragon truly was immense, and Peregrine was so small that he fit perfectly. It seemed to him that he could sit there forever and never once feel uncomfortable, like Sebastian had been made to hold him, and Peregrine to fit in his arms.

"We will rest here for quite some time," Sebastian said after the silence had stretched on long enough. "You are not yet well enough to travel. My brother Everard, the doctor who saw to your wounds, says you've sustained injuries that not even his magic can fix, but he's cured the worst of it. You are well now and you will not die. I will not let you, for you are mine."

Peregrine did not speak, for it would mean disobeying his lord, so he kissed Sebastian's collarbone to show his willingness to be claimed.

"You will have scars," Sebastian told him, and tenderly touched Peregrine's chest. "Everard says they will fade in time, but they will never disappear. They will decorate you like jewelry, each a badge of honor. Not many can say they've survived a fight with a dragon, but you will wear the proof on your skin and by doing so, prove without speaking that you are fierce and resilient—the perfect mate for me."

Sebastian had ordered silence, but upon hearing what he had to say, Peregrine could not keep quiet. "I am the son of a Disgrace, my lord. Young men like me do not make mates for dragons."

"No. You are my mate. Your lack of a mark will not make me question what my heart knows is the truth." Sebastian kissed Peregrine's curls and said into his hair, "Mine. Mine forever. My mate. *Mine.*"

With that said, Sebastian eased Peregrine into bed one kiss at a time until they lay beneath the sheets together. Held as close as he was to his dragon, Peregrine did not miss how Sebastian's erect cock pressed into his thigh, but despite his arousal, Sebastian did not try to breed him. They kissed and touched each other until Peregrine came prettily into his hand instead.

"My mate," Sebastian purred as he licked up the mess. "I will take care of you always."

Foggy-brained from his orgasm and still addled from the remnants of a fever, Peregrine dared to ask, "Does that mean my lord will fetch me water? I'm afraid if I go too much longer without it, I may perish."

As soon as he said it, Peregrine regretted how bold and assertive he'd sounded, but before he had a chance to apologize, Sebastian's face lit up as though he'd declared his eternal love. "Yes. Of course. At once."

Sebastian kissed Peregrine briefly on the nose, then rose from the bed and left the room to embark on his given quest. Peregrine stared after him, heart pounding from the rush. Not many survived a dragon attack, true, but even fewer could claim they'd ordered something of a dragon and walked away with their lives.

It would be the first time of many in the two weeks that followed that he would ask Sebastian to do his bidding, but with his heat creeping ever closer, what he planned to give in exchange more than made up for his hubris.

15

SEBASTIAN

1508

Sebastian was pleased with the palace he'd bought off a local official. It was large and airy, surrounded by private gardens, making it feel isolated, but was actually only a short walk to the nearest marketplace, which the people in this area insisted upon calling a bizarre. Sebastian supposed some of the things sold there could be considered strange, but mostly the marketplace had commonplace goods, like produce and meat and household items. Bizarre or not, however, it was convenient to be near one. The servants never had to travel very far to get anything that Peregrine might want or need.

The servants Sebastian found were not Attendants, but were nearly as good as them. Alistair, who spoke several languages, had been of tremendous help in hiring them on. Several of them even spoke some English, having worked for noble crusaders in the past. Apart from having saved Peregrine, it was about the most useful Alistair had ever been in his entire life, although the gift of the small tortoise came a close third. Sebastian might have been jealous if it weren't for the frank pleasure the small animal seemed to bring his mate.

Sebastian gazed at Peregrine's sleeping figure, covered only in thin, gauzy silk, and let out a small huff of smoke at that thought. Peregrine wasn't his mate. There was no mark. Likely there never would be one. Mates were extremely rare. Sebastian had only seen a handful in his entire life and had heard of maybe a score of them. The chances that this fragile omega—the son of a Disgrace, no less—would be his mate was smaller than he could calculate, and Sebastian was quite good at calculations. Nevertheless, Peregrine felt like the mate of his heart, and surely that was more important than any mark. He skimmed his hand over Peregrine's arse, torn by lust and worry. The weight Peregrine had put on over the course of their journey had been shed during his recovery, and he was so very thin.

True to form, Everard chose that moment to enter the bedchamber, an embarrassed Alistair in tow. Sebastian growled at them, smoke pouring from his nostrils.

"Now, now, brother," said Everard. "No need for that. I've come by to visit my patient one last time."

"One last time?" Sebastian asked, brows raised.

"Indeed. If your omega is well enough, I shall leave and take our scapegrace of a brother with me."

Alistair bristled. "I say. That's uncalled for."

Everard and Sebastian ignored him. Their eyes were on Peregrine, who sat up with a yawn and a stretch.

"Are you leaving, then?" Peregrine asked.

"If you are well enough to be left to my brother's tender mercies, then yes. I shall, of course, leave very strict instructions for you both, but I do think the danger is over." He held his hand to Peregrine's forehead, and Sebastian had to hold himself back from eviscerating him on the spot. "No more fever. That's very well. Eyes are focused. Your wounds have mostly healed and seem free from rot. Even your appetite is improved, if the servants are to be believed."

Peregrine nodded his head solemnly. "Indeed, Sir Dragon. I feel very much improved. I must thank you again for saving my life."

Everard waved the gratitude away. "Oh, I did it for purely selfish reasons. Sebastian is so very difficult when his playthings get broken. Healing you was by far the most convenient course of action."

Sebastian growled again, but Peregrine put his hand on Sebastian's leg and smiled sweetly up at Everard. "I am quite grateful for your shameless self-interest, then."

Everard quirked half a smile back.

"I helped, too," Alistair pointed out. "I kept him from dying."

"And I thank you for that, Sir Dragon," Peregrine told him with a dimpled smile.

Sebastian found himself wanting to defenestrate both of his clutch-mates.

Everard gave both Sebastian and Peregrine a long, searching look, then pointedly sniffed the air. "Ah, yes. I do believe we shall take our leave of you now."

"But—" Alistair protested.

"Now," Everard hissed, "and I do not mean a second longer. Come, brother, it's time we set out on this journey of yours to… what was the name of the city again?"

"Tehran. I think I've told you only a million times."

Everard pushed his brother to the door. "Exactly that. Now go to your room and make sure you have everything packed."

"I'm not a whelp," Alistair protested as Everard pushed him out the door and closed it behind him.

Everard leaned against the closed door. "I will leave instructions with the servants," he said, "since you won't be able to. I'm sure this isn't the first heat they've had to deal with, but it seems prudent all the same. But, dear brother," he pointed a finger at

Sebastian, "I do believe it shall be your first time, so here is what you should know. Peregrine will not want to eat, but you will have to make him. You must ensure he is given water, as he is likely to reject that, too. There is no need to gorge him, but regular maintenance is necessary for his continued healing. A bellyful of semen will not suffice. Am I understood?"

Sebastian shot a jet of flame at Everard that he easily dodged.

"Right then," continued Everard. "I'm off. And, by the way, you're welcome for me spiriting away our brother and taking up the mantle of minder. Which is to say, you owe me." Then, before Sebastian could respond, he opened up the bedchamber door and slid through it, shutting it behind him with a decided thud.

Peregrine rolled on the bed so he could look up at Sebastian. "My heat?" he asked. "However could your brother detect it when I cannot?"

Sebastian kissed the top of Peregrine's head, amongst his curls. "Everard has the ken of many things only he understands. But, damn his eyes, he's rarely wrong."

"We should rest then," Peregrine said decidedly. "If Everard is right, we shall need it. And if he's not, well, I think an afternoon nap sounds lovely. Don't you?"

Sebastian looked into Peregrine's crystalline blue eyes and thought there was nothing at all he could ever deny him.

Except his eggs. Should he fall gravid with a clutch.

Sebastian didn't like that thought one bit, so he pushed it to the back of his mind where it could not so easily prey upon him.

That night, Sebastian was woken by Peregrine thrashing beside him. He had kicked the thin silken bedclothes to the floor and yet still he dripped with sweat.

"So hot," he moaned.

Sebastian, in his much younger days, had secretly been with an omega in heat. A wild omega, not one from the Pedigree. It was frowned upon, but he'd been young, and allowances were made for the immaturity of youth. He had no way of knowing if his experience with Peregrine would be at all similar. Pedigree omegas were supposed to be different from the norm, but he was unsure as to how. Perhaps it was something he should have asked Everard, but his brothers had already departed and Sebastian wasn't about to leave his omega to hunt them down. He'd have to discover it for himself.

"I know, sweet," Sebastian replied, remembering how the long-ago omega had seemed to burn from the inside out. "Let me help."

He gathered Peregrine in his arms. The poor boy was drenched in sweat and hot to the touch. Sebastian might have worried it was from a resurgence of his earlier fever if it weren't for two things: Peregrine's pretty cock was erect and leaking, and the room had begun to smell of heat. It was honey, sweet summer apples, and ripe quince, and it made Sebastian's mouth water.

With Peregrine clutched to his chest, Sebastian abandoned the bed.

"Where are you taking me?" Peregrine asked, sounding pitifully afflicted.

"Somewhere cool."

Before Peregrine could ask another question, Sebastian strode out of their bedchamber and into the adjoining courtyard. In the middle of it was a shallow pool with a fountain. With no ceremony, Sebastian climbed in and took Peregrine with him. The water was fragranced with jasmine and was deliciously cool to his skin. It wasn't much, but he hoped it would bring Peregrine peace. What he should have had was piles of gold for Peregrine to luxuriate in, but it was all packed away. A serious oversight, despite Everard's warning.

I'll do better next time, he thought.

Still, as unsatisfactory as the water was in comparison to a proper hoard, Peregrine did seem to settle. He sank into the water and sighed, then looked up at Sebastian from beneath lust-lidded eyes. "I need you inside of me, my lord. Please."

"Mount me, then." Sebastian lifted Peregrine easily and gripped his buttocks, spreading him open. He sank his thumbs inside of him, and the boy cried out in pleasure and frustration.

"*More. Now.*"

Sebastian surged up, causing Peregrine to gasp as his slick channel was filled with Sebastian's cock. He very delicately wrapped his arms around Sebastian's neck and began to sway his hips, taking more and more of Sebastian into himself until all Sebastian could feel was the squeeze of his hot body as it bore down upon him.

It was greedy. Elegant, yet crude.

Perfect.

And as Peregrine began to bounce, it was almost more than Sebastian could take.

With a groan, he let his head roll forward and gave in to the pleasure of it all. Pedigree omegas *were* different. The lessons Peregrine had been taught had been so deeply internalized that even now, lost as he was to instinct, he knew how to bring Sebastian unparalleled pleasure. The way he rode, the tension in his body, and even the way he held himself so moonlight glinted in his hair and shone along the curve of his arched body was perfect. Sebastian had only just started, but he was already close to orgasm.

"I need your knot," Peregrine gasped as he worked Sebastian's cock, water splashing with every movement. "Breed me. Knot me. I'll die if you don't."

"No dying," Sebastian growled. "I won't allow it. Not ever. You are mine."

He took hold of Peregrine's hips then fucked up into him hard and fast, with absolutely no restraint. Peregrine's head lolled back and he screamed with pleasure.

Mine. Take. Breed. Claim.

143

Sebastian came inside his Peregrine, his knot inflating, binding them together.

Forever, his dragon proclaimed. *Mine.*

The hours melted into one another as Peregrine's heat held them in its grasp. Servants brought them food and jugs of cool water and sweet wine, leaving it discreetly outside their bedchamber door.

Sebastian fed Peregrine, bathed him, fucked him, and curled around him when they exhausted themselves. The time seemed to fly by, but also stretch into infinity.

Finally, though, the spell lifted, and Sebastian found himself waking up next to the slumbering body of his sated omega. He felt the stirrings of hunger, but had no desire to leave Peregrine's side.

Slowly, Peregrine stirred, then stretched his limbs like a cat. "It feels like my heat is over," he said with wonder. "How many days went by? Five? Six?"

Sebastian chuckled. "Three."

"Impossible. My heat never fades that quickly."

Sebastian laid his hand on Peregrine's taut belly. "I think," he said slowly, feeling like he might burst from pride, "there might be a reason why."

"Oh," Peregrine said. Then his eyes went wide. "Oh!"

He wrapped his arms around Sebastian, then burst into tears. Sebastian wasn't good with crying, but he went with his instincts, which were to hold Peregrine close and promise him things that somehow, someway, he'd find a way to fulfill.

16

SEBASTIAN

Present Day

"Sebastian, darling, we need to talk."

That was all it took for Sebastian to know he was in trouble. He reluctantly looked up from the figures he was studying on his computer, one brow raised.

"Oh, put that look away, dearest," Perry chirped. "Trying to look innocent will do you no good, you know."

"I wasn't trying to look like anything," Sebastian complained.

"Nonsense. You've been secretive and tiptoeing around me and I do not care for it one bit. And now Williams has told me she's under orders not to drive me anywhere? I wish to go shopping, darling. How am I supposed to get out of the house if not driven?"

Sebastian ignored the main gist of his mate's complaint and said, "There isn't anything you can't buy online."

Perry smiled, but it was hard and tight. Internally, Sebastian winced. "Oh, of course I can buy anything online, but I can't precisely shop, can I?"

Sebastian tried to puzzle that one out and lost, so he ignored it as well and just looked at Perry, trying, and likely failing, to seem patient.

"I see," Perry said, his tone darkening. He tapped a finger against his upper lip. "Well, Everard said that very gentle exercise would be good for me. I think I should like to go for a walk. It's quite mild out for the time of year, you know, and it would be a shame to waste such a great opportunity to go outside. I'll take the children to the park and sit while they play. I'm sure they'd be delighted, and I can't see Everard objecting to it."

A walk. Good lord. What a terrible idea. Their neighborhood was a gated community with security. Under normal circumstances, a short walk would be just the thing, but not now. Not with Bertram's little security problem endangering the family. Raven's hostility toward the most vulnerable of the Drakes meant that eight small boys and an unaccompanied pregnant omega would be too tempting a target. The very idea made Sebastian's blood run cold.

"No," he said. "I forbid it. I have built the whelps a jungle gym. It will be sufficient."

Perry opened his eyes wide. "I beg your pardon."

Heat flooded Sebastian's face, but he ignored it. He hated to make Perry angry or deny him anything, but this was too important. "No," he repeated. "It's not safe."

"I see," Perry said darkly. "Why, pray tell?"

Sebastian studied his computer monitor in the hopes it might give him a good answer to Perry's question.

It did not.

Perry came closer and leaned across the desk toward him in a series of dainty clinks and bright jingles. The small diamonds on one of the bangles he wore glinted brilliantly in the sun. "I need you to talk to me, darling," he said. "You must see that. You can't just wrap me up like a precious bauble and tuck me out of sight."

The hell I can't, Sebastian thought, but wisely didn't vocalize.

"Seb, darling, please."

Sebastian sighed. He was defenseless against Perry, and Perry knew it. "There are things I'm not supposed to discuss," he hedged. "I just want to keep you and our children safe. *All* of our children."

Perry's hand drifted down to his rounded belly. "Does this have anything to do with Bertram?"

That made Sebastian freeze in place. "Bertram? Why on earth would it have anything to do with my brother?"

After a tense moment in which Perry's lips tightened, he went to sit in one of the study's more comfortable leather chairs. It was made large to accommodate Sebastian's frame, and when seated in it, Perry looked like a child. Sebastian told himself to be careful. Youthful appearance or not, his mate was no child and had not been one for a very, very long time. Perry was intelligent. Frighteningly so. And Sebastian knew no other man—or reptile, for that matter—who possessed such uncanny insight. Sometimes, though, like now, Sebastian thought he was too smart for his own good.

"A little bird told me," Perry said at last.

Sebastian's eyes narrowed. "A little bird? Which little bird?"

"It doesn't matter. The important part is that I have reason to believe that you think I'm in danger and that Bertram is not to be trusted."

Misha. The informant could be no one else. He'd been there to witness Sebastian and Bertram's argument after the rescue of his clutch, and with a devious mind like his, must have seen it as an invitation to figure out what their little spat had been about. With his aptitude for technology and his sharp intellect, it was no wonder he'd discovered what it had taken Sebastian half a millennium to figure out—that Bertram's erratic behavior was linked to his ties with a certain troublesome omega.

One who, it seemed, never aged, and had not died despite being hundreds of years old.

"I'm keeping an eye on Bertram," Sebastian said. "As is

Reynard. And probably Everard, since he can't keep his snout out of anyone's business."

Perry's hand went back to stroking his stomach. A frown marred his lovely face. "So Bertram really isn't to be trusted, then?"

Sebastian frowned as well, contemplating how to explain his vague feelings and suspicions with Perry. "You know I would do anything for you."

"That is not an answer, Sebastian Drake."

"Then allow me to explain what I mean." Sebastian folded his arms on his desk and looked Perry in the eyes. "Think of what my brothers would sacrifice for their mates. Everard especially. What might he do to save his troublesome omega-beta?"

Perry bit his lip. "I think he might burn the world to ash to save Harry."

"Indeed. And of all my brothers, the one Everard most closely resembles is Bertram. They're both ruthless, clever, arrogant, single-minded, and pigheaded."

Perry gave him a wobbly smile. "That describes most dragons, darling."

Sebastian's lips twitched. "I suppose. But I think you know what I mean."

"I do."

"And what would Everard do if Harry went mad and started doing horrible things?"

Perry gasped. "Harrison would never! You bite your tongue."

Sebastian raked a hand through his hair. "Or Alistair? What would he do to save Ignatius? Or Father, for that matter. Can you imagine what he'd risk to keep Walter safe?"

"You can't be suggesting what I think you are," Perry said, sounding a little shaky, which was why Sebastian had not wanted to have this conversation in the first place. But it was unavoidable now. The truth would come out one way or another, and he'd much rather it be through channels under his control than those of anyone else.

"Unfortunately, I fear that is the case." The admission wounded Perry very much indeed. He frowned and lowered his gaze, near breaking Sebastian's heart, so he hastened to add, "Perry... you misunderstand. Bertram would never hurt you. He can be trusted to keep you safe, and he has a vested interest in making sure our current threat can't touch you. You needn't worry on that score. But..." Sebastian trailed off, not wanting to say what had to come next. What Perry, indeed, deserved to know, if he hadn't put the pieces of it together already.

"But if it comes down to my safety," Perry murmured, as though he was pained to put it into words, "or our child's safety, or the safety of our whelps, Bertram is not to be fully trusted. Not if... someone else... comes between us."

"Yes," Sebastian said with a heavy heart. "I'm afraid that's the case."

Perry frowned thoughtfully. "Has your brother found himself a mate and told no one?"

Sebastian would have loved to flat-out deny the outrageous statement, but knew Perry would see right through it. "I don't know," he admitted. "Not for certain."

Perry made a noncommittal noise. "Perhaps a better question is, who mated first in your family. You, or Bertram?"

"I don't know," Sebastian repeated. It was the truth. "I threatened to kill him, Perry. This mad omega who stalks our family. And I meant it. For you, I would snap off his head and feed on his still-beating heart."

Perry turned a delicate shade of green. "Please don't talk of eating relatives. Not even mad ones. My stomach is not up to it. The babe is squeamish, I'm afraid." He smiled worriedly down at his belly. Then his eyes flew up to stare into Sebastian's. "Oh," he said, horror dawning on his face. "Oh." Then his face crumpled and he began to cry.

Sebastian leapt out of his seat, took his mate into his arms, and held him close. "Don't cry. Please don't cry. I can't bear it when you do."

"I think Ignatius is right." Perry sniffed. "You are a lot of stupid lizards."

"What do you mean?"

"I've been cooped up in this house for ages and on the verge of going mad myself. And I've been very angry with you about it, darling, which I see now was unfair. If you had explained to me the reason why it was so important I stay in, I would have understood. Of course you don't want us in harm's way, but it goes so much deeper than that, doesn't it? For if your brother truly is mated to this mad omega and you are forced to kill him to save our lives, his ties to your brother mean you may end up killing Bertram as well."

"So you understand then," Sebastian whispered into Perry's curls. "I would do anything to keep you safe, Perry. Anything. Even that. But I do not wish to kill my brother. As misguided as he is, he is a Drake, and he is family. So will you keep safe? Will you do it for me?"

Perry was quiet for several moments. At last, he said, "Am I safe when I'm with you?"

"Always," he vowed. "Forever."

"No matter where we go?"

Sebastian wasn't sure he liked the sound of where his mate was going. "Perry," he said in a warning tone.

Perry disregarded it. "Please answer. Can you keep me and the children safe wherever we go?"

"Yes, but only because I will not allow you to endanger yourself or our family. Not even if I am there beside you."

"Will you allow us a trip to the park?"

Sebastian thought of how vulnerable they would all be. Nine souls he needed to guard and only one of him. It was the stuff of nightmares. Nevertheless, he wanted to make Perry happy.

"Give me a day," he conceded. "Or two. I'll see what I can do."

It ended up being three days. There was travel to arrange. Plans to disrupt. Hoards to secure. But in the end, they all came, just as Sebastian had asked. All that was left was for Sebastian to inform Perry that their plans could finally proceed.

He looked all over the house and finally found Perry in the atrium, sitting next to his tortoise. The creature had become quite massive over the last half millennium and was much larger than Perry, although that wasn't much of a feat. Despite Sebastian's attempts to put some meat on his omega's bones, Perry had stayed slender all these years, although never as miserably as he'd been when they'd first met. Pake, however, had grown into a formidable creature that even Sebastian would pause before trying to lift.

He was, in a word, a boulder.

An ancient, plodding boulder.

One who spent most of his time sleeping, but who was doted on all the same by Perry, who loved him to the moon and back.

Perry did not look up when Sebastian entered the room, but he no doubt knew he was there, as Sebastian had brought along the whelps, and they were a noisy bunch.

As the children flew across the room to join their father and his tortoise, Sebastian called out to his mate. "My love, I have a surprise for you."

Perry did look up then, but his eyes were dreamy, as if he'd been lost in a fantasy. "What sort of surprise?"

The children all settled around him and began to stroke Pake's moss-covered shell. Pake stretched his neck to look at the whelps on one side of him, then the other, before affectionately rubbing his head against the nearest whelp, Hadrian, who laughed and returned the gesture.

"The good kind," Sebastian assured him. He came to stand by Perry and took his hand, lifting him up. Perry, ever sweet, did not resist, and allowed Sebastian to lead him across the atrium toward the door.

"Where are you taking me?" he asked.

"The blue room," Sebastian replied. It was Perry's favorite parlor. "Come along, boys. Leave Pake be. It's time for the surprise."

Very little was able to pry the boys away from Pake when the tortoise was awake and active, but this did the trick. All eight of them scrambled to catch up, tripping over themselves in excitement. Even Cornelius, who was the most serious of the bunch.

"You're being very mysterious, Seb darling," Perry noted.

"For only a few minutes more, I assure you." Their small parade came upon the door to the blue room. "I have been hard at work to grant your request, and have found a solution we all can live with." He bent down and looked at the boys. "Would you like to go to the park?"

A deafening chorus of yeses followed. Maximus went so far as to punch the air. It was all too much. Sebastian held up his index finger in warning and the boys quieted at once.

"Now," Sebastian said, "you must listen closely to me. There are rules. No wandering from the playground and going off on your own. Any whelp who tries will forfeit his dessert tonight, and I've heard rumors it's chocolate cake."

The boys let out an appreciative and slightly awed, "Oooh."

"If you are told to do something, you do it. When it is time to go home, there will be no whining. Do I make myself clear?"

Eight small, dark heads nodded solemnly.

"Good. Now it's time to reveal the surprise."

Perry laughed. "I don't see what more you could give me. You've already given me exactly what I wanted, dearest."

"Sometimes," Sebastian intoned, "what we want and what we need aren't exactly the same thing." Then he opened the door.

The blue room was quite gorgeous. Its walls were painted a robin's-shell hue, and its furniture upholstered with fabric a few shades darker to create interest and draw the eye. Some of Perry's most treasured paintings from the 1800s hung on its walls in elaborate, gilded frames, but today they weren't the most valuable things in the room, for in its armchairs and on its couches sat five handsome young men, all of them with dark hair and eyes of varying shades of purple.

Sebastian and Perry's first clutch.

Perry clasped his hands to his mouth as tears formed in his eyes. "Oh. I... I don't... *boys?*"

Kian was the first to step forward. He hurried to Perry and hugged him hard. "Papa. I've missed you so much."

The other four pushed in for their hugs as well, even Arsaces and Sargon, who lived in Aurora.

Perry burst into tears, frightening the younger boys, but Sebastian squatted down to their height to reassure them. "They're happy tears, boys. Everything is fine, I promise."

It was not exactly the truth, but it would do. The boys need not concern themselves with matters beyond their control. To them, their brothers' visit wasn't anything beyond a happy coincidence, and Sebastian would do all he could to make sure it stayed that way. They did not need to know that their brothers had come to help keep them safe.

Amidst a flurry of hugs, a small voice piped up loud enough to be heard by all. "Are we going to the playground or not? Because you said we were." It was, of course, Cornelius, who took all things so seriously.

Perry laughed, but it sounded a bit watery. "Yes, my darlings. Go grab your coats and let's go."

17

PERRY

Present Day

The Drake family filled the playground nearly to capacity. Between eight boys and their five adult shadows, the jungle gym was overrun. It was a blessing the children hadn't decided to bicker over the swings. Originally there had been six of them, but after a squabble last year, there were only five.

Five, and one sad, melted rubber blob.

The children did sometimes like to stand on it and swing upright, but with their older brothers present, they gave it a wide berth. Perry had scolded them within an inch of their lives after the incident had occurred, but there was no shame quite like the disapproval of an older sibling, and the boys did so idolize their adult brothers.

"Papa!" Octavius called from the very top of the jungle gym, near the largest slide. He bounced up so his feet were slotted between the balusters of the security railing surrounding the slide's platform and waved high over his head so Perry would see. "Papa, look, I'm going to fly down the slide! I'm going to go so fast, I'll be a blur. Watch me!"

Osric, who'd followed him all the way to the top of the jungle gym, leaned down to whisper something in Octavius's ear that made the boy clap both hands over his mouth.

After a moment of intense dread, he popped back up and cried, "By fly, I just meant I'll go really fast! Not anything else! Everyone knows boys can't fly."

With that said, Octavius flung himself down the slide in an apparent attempt to escape rebuke for his indiscretions.

He was, indeed, quite the blur.

Osric sighed and followed him down much more slowly. Even with his legs folded to his chest and his hips angled slightly to the side, he was too large to make the journey without getting stuck multiple times. Of all the older boys, he resembled Sebastian the most. Perry was very proud of him. Being so large was no easy thing. In this day and age, where eating people was slightly more frowned upon, sustaining such musculature was a near impossible feat.

While Perry watched the children play and the older boys shepherd them, Sebastian came back from scouting the perimeter to sit beside him on the park bench. Once he was seated, he tucked Perry protectively beneath his arm. "Is it everything you dreamed it would be?"

"No. It's even more wonderful." Perry snuggled closer to Sebastian and rested his head on his chest. "I haven't a clue how you arranged for the older boys to come home, but it's made me uncommonly happy. Do you know if they'll stay for long? I miss them so. If I could, I'd keep them here with us forever."

"I've asked them to stay for a time." While Sebastian spoke, his eyes were on the playground, ever watching the children. "Some will need to come and go, but with any luck, we should have at least a few of them with us on any given day."

"For how long?"

"For however long it takes."

While Sebastian spoke plainly enough, Perry was attuned to

him more than most, and he heard the pain behind his words. And try as he might to cover up his emotions with impartiality, hints of what Sebastian felt trickled into their bond. It made it far too obvious what he implied.

Sebastian was preparing himself for the death of his brother.

It wasn't something Perry cared to think about, but it was a possibility he had no choice but to confront.

"All will be well, Sebastian," he whispered, and laid a hand delicately atop Sebastian's thigh. "Life always has a way of going in directions we never imagined possible. Perhaps now is one of those times."

"Therein lies the problem—now is one of those times."

Perry frowned. "Have faith, my love."

"I have it." Sebastian pressed a kiss to the top of Perry's head and spoke into his curls. "I believe that no matter what happens, the choices I make to protect you and our children will be correct."

Before Perry could respond, a young voice distracted him.

"Papa! Papa! Look!" Hadrian shouted from the monkey bars. To Perry's immense displeasure, he was hanging from them upside down by his legs. "I'm a bat!"

"Yes, darling! And what a bat you are. Kian, please see to it that our adorable bewinged mammal doesn't take a tumble... or decide to try his hand at making guano."

"I will," Kian vowed. "All will be well."

Sebastian blew air through his nose. "Say what you'd like, but resemble me as they might on the outside, the boys take after you."

Perry arched a brow and pushed back from Sebastian's chest to look him in the eyes. "Are you calling me a bat, darling?"

"No." Sebastian drew Perry effortlessly onto his lap. "I'm saying that you are the reason our grown sons are kind, compassionate, giving young men who have made, and will continue to make, an impact on our world."

"Funny." Perry carded his fingers through Sebastian's hair, a hint of a smile perking his lips. "Those are exactly the reasons I'd say they take after you."

Sebastian, eyes aflame with unmet desire, cupped Perry's face with both hands and drew him into a passionate kiss.

"Gross!" one of the younger boys shouted.

A chorus of agreement followed, which devolved into the younger boys running at top speed across the playground, gagging, while their older brothers ran after them in a fruitless quest to get them to stop.

"I suppose we should be more mindful," Perry conceded as he slipped from Sebastian's lap back onto the park bench. "We are in public, after all, and while our brood has chased off everyone with common sense, there could still be a passerby who spots us and causes a fuss, sure to the very fiber of their being that you, you very naughty dragon, are getting ready to be inappropriate with the teenage babysitter."

Sebastian snorted. "What a day that was."

"I'll never forget the look the police gave you when you told them I'd fathered every boy in the park."

Sebastian laced their fingers together. It was about as close to a smile as he'd come while in public, and while it was a small act, it made Perry's heart race madly. Sebastian, his handsome, stoic dragon, had chosen him, and continued to choose him every day. In five hundred years, that hadn't changed. Through tremendous loss and gain, he remained true.

"One day," Sebastian said quietly, "there will come a time when you and I can come here again without having to call our sons in from across the land. When that time comes, all will return to normal. I vow it."

"I know." Perry rested his head on Sebastian's shoulder, eyes on the playground, where Hadrian and Maximus were digging a brother-sized hole in the sand. Cornelius, clueless, supervised. "I don't like to have my freedom taken from me, but I'm aware you

157

wouldn't do it if it weren't absolutely necessary. But will you promise me just one thing?"

"Speak it and we'll see."

"Will you please, *please* keep me informed as to the situation? I know you fear I won't fare well in my delicate state, but I'm stronger than you think. I'd much rather be nervous and well-prepared than unaware and at risk."

Sebastian's grip tightened. It wasn't painful, but it was a near thing.

"Please, Sebastian?" Perry whispered. "It's all I ask."

For a long while, Perry received no reply. When it got to the point where a response seemed unlikely, he frowned, but before he could voice his displeasure, Sebastian lifted his hand to his lips and kissed it. "Very well. Should anything happen, I'll be sure to let you know."

"Thank you."

"Anything for you, Perry." Sebastian lowered their hands to rest in the scant space between their bodies. "You've given me everything. I can only dream that one day I'll be able to pass back a fraction of the happiness you've brought me. If this is what makes you happy, so be it."

"Papa?" a new voice asked. It came not from Sebastian, but from the young boy who'd bounded up to the bench while Perry hadn't been looking.

It was Elian, whose trousers were grass-stained and whose palms were dirty. He looked as apprehensive as he sounded, which was never a good thing. The boys, by virtue of their father, were not the timid sort.

"Yes, darling?" Perry asked.

"Cornelius is stuck in a hole and Maximus and Hadrian can't get him out. Can you help? He says he needs to use the bathroom."

"Oh, dear." Perry slipped his hand out of Sebastian's and rose, but Sebastian was quicker, and he was off across the playground before Perry could so much as take Elian's hand. He joined a flustered Arsaces by the burial mound, dropped to his knees, and dug into the sand like a hound through dirt. The boys had been particularly industrious, so there was a fair amount of sand to move, but Sebastian made quick work of it.

Once Cornelius had been excavated to a satisfactory degree, Sebastian lifted him out of the hole. Cornelius promptly darted behind the nearest bush to do what it was young boys in bushes did.

"You're a good boy for coming forward and telling us, Elian," Perry told his son. He bent down to kiss him atop his head, which smelled of sunshine and faintly of shampoo. "Your brother will remember your kindness, and so will I."

"You're not gonna get mad at Maximus and Hadrian, are you?"

"Did they put Cornelius in the hole against his will?"

"No."

"Then no, darling. There's nothing to be upset about." Unusual movement in the area of Cornelius's chosen bush drew Perry's eye. Octavius had joined him. Osric, arms crossed and expression stoic, stood with his back to them, the perfect image of a bodyguard. "Although I do think that perhaps it's time to leave. That poor bush deserves a repose. We'll take our business home to the toilet, where it belongs."

Sebastian, whether through suggestion via their bond or his own parenting instincts, began to herd the remaining boys in the direction of Perry's park bench.

"But I don't need to go." Elian looked up at Perry imploringly. "Can I please stay? You can stay with me. Father can take everyone else home to use the bathroom and we can stay and play. Just you and me."

"You have no idea how much I'd love that, darling, but it simply cannot be." Perry held out his hand, which Elian took. At eight years old, the boys were rambunctious, but they had yet to reach the age where they shied away from his affection. It would be upon them soon, though, so Perry intended to cherish every hug, kiss, and held hand he had left. "Now that your older brothers are home, perhaps we can come to the park more often, but we can't stay here today all by ourselves. You wouldn't want to waste the time we could spend together with brothers, would you? They're so rarely able to visit."

"Oh. You're right." Elian gave him a large, gap-toothed smile. "Next time we come back, I want you to push me on the swing."

Perry smiled. "That does sound like fun, doesn't it?"

The other children began to arrive, and soon enough all eight had been assembled. Perry and Sebastian took the lead while the older boys walked behind to make sure none of their younger brothers wandered off along the way. Apart from a little rough-housing, the way home was uneventful, and all eight boys and their five adult brothers arrived in one piece.

No sooner had they arrived, than they scattered and were gone.

In the quiet that followed, Perry heard Sebastian approach him from behind. It came as no surprise when he slipped his arms around Perry and drew him close.

"I love you, Perry," he whispered into Perry's curls. "My heart. My soul. My perfect mate."

Perry had heard such declarations often over the last five hundred years, but they never lost their sparkle. Entire millennia could come and go and he imagined they'd always feel this way— bright, exciting, and new.

"And I love you, Sebastian," he whispered back, lifting his chin to allow Sebastian to kiss him, which he did. "We've weathered hell and come out stronger for it. Whatever happens, we will weather this, too."

Sebastian grunted in agreement, then scooped Perry into his arms and carried him off to where no whelp would find them. With some luck, the dangers plaguing them would lose their way, too.

In the months following the trip to the park, the lair felt less like a prison, but even with his older children home, being cooped up began to weigh on Perry, who knew that life continued on without him beyond the walls of the estate. He thought often of Grimbold Drake, patriarch of the Drake family, and his new mate, Walter, who was expecting a dragonet, and also of Finch, who'd absconded to parts unknown after last Perry had seen him. It bothered him to no end that he wasn't able to check on Hugh, who he was sure was distraught, or wrap sweet Walter in his arms and assure him that a dragonet was not a curse, but a gift to be cherished.

It bothered him even more to think he wouldn't be able to attend the birth of Grimbold and Walter's daughter and personally extend his congratulations, as was proper.

The only things that made confinement bearable—apart from his boys, of course—were the small acts of kindness Sebastian bequeathed onto him every day. There was always something. One day it was a box of sweets left on his bedside, the next a golden anklet studded with pinprick diamonds. Sometimes it was soaps and fragrances, new riches to add to their hoard, or colorful embroidery silks for the tapestry he was working on. On one very particular occasion, it was a love note with a very bad poem written in Sebastian's hand.

Perry loved it most of all.

On this particular night, though, Sebastian's act of kindness was not material—he sat at the foot of their bed after a particularly long and tiring day and rubbed Perry's swollen feet and ankles. He used far too much of a lavender-scented cream to do it. Perry would have to sleep in socks so as not to ruin the bedding, but it was a small concession. Perry wouldn't trade the massage for anything.

Sebastian was not much of a conversationalist, so while he worked, Perry filled the silence for him.

"Kian is leaving tomorrow, and says he'll be gone for a few days—perhaps up to a week. He alleges there's business he must tend to in England, of all places. Can you believe it? I haven't a clue why the English Drakes would need our American boys to step in and handle matters for them, but I suppose I've yet to hear the full story and therefore shouldn't pass judgment."

"There are other Amethyst families in England as well, Perry. Not just the Drakes."

"Yes, but the Drakes are the ones out of all of them who will get done what needs to be done. It seems strange to me that the English branch of our family would be indisposed. Why call in Kian to settle things? It's all very odd, if you ask me."

"Kian is more skilled than any English Drake. All of our boys are."

"True."

"That's not really what's on your mind, is it?"

Perry fanned his toes, then wiggled them. His gaze passed from his foot up Sebastian's bare thighs to his chest, which was likewise bare. It was a short journey from there to Sebastian's unreadable face.

"No, I suppose not," he said after a moment spent in admiration of his lover. "I know that Kian is more skilled and therefore in demand, but… I can't help but daydream there's more going on than meets the eye. I'm bored with being trapped here, Sebastian. I want to know what's changed since I lost my freedom. What of Walter? He must be distraught I'm not available to visit. Has his pregnancy been going well? He's two months short of giving birth, if my memory hasn't failed me. Tell me it's been easy for him. The poor boy deserves only the best."

Sebastian added a pump of lotion to his palm.

Socks were now a certainty.

"I don't know."

162

"What do you mean, you don't know?" Perry propped himself up on his elbows. "He's your father's mate."

"Yes."

"Which means the babe he's carrying will be your sister."

"Yes."

"So matters pertaining to the pregnancy must concern you." Perry hesitated. "Right?"

Sebastian shrugged and worked his thumb into the arch of Perry's foot. The pleasure brought by his touch was otherworldly and likely heightened by an infusion of emotion through their mate bond. It struck Perry in such a visceral way that he dropped from his elbows to the bed and relaxed as it washed through him.

Unfortunately for Sebastian, it was not enough to distract him from the conversation.

Once the pleasure receded, Perry propped himself back up and set his sights on his mate. "Sebastian? Answer me, please."

Sebastian's typically stoic expression drooped with reluctance. He looked, very much, like one of the boys when asked to clean up their Legos.

At last, he said, "I assume the pregnancy is going well enough. If it weren't, one of my meddlesome siblings would have informed me otherwise."

"But you don't know for certain."

Sebastian's expression drooped further. "I suppose," he said, "I could ask."

"Oh, thank you, darling!" Careful of both his lotion-slathered feet and the babe he carried, Perry flew up and peppered Sebastian's face with kisses. With his legs up it was a little awkward, but Sebastian helped by drawing him onto his lap and supporting the backs of his thighs while the kisses Perry gave went from innocent to amorous. "Please do. I simply must know. I can't stand to think of poor Walter suffering all on his own."

Everything ground to a complete stop, and Sebastian gave him a warning look that could have stopped traffic.

Perry chuckled and hastened to add, "Not that I'll be heading out of the lair to visit with him, of course. You'll be the one doing that. I'll remain where it's safe so the worst won't come to pass. But if I know, I can send Walter a gift basket. Wouldn't that be nice?"

Sebastian grunted in acknowledgment but didn't otherwise comment.

"And what of Hugh?" Perry continued. Now that the moment was broken, it seemed as good a time as any to ply Sebastian for more information. "And Finch? Has anyone discovered his whereabouts? Is Hugh in good spirits despite the loss?"

Sebastian growled low in his throat. "And how do you know there's something amiss with Hugh?"

Oh, what an oversight. Perry bit his lip. "Oh. Well. Yes. It is strange, isn't it? I promise I haven't been out and about, Sebastian. I've been here this whole time. I wish I could explain it to you, but I'm not sure you'd understand. You could say it's an omega thing."

Sebastian's eyes narrowed with suspicion, but after a moment, he shook his head. "You're safe, so it's no matter. Hugh is fine. He was abroad the last few months chasing his omega secretary across territories both allied and enemy, but has finally come home thanks to Everard and Geoffrey."

"Chasing?" Perry's eyes widened. "Sebastian, what do you mean?"

"I misspoke. 'Gallivanting' would be more appropriate. The omega he was after abandoned his station and fled to England, from what I heard, where he found employment with one of the English Drakes. Hugh set off without a clue to his whereabouts and his antics near started a war."

"Oh, dear."

It was clearer by the second why Kian was being called to England, and it made Perry wonder if Sargon, who'd been absent for the last week with important matters pertaining to the council, was currently abroad as well.

"But what's done is done, and with him home, there's no more risk. The omega was recovered and brought back to Aurora, too. Apparently, he's pregnant with Hugh's child."

The news of Finch's pregnancy warmed Perry, and he smiled. "I thought so."

Sebastian raised an eyebrow. "An omega thing, you said?"

"Mm." Perry kissed along Sebastian's jaw. "Quite."

"You know too much, Peregrine." Sebastian turned his head to meet Perry's lips and kissed him deeply. Beneath him, Perry felt Sebastian's cock harden. "What am I to do with you?"

"Love me," Perry urged. "It's all I ask."

"Always and forever, in this lifetime and the next."

Sebastian proved his vow that night one rolling thrust of his hips at a time, and Perry, swept up in the pleasure of it all, knew that Sebastian would always be true to his word.

18

PEREGRINE

1508

For three days, Peregrine waited for his heat to return, sure that there had to be some mistake. It was natural for an omega's heat to wax and wane throughout their cycle, and while his previous heats had only offered brief moments of clarity—long enough to eat or drink or otherwise care for his essential needs—Fenja, from his cloister, routinely broke from her heat for up to a day before succumbing to it again. It stood to reason the same could happen to him.

But wait as he might, his heat never returned.

On the night of the fourth day—the seventh of his heat—Peregrine stood on his toes to peer into his bedchamber's large looking glass, intending to examine his face. Was he glowing, or was it a trick of the candlelight?

It was impossible to tell.

"Peregrine," his lord Sebastian beckoned from their bed. "Come."

Peregrine spared himself one last glance, then broke away from the looking glass to approach the bedside, where Sebastian was lying naked in wait. The dragon was truly a study in anatomy, with his large and perfectly sculpted muscles, broad frame, and staggering height. It seemed impossible that someone as small and dainty as Peregrine would be able to successfully breed with such an impressive individual, but...

Perhaps he had.

Perhaps he really was with egg.

"Come," Sebastian repeated. He smoothed a hand down his thigh, indicating where Peregrine should sit. Peregrine climbed onto the bed, then atop his dragon. By now he was familiar with Sebastian's wants and needs and didn't waste any time before taking the dragon's cock in hand and lowering himself onto it.

As Peregrine sank onto his lord, Sebastian grunted with pleasure.

"Yes." Sebastian gripped his hips and held him steady, then began to thrust up into him. Pleasure speared through Peregrine, and with a cry he squirmed and writhed as Sebastian claimed his body.

He was big.

Too big.

But perfect.

It shouldn't have been possible that a thing like that could fit inside of him, but it was, and Sebastian bred him often to remind him of it.

When the pleasure became too much to bear and Peregrine was reduced to mindlessness, Sebastian rolled them over and screwed him into the mattress until Peregrine came and clenched around his dragon's cock as if to forbid it from ever leaving. The increased tightness spurred Sebastian on, and he bucked wildly until his knot swelled and locked them both in place.

"*Mine*," Sebastian rumbled as he threaded his fingers through Peregrine's curls and kissed from his neck to his jaw to his lips. "Mine forever. Mine. All mine."

"Yours," Peregrine gasped through their kiss. "Yours forever."

He wrapped his arms around Sebastian's neck and kissed and kissed until Sebastian's hips began to move again, working his knot deeper, bonding them more. Peregrine's legs, which were hooked over Sebastian's hips, drooped. It was too much work to keep them up. Orgasm had left him too boneless, and his attentions were now focused elsewhere—namely on his racing heart.

Sebastian wanted him.

And against all odds, he'd left Peregrine with egg.

"Our clutch will be large and strong," Sebastian growled into Peregrine's mouth. "Mighty warriors, every last one."

"I vow it, my lord."

"And I will mate you, Peregrine." Sebastian continued to thrust. With his knot lodged so deep and swollen as it was, he wasn't able to get much movement, but even with thrusts no more than a fraction of an inch, he brought Peregrine pleasure. "I will mate you and make you mine, and no one will take you away from me. No one. You will be my wytad, and I will keep you and our eggs safe."

Peregrine kissed Sebastian with increased fervor, and when Sebastian's knot began to deflate, he worked his hips to tempt Sebastian to take him again. It didn't take long for Sebastian to understand, and they came again a half hour later, leaving Peregrine exhausted, sweaty, and utterly addicted to the dragon who promised such pretty, impossible things.

The palace Sebastian had secured for them was larger than Peregrine's cloister and more magnificent than any building Peregrine had seen to date. There were more rooms than he could count, and even the smallest of them was bigger than the largest room back home. What was more, each bedchamber had its own garderobe that eliminated the need for chamber pots—a luxury indeed. Although, Peregrine had to admit, it was a little strange to have to step out of a room to relieve oneself.

Each of the rooms in the palace—garderobes included—was ornate. The walls, floors, and ceilings were decorated in the same arabesque style as Peregrine's bedchamber and the windows and doors were all fancifully tall and domed at the top, meeting in the center at a sharp peak. The colors were bold and beautiful. Rich blues and reds and yellows, and, good lord, the gold. So much gold. It glittered and gleamed and seemed to please Sebastian very much, which meant that it pleased Peregrine, too.

In Peregrine's favorite room, however, there was not a speck of gold in sight. In this room, no color had been worked into the design of the walls, floor, or ceiling at all, because it came from another source: the stained glass on all three exterior walls. When the light hit it just right, its vibrant colors bled across the floor and seemed to color the air itself. Peregrine had never seen anything so beautiful.

What a world they lived in, where men could make something so beautiful from nature. And what a life Peregrine lived now where he could be at his leisure to enjoy such luxuries.

It hardly seemed real that a few months ago, he'd been half-starved and convinced no dragon would ever come for him.

Sebastian had proved him wrong in every sense of the word.

With Alistair and Everard, the doctor, both gone and Sebastian often out and about to see to it that they were granted sanction for their clutch, Peregrine spent a great deal of time sitting in the stained-glass room and appreciating the windows. Pake, by appearances, seemed to enjoy them, too. In particular, the tortoise enjoyed when the design from the windows was projected onto the floor. When that happened, he'd spend his time plodding from one colorful section to the next, stopping to stand in each for several moments before moving on. Peregrine considered it evidence of tremendous intelligence and encouraged Pake to continue the behavior by feeding him leafy greens whenever he played in the light.

Pake had not grown much in the weeks since Peregrine had come into his possession. The tiny tortoise was still small enough that he could sit quite comfortably on Peregrine's palm and still have space to walk around. Peregrine had no idea how large he'd grow, but he quite liked how small and sweet Pake was. Perhaps, he thought one day when lying near the stained glass, it was why Sebastian liked him. Like Pake, he was small and sweet, especially when compared to the dragon.

Whatever the reason, Peregrine was glad he'd caught Sebastian's eye. His lord wasn't a man of many words, but he was virtuous and loyal. Peregrine didn't doubt that he meant what he said when he promised that they would become mates. The problem was, Peregrine had no clue how to go about doing it. Mates were so incredibly rare that it was a surprise Mistress Fokje had thought to mention their existence at all.

"What do you think, Pake?" Peregrine asked aloud one day while he lounged in the glow of the stained glass with his tortoise. "Will my lord and I truly be able to mate, or is it all a tall tale? I do so wish it to be real. Can you imagine it? A Disgrace like me, mated to a dragon? I would never in my wildest dreams imagine it possible, but I would never have imagined I'd be with egg, either, and yet…" He set a hand on his stomach. "I very well could be."

Pake lifted his head slowly and blinked at Peregrine.

"Yes, you're right." Peregrine used a single finger to pet Pake on his head. "It is silly to dwell on it, but it can't be helped. If we don't mate, I'll be sent back to my cloister after I lay and I'll never see him again."

Pake, as slow and steady as always, stepped forward and fit himself into the space under Peregrine's chin.

"What should I do?" Peregrine asked as Pake settled. "I don't want to lose him. I want to stay forever and give him every clutch his heart desires. But how?"

The door opened, startling Peregrine. It was one of the servants, a young woman with a sweet face and pretty brown eyes who bowed her head when Peregrine looked her way. Peregrine didn't speak her language, which was unfortunate, as he wished he could tell her that she needn't respect him as she did their lord, but he did his best to convey how he felt in the kind way he treated her and by the tone of his voice.

"Hello." He took Pake in one hand and sat up. "Is everything well? Is there something I can help you with, or did you want to sit here with me and enjoy the window, too?"

The woman bowed her head and stepped forward, then set a box at Peregrine's feet and exited the room. Peregrine looked after her, neck craned, but when she didn't return, he set his sights on the box. It was long and not very tall. When he touched it, he found it not all that heavy. "How odd."

Peregrine set Pake down to enjoy the light from the stained glass on the floor and worked the top of the box open. It contained fine silk. Atop it sat a note.

Peregrine,

A dragon's mate deserves to look the part.

-S

Peregrine covered his mouth in awe and looked down at the parcel. The silk was plain, but he supposed he could fashion it into a nice enough tunic given time. It would be of far higher quality than any of the tunics he'd worn while in the cloister—that was certain.

He set the note near Pake and went to remove the fabric from its box when it tinkled in the same way fine jewelry did. Stunned, Peregrine dropped the entire thing and poked at it.

There was something inside.

"What's all this?" he asked, but no one was there to answer. It would be up to him alone to find out.

Peregrine unfolded the silk with trembling fingers and found not more raw fabric beneath it, but finely crafted garments made from airy fabrics that would do well to keep the body cool even in the midday heat. They were not in the styles he'd seen most commonly in Ljouwert, and while they seemed very strange and foreign, he assumed they were fashionable in their current corner of the world.

Included with his new clothing was a king's ransom of golden jewelry—jeweled necklaces, engraved bangles, and delicate anklets. There were some pieces Peregrine had no idea how to wear, but suspected were for other parts of his body—his ears, his chest, his hips. Were he to sell what he found, there would be nothing stopping him from setting off into the world and living a life of luxury wherever he pleased.

But Peregrine didn't long for freedom.

Not anymore.

The adventure he'd found with Sebastian was better than any he could have dreamed of having on his own.

"Oh, Pake," he whispered, and held out his hand for his tortoise, who climbed with some effort onto his palm. "Look at it. Look at all of it. Can you believe it? There's so much."

Pake opened his mouth and closed it gently around Peregrine's little finger, as if to give him a hug.

"My lord wants me to have it." Peregrine lifted one of the garments out of the box and laid it across his lap. It appeared to be fitted to his exact measurements, although he hadn't the faintest clue how. Sebastian did not seem particularly mindful of such details. "What should we wear, Pake? All of it is so lovely."

Pake closed his mouth around Peregrine's pinkie a second time.

"Oh, you are quite the visionary, aren't you?" Peregrine lifted his friend and kissed him on his head. "Yes, I think that will do nicely. Lord Sebastian will be quite pleased."

Peregrine dressed in one of the outfits afforded to him and found it both billowy and comfortable, if rather sheer. It seemed to him as though the clothing belonged either above or below another layer, but none of what he'd been given was a match.

It made little difference.

Pedigree omegas were taught not to be ashamed of their bodies, and while Peregrine did not very much like the claw marks that now scarred his chest, he otherwise found the outfit to be charming.

It took him a much longer time to dare touch the jewelry, and in the end he only summoned the courage to do it after Pake climbed into the box and tried to eat one of the earrings.

"No," Peregrine scolded, and set the naughty tortoise aside. "We do not eat the jewelry. It belongs to our lord, the dragon."

Pake wandered off. It seemed he cared not for dragons or their treasure, but rather for things to fit in his mouth. It was, therefore, imperative that Peregrine move the jewelry out of his reach… and there seemed no better way to do it than to put it on himself.

It was such a selfish pleasure, to be a Disgrace adorned with riches the likes of which few other omegas would ever see, but Peregrine had been given it freely and instructed to put it on. So put it on he did.

The gold chilled his skin and the gemstones were both heavier and smoother to the touch than he'd imagined. When he rose, his bangles clinked together and the dainty chains he wore tickled as they tumbled into place. They made music when he walked—soft clinks and jingles that sounded like luxury brought to life. While it was embarrassing to think of a lowly creature like himself worthy of wearing such finery, he supposed that it was fitting—

dragons were being made inside of him, and they deserved to be surrounded by riches.

"Let's return you to the courtyard, Pake," Peregrine said, and scooped Pake up. "I haven't a clue if our lord is home yet, but if he is, I should thank him. It's only polite."

Pake answered by mouthing Peregrine's thumb.

Peregrine took it to mean he agreed.

Sebastian was not in the courtyard. Peregrine found him disrobing in their chamber, back to the door, two hours later, having just returned home from the bazaar.

"My lord," Peregrine said softly as he closed the door. "Thank you for the gifts today."

Sebastian looked over his shoulder and seemed about to speak, but when he spotted Peregrine, his eyes went dark with desire and whatever he was about to say was forgotten. With one smooth movement, Sebastian stripped off the tunic he'd been untying and came to Peregrine bare-chested, his excitement burgeoning.

"Peregrine," he uttered, and traced his knuckles over Peregrine's cheek. "You are stunning. More beautiful than I could have imagined."

"Thank you, my lord."

"You will wear my gold forever." Sebastian's hand lifted to the chains hanging from Peregrine's ear and the thick golden cuff that held them in place. "I will get you more. Much more. When others look at you, I want them to know you are loved by a dragon. I want them to see plain as day that you belong to me."

Peregrine nodded and nuzzled into Sebastian's hand. "Yes. Of course."

"Come." Sebastian took him by the hand and brought him to the bed. He removed Peregrine's clothing but left the jewelry in place. All of it. Even the elegant chain looped over Peregrine's hips. "Gorgeous," he whispered, and pushed Peregrine onto the bed. "Stunning. Divine. My omega. Mine. Mine."

Sebastian's hot mouth surrounded Peregrine's flaccidity and sucked him in, and suddenly Peregrine was drowning in pleasure. It burned through him like dragon fire and ate him to the core.

"My lord," he breathed. "*My lord.*"

"Sebastian," rasped the dragon who'd given him everything, and now gave him so much more. "I am Sebastian. You will call me Sebastian. For as you are mine, I am yours, and you will call me by my name."

"Sebastian." The word was like a prayer, and it lifted to the heavens from his tongue. "Don't stop. Please, don't stop."

Sebastian didn't. Not until Peregrine went rigid and came into his mouth. Once he had, Sebastian pulled away to speak. "You have given me everything, Perry," he said, setting a loving hand on Peregrine's stomach. "Now it's time I do the same for you."

New gold was brought into the palace every day, most of which ended up in Peregrine's possession. Brooches and hair clips and rings. Necklaces, body chains, and more. Peregrine wore it all and cycled between pieces depending on his mood. There were diamonds and sapphires and emeralds to choose from. Fat rubies and smooth black tourmaline. Some of his jewelry had no gemstones at all, but was made of gold in colors Peregrine had never seen before—whites so intense they resembled snow and dusty colors that verged on pink.

Sebastian had more light, airy clothing commissioned, and soon Peregrine had a wardrobe so large, it necessitated its own chamber for storage.

Weeks passed. Sebastian made love to him every day, often more than once, and vowed all kinds of impossible things—that they would mate; that Peregrine would be his forever; and that it didn't matter what anyone said about his parentage, Sebastian would defend him until the end.

But when one month became two, and then neared the end of three, a mate mark had yet to appear, and Peregrine began to worry. If he and Sebastian were not mated, his eggs would be taken from him and he would be sent away. Should he stay, he would bond with them and go mad, as had happened to every omega before him, and as would happen to every omega after.

Sebastian appeared to have arrived at the same conclusion. While stoic, Peregrine had become familiar enough with him to read the subtleties of his body language, and he could tell his dragon was in distress over their failure to mate.

"It's possible," said Peregrine quietly one evening after they'd made love, "you'll need to send me away."

"No. I shan't do any such thing."

"You might need to."

"No, Perry."

"But—"

"No buts." Sebastian sounded insistent, but he stared through the ceiling as though it would offer them the solution to their problem. "You are mine. I will not send you away."

"Then I will go mad."

"You won't."

"It's the law of nature, Sebastian."

"Then I will fight nature tooth and nail, and when I win, I will force it to change." A curl of smoke escaped Sebastian's nostrils. He snorted to chase it away. "I refuse to lose you. You are my treasure, and I will not give you up."

But by the end of the month, there was no mark, and nature refused to be conquered. Worse, one night Peregrine woke from his sleep to find it had attacked—labor pains tore through him. He was without a mate, but his clutch was ready to be laid.

19

SEBASTIAN

1509

Sebastian didn't like being separated from Peregrine for even an instant, but this was a task that he could not entrust to anyone save himself. It was far too important to leave to a servant.

He reached into the dovecote and grabbed a pigeon, pleased to find it was Nisaba. She was the most reliable of the lot. He took his message, rolled it into a tube, and put it in a small container he fastened to her leg. Sebastian lightly threw Nisaba into the air and she took off, flying east toward Hillah, where his brothers had taken lodging while Alistair poked about in the ruins of Babylon. She would find his brother and he would come.

Peregrine would not die. Sebastian wouldn't allow it.

The trouble had begun that night while he and Peregrine lay in their bed. There had been no sound that emanated from his omega, but somehow, Sebastian had still woken up. To his distress, he'd not found Peregrine cuddled up against him, but rather a distance away, where he lay rigidly on his back and shook.

"Love, what is it?" Sebastian lit the fat candle that sat on a table by the bed to see Peregrine more clearly. His omega's pale skin had bleached to the color of old parchment and looked just as fragile, and his teeth worried at lips nearly as pale. His eyes were squeezed tightly shut. Silent tears streaked his face.

Alarmed, Sebastian pulled Peregrine into his arms. The movement made Peregrine cry out, sounding like a small, wounded animal. The mattress showed a dark red stain that looked almost black in the candlelight. Peregrine was wet with blood.

"It hurts," Peregrine moaned. "It hurts so much."

Labor was supposed to hurt, Sebastian was sure, but the blood... was it normal? He couldn't be sure, but he had a sinking feeling that it was not.

What was he to do?

He'd hoped for a clutch when Peregrine's heat had ended prematurely, but not at this kind of cost. Eggs without their father meant nothing to him.

"How can I help you?" he asked, never having felt more helpless in his entire life. He'd foolishly allowed Everard to leave with Alistair and had failed to send for him, even after Peregrine had fallen pregnant, wanting as much time alone with his omega as possible.

Now his avarice would cost him everything. It could very well be too late. If he was right, and this bleeding was abnormal, there was a chance that Peregrine could die.

With Peregrine in his arms, Sebastian walked to the bedroom door, opened it, and bellowed for the servants. Then, leaving the door open, he went into the courtyard and to the pool. Once there, he lowered both himself and Peregrine into the water. Despite the chilly night air, the water was still warm from the day's unforgiving sun.

Peregrine's trembling eased.

"Is this any better, love?" Sebastian asked.

"Some," Peregrine whispered. "The water helps a little. And you. You help. It doesn't hurt so bad when you hold me. But this can't be safe. Not for the eggs. You should take me and—"

"Hush," Sebastian crooned. "Focus on me. Forget all else."

Peregrine frowned, as if he thought the order impossible to follow. "I'll try, but—" He broke off speaking and began to scream. Around them, the water in the pool began to take on the color of blood.

I'm going to lose him, Sebastian thought. *He's going to die and already I don't know how to live without him.*

He felt like opening his own mouth in a bellow at the agony of the thought, but that was halted when Sebastian saw several servants hurrying their way. Men and women. Nearly all omegas, but some betas. They chided him in a language he couldn't understand, but it became evident that they meant for him to bring his ailing omega out of the pool.

Peregrine grasped Sebastian tighter. "They can't see the eggs. Not one of them can be trusted with the secret."

Sebastian's heart felt like it was breaking. "Don't fret, love. I will speak to the council and right all wrongs. You are more important than keeping the secret safe."

"But..." Peregrine began, then stopped. Pain racked his features, and he did not pursue the conversation any further than that.

Not having any idea of what the correct path was, Sebastian ended up surrendering to the bullying of the servants. He didn't like feeling helpless. He didn't like it one bit. But what was happening to Peregrine wasn't an alpha problem or even a dragon problem—it was an omega problem, and Sebastian had to hope that the omegas surrounding them would have more of a clue than he did how to fix it.

Sebastian carried Peregrine back into their bedroom. The bedclothes were gone and new ones put in their place. Instead of fine white sheets, the bed was now covered with thick brown blankets. The servants mimed Sebastian laying Peregrine down onto the newly made bed, which he did, noting while he did so that the blankets were soft as down. They had been made from lambswool, he thought, and that of a remarkably fine quality.

Once Peregrine was on the bed again, crying and moaning softly, a few of the servants chattered at Sebastian and pushed him away. A snarl built up inside of Sebastian at the mistreatment, but he held it in. He would be strong, if only for Peregrine's sake.

While the servants tended to Peregrine, Sebastian went to do the only thing he could think to help—he penned three words on a piece of parchment, then sought the dovecote.

Come at once.

If Everard received the message in time, perhaps Peregrine might be saved.

Everard arrived a day and a half later, just as the sun was setting. He marched into Sebastian's home without any announcement, made his way to the bedroom, and shooed out all the servants with little regard to their protests.

"He still lives, I see," Everard noted as he inspected a haggard Peregrine. "That's promising."

"Can you fix him?" Sebastian asked, desperate past the point of rising to any of Everard's barbs.

"Let me see." Everard put one bare hand onto Peregrine's pale brow. "He's feverish. That probably means rot." He lifted the blanket that covered Peregrine's hips and made a face of disgust. "That smell is worrisome." He moved Peregrine's body so that he lay prone. The omega didn't protest. He was entirely too weak.

180

"What ails him?" Sebastian asked. "None of it makes any sense."

"There is rot inside of him," Everard murmured. "His inner tissues are damaged, and it will require magic to fix. Quite a lot of it. He's also lost far too much blood. I will need to get to work immediately to see if I can fix this, but I fear it might take a miracle."

Sebastian's heart bled, and as much as he did not want to ask, he had to know. "And the eggs?"

Everard lifted his gaze and looked Sebastian in the eyes, a pitying look on his face. "There are no eggs, brother. There never were. Now, leave me to work my magic. The babe is gone, but with some luck, I will be able to save your omega."

2 0

SEBASTIAN

Present Day

It was good to have the boys around. They all came and went, except for Arsaces, who had volunteered to temporarily move in to assist with the "adulting," as he insisted upon calling it. Relying on one's children did seem, at some level, to be wrong, but the part of Sebastian that needed to protect Perry at any cost welcomed the assistance. With Arsaces there to take on Sebastian's other responsibilities, he was able to better focus on what mattered most—Perry and their whelps.

At five months into his pregnancy, Perry had begun to show. Sebastian could not remember a time when his pregnancy had been so pronounced, although he supposed it was possible that it had happened before. Whatever the case, it was not common, and it gave him hope that perhaps this time, it would be different, and nothing—not nature or crazed omegas—would take their child away.

On this particular day, Perry lazed in the atrium, reading Kafka's *The Metamorphosis*, while the children ran to and fro. Maximus, who was the largest of the bunch, had climbed onto

182

Pake's back. The massive tortoise plodded forward slowly, seemingly as delighted by the arrangement as the whelp who rode him. A pity he'd been too small to do it when their first clutch had been young—the whelps would have loved it, Sebastian was sure. Childhood in the 1500s was not as entertaining as it was today.

"Be careful of tiring Pake out, dear," Perry called after Maximus as the tortoise carried him off. "He is quite old, you know, and may very well fall asleep if you push him too hard."

"You've done it now," Sebastian murmured in Perry's ear as their seven other children rushed off in pursuit of their pet. "All the boys will want a turn. Poor Pake, having to ferry eight-year-olds around the atrium."

"He loves it and you know it."

Sebastian stroked Perry's belly. "And soon he'll have another to ferry. Do you think he'll love this one, too?"

Perry's cheeks went a pretty pink, and he slid his hand over Sebastian's. "Yes," he whispered, and kissed him sweetly. "I think he will love this one very much, too."

The children had all left their line of sight, and by the sounds of their laughter, were rather far away. Sebastian took advantage of their absence, rekindling the kiss and fanning its flames until Perry gasped and pulled back. "*Sebastian...*"

"Yes?"

"We mustn't."

"Here, perhaps, but there are other rooms. The children are old enough that they can be left unattended for a short while."

Perry glanced toward the last known location of their brood, then cozied up to Sebastian, sliding one of his legs down Sebastian's thigh. "You are very naughty, Sir Dragon."

"And you are incorrigible."

Perry dimpled. "Quite. Now, are you going to keep telling me what a bad, bad boy I am, or are you going to capitalize on it?"

At that exact moment, there came a great many groans of disappointment from the boys. Perry, ever intuitive, wiggled away, and not a second too soon—the boys trudged by dejectedly a moment later.

"Why the long faces, dears?" Perry asked sweetly as they passed.

"Pake fell asleep," pouted Elian, who looked most dejected of all. "Maximus was the only one who got to play."

"There will be other days." Perry looked pointedly at Sebastian. "Isn't that right, darling?"

Sebastian did not like what he was inferring one bit, but he agreed for the sake of the boys. "Yes. Quite."

"Very good." Perry winked at him salaciously, then, with some effort, climbed to his feet. "Since Pake is sleeping, why don't we all go play on the jungle gym your father built for you instead?"

"Can we go to the park?" Octavius asked.

Perry shook his head. "I'm afraid not, darling. Not today. The jungle gym will have to suffice."

There was a little bit of grumbling, but nothing unreasonable. Sebastian felt a bit like grumbling, too, but he held back. His tryst with Perry would have to wait, but it would happen. All he had to do was be patient.

Before leaving with the boys, Perry turned so he was facing Sebastian and rested one hand on his belly. He smiled. "Will you come out with us, darling? I do feel terribly about having to interrupt what should have been a lovely afternoon of you spiriting me away, but needs must. Regardless, I would very much like to have you with us, and I'm sure the boys agree."

Sebastian grunted in response and stood, and Perry, never one to be discouraged, circled round to tuck himself under Sebastian's arm. How magical it was that even after all the centuries they'd been together, he still made Sebastian's heart trip within his chest.

"Come, now," Perry said, guiding Sebastian forward. "I'm a trifle worried what mischief the boys will get up to if left unattended. The jungle gym is sturdy, but it is not infallible, and I doubt it was constructed with young dragons in mind."

It was certainly not, but it did not stop their boys from having a good time. They swung and climbed and chased each other, and their laughter was exactly what Sebastian needed to remember why it was so important to do what he was doing. If anything should happen to them, he would never forgive himself, and should anything happen to Perry... well, if he survived, his heart would never recover.

That night, Perry sat in the middle of their hoard bed working on a crossword puzzle. He wore a pale pink silk robe and nothing else. Sebastian, meanwhile, perused the hoard's pathways looking for just the right trinket. It didn't take long before one caught his eye. It was a long strand of marble-sized pearls with a clasp that held a large sapphire. The stone, however, was of an unusual shade of blue that was nearly purple. Perfect.

Sebastian brought the necklace to his mate, then adorned him with it. The pearls were just a shade lighter than Perry's skin.

"I take it you aren't interested in a quiet night in?" Perry asked, raising a brow.

"A night in, certainly." Sebastian slid the silken robe down Perry's shoulder then kissed the warm skin he'd revealed. "Quiet? I think not."

Perry's lips curved into one of the special smiles he reserved only for Sebastian. "So we meet again, Sir Dragon. I thought I might have lost you forever after we were forced to part ways in the atrium, but here you are. In bed with me. Pushing down my robe. Whatever should I do?" Perry held the back of his hand to his forehead in imitation of a swoon. "If I don't act promptly, I'll be ravaged, no doubt, but alas, I seem unable to move. It must be the doing of this lovely necklace. Gold is nothing if not my undoing. Your fiendish machinations will be the end of me."

Sebastian's cock twitched at the game his mate was setting up for him, and off he went to find more treasure to give to Perry. And not just any treasure. What he needed was finery befitting a prince.

Prowling about the hoard, Sebastian looked for just the right pieces. He found an arm cuff made from gold and studded with pearls and diamonds, a smooth platinum collar, several rings encrusted with a rainbow of stones, and something else he'd had commissioned for Perry centuries ago and forgotten existed. Loaded down with treasure, he made his way back to their bed.

Perry had set his puzzle aside and removed his robe, enterprising omega that he was. His eyes were closed and his hands gently stroked his small belly. Sebastian let his treasures fall onto the bed, for the moment unheeded, as he leaned forward to join his hands with Perry's.

Under his hands, he felt a flutter of movement. Something else, as well. It was a little like an egg bond, but infinitely fainter. The mere suggestion of a connection, but Sebastian swore he felt it.

"The babe quickens," he said.

Perry's eyes shone with tears. "You feel it, too? Our baby. I'd half-convinced myself I was imagining it. Making up phantom movement."

"No, I felt him. He's very strong. He's a fighter, just like his Papa."

A dreamy smile slid over Perry's face. "Her. She's a fighter."

Sebastian wasn't sure what to do with that information, but Perry was intuitive in the extreme, and he was very seldom wrong. So they would be having a girl, then. A daughter. Boys were all he knew, and alpha boys at that. But, slow and stolid as he was, Sebastian would learn.

"I love you," Sebastian said. "You, the babe, and all our children." He cupped his beloved's cheek. "But most of all, you. Always and forever, you."

PERRY

Present Day

Sebastian Drake was not known to be a gentle dragon, but the care he afforded Perry's belly suggested otherwise. Though his fingers were calloused and leathery and his hands designed to crush rather than cradle, he was delicate in his affections. And so it was that when Sebastian cupped Perry's cheek and vowed his love, Perry didn't doubt it any more now than he had five hundred years ago.

"If I were to explain how much I love you, Sebastian Drake," he replied in a voice meant only for Sebastian's ears, "I would have to speak without end for every second that remains of our very long lives, and even then it wouldn't be long enough."

The dark pools of Sebastian's eyes flared with arousal, and so, like any Pedigree omega worth his designation, Perry climbed prettily onto his lap and loosely wrapped his arms around his dragon's neck. Sebastian's dick stiffened. It was to be expected. He was, after all, a predictable sort of dragon, which was half of his charm. Perry wouldn't change him for a thing.

"The babe," Sebastian muttered, but his hands were already on

Perry's hips, and if the tone of his voice was any indication, he was well on his way to being utterly seduced. "You're in a delicate state, Perry. We shouldn't."

"Nonsense." Perry kissed the corner of his lips. "I know my limits. I will not test them."

"And if you've misjudged?"

"You wound me, Sebastian." At that, Perry put his hands on Sebastian's broad shoulders and pushed him flat onto the bed. "I've loved a dragon for half a millennium. Don't you dare tell me I don't know how to ride."

There was no shortage of lubricant in Sebastian Drake's lair. It was hidden in drawers with whelp-proof latches and kept on high shelves not even Perry could reach. There was even a bottle of it hidden under a fake rock in the atrium, and sometimes Perry carried small packets of it with him when he anticipated that Sebastian might be feeling more amorous than usual. Needless to say, any room containing a bed was well-equipped, and their hoard room was the best equipped of all. It took Perry all of a second to locate the nearest dispenser and slick his palm, and a second or two after that, Sebastian's burgeoning erection was coated and glistening.

"You mustn't," Sebastian grumbled even as he lifted Perry up and helped him into position over his dick.

Perry, head thrown back artfully in pleasure, slid down his shaft so it was buried between his cheeks, but not yet inside him. It was pointless to argue with a dragon—or, at least, a Drake—so he didn't try. Rather, he moved his hips and pleasured Sebastian without penetration. He would not go any further without Sebastian's consent.

"Perry." Sebastian's grip tightened, the pointed tips of claws at the very start of their transformation sinking into his skin. Scales plunged down Sebastian's shoulders and up his arms, along the length of his neck to his jaw, and over his collarbones down his chest in a patchwork V. "*Perry.*"

"Will you let me ride, Sebastian?" Perry asked as he lifted himself into position, allowing the head of Sebastian's cock to butt against his tight hole. "I shan't do it unless you allow me, but I crave it. I am a terribly bad, naughty boy and I need you, Sebastian. I need you more than words can say."

Smoke escaped Sebastian's nostrils, and he answered by pushing Perry onto his shaft, forcing his way inside.

The pleasure was immediate and immense. Perry gasped and lurched forward to brace his hands on Sebastian's scaled stomach, then, once he'd found balance, he began to ride. If Mistress Fokje were to see him now, she would tan his hide for how much he gave in to his own pleasure, but Perry's old teachings from the Pedigree had long ago been overwritten by his centuries of experience as Sebastian's lover. No matron knew better than he did what his dragon liked, and in Sebastian's case, what he liked best was when Perry was greedy.

"Ravage me, Perry," Sebastian growled. The points of his claws raked down Perry's hips to his thighs, nearly deep enough to draw blood. "Take it. Take all of it. Make me yours as I make you mine."

Pleasure like lightning forked down the length of Perry's spine and struck a deep, forbidden place low inside of him that tightened his balls and thickened his own erection. There was no beast inside of him in the same way there was inside of Sebastian, but in moments like these, it felt very much like there was—like he was some wild thing that existed beyond the niceties of humanity. Like he could take, and take, and take forever and still never have enough.

"*Take,*" Sebastian demanded, his voice more dragon than man. "*Claim.*"

And Perry, snarling and breathless, did just that.

He rode savagely until Sebastian's knot stopped him and

continued on after that, working his body with what little movement the knot afforded him to bring himself all the pleasure he could.

Orgasm came quickly. It always did when his lover's cum flowed into him. The heat of it made sex that much better, and Perry never lasted long after that. Exhausted, he slumped onto Sebastian and allowed himself to be rolled to his side. Once settled, Sebastian kissed him until his knot receded and their shared excitement had burned to ash.

"I love you," Sebastian said, and tenderly laid a hand over where their child quickened. "I am yours forever, come what may."

"How fortunate," Perry whispered as he kissed Sebastian with all the affection a heart could hold. "For I plan on loving you forever, my dragon, no matter what is or what shall be."

Sebastian was always quick to fall asleep after sex, but such was not the case for Perry, whose thoughts were entirely too busy to be put to bed. Some nights he didn't sleep at all, and over the last few months, burdened with worry over the unborn babe, such times were far more common.

Tonight, it seemed, was one such night.

Perry tossed and turned, but no matter which way he lay, there was no comfort to be found. At last, with a sigh, he pulled back the sheets and left Sebastian to slumber. It wouldn't be fair to wake him with his restlessness. A good dragon deserved good sleep. Perry would not bother him.

It was an inconvenience to cross the main chamber of the hoard without making noise—coins and other golden trinkets always seemed to be underfoot—but Perry was nothing if not patient, and he picked his way across the room with the precision of a cat stalking its unsuspecting prey. The door to their hoard, while heavy and well-secured, opened silently, and so out into their lair Perry went. He had no clear destination in mind, but it made little difference. With some luck, a walk would help clear his head.

At this hour, the boys were all asleep and the staff had long ago retired to their quarters, so the halls were quiet and the lights were out. Perry picked his way through the dark to the foyer, where he'd once spied on Bertram from on high. Now, however, there were no pesky brothers to scrutinize. There was only moonlight, which streamed in through the tall sidelight windows and fell across the floor in narrow strips. Perry leaned on the railing of one of the twin grand staircases and watched it for a moment, lost in thought over what he'd learned and what it meant for his family, then wearily made his way across the foyer and through the streams of moonlight. In it, the sheer robe he was wearing sparkled. It had been a long time since he'd lived in poverty, but moments like these would forever be magical. It was simply unfortunate that those who lived in fairy tales were so often bedeviled with curses.

The baby kicked as though frightened by the thought, and Perry smoothed a hand over his stomach to soothe her.

Never fear, little one, he thought. *Your father and I are here, and we're doing all we can to break this wretched curse forever.*

From the foyer, Perry walked into the sitting room and went to peruse the books in its small library by moonlight. The titles in it were eclectic, to say the least—the bottom shelves were occupied by picture books and novels written for beginner readers while higher shelves were filled with pulp fiction, the kind that sucked you in and refused to let you go. Perry traced his fingers along spines of books Sebastian had gifted him years ago—ones he'd read and loved and kept for nights like this when real life was too wretched to bear. But none of them spoke to him, and so he continued on his walk.

Perhaps he'd have better luck in the study, where their older books were kept. Perry seldom touched them for fear their old bindings would give, but if damaging a book meant he might sleep tonight, it was worth the sacrifice. Ignatius, he was sure, could refer him to someone who specialized in repairing "antiquarian" titles. Not that he approved of the designation. The books were a few hundred years younger than he was, after all, and Perry did not consider himself an antique.

Perry was halfway to the bookshelf when he came to an abrupt stop.

There was something moving behind the drawn curtains of the window across the room.

Had it been any other time, Perry wouldn't have thought much of it. Yes, the boys were good sleepers, but there was always the chance one of them had woken up and decided to brave the dark on a late-night adventure. Likewise, sometimes the servants did walk around after hours, whether to chase off insomnia or indulge in moonlit trysts—or sometimes perhaps both—but in all his years, Perry had never seen an affair that looked quite as insidious as this. There was no rhythm to it. The curtains swirled like they were being disturbed by a breeze, but that was impossible— the windows were shut and locked, and no other set of curtains in the room were acting in the same way.

It was, Perry knew, quite foolish to approach a potential threat while unarmed and pregnant. The proper course of action would be to return to the hoard room, wake Sebastian, and allow him to deal with it. With claw and tooth and scale, he could defend himself against attacks that Perry couldn't. But there were things Sebastian was hiding from him. He'd hidden the truth for hundreds of years, disappearing on business of his father's design only to come home and never speak of what had transpired, even when Perry had asked. And now there was this business with

Bertram and his omega. Sebastian had known about it, but hadn't told Perry until he was directly in harm's way. If he went to his dragon to tell him about the strange happenings in the room, it could very well become another mystery—yet another piece missing from a puzzle Perry was eager to solve. So he approached the window, steeled himself, and yanked open the curtains.

There was nothing there.

"It's all in my head, isn't it?" Perry muttered to himself as he dropped his arms to his sides. "Maybe Sebastian is right to hide what he does from me—the stress is eating away at my brain."

But as he spoke, a breeze teased its way inside of his robe and ghosted along his skin. Perplexed, Perry stepped into the space in front of the window and discovered two things at once.

The first: the window was unlocked and remained open by a sliver.

The second: there was something there after all, and he'd gone and stepped on it.

To keep from making a sound, Perry clamped a hand over his mouth and quickly backed away from the window. There, on the floor, heretofore unseen, was a small dragon scale. Much like the hardwood, it gleamed in the moonlight and was so thin and flat that Perry hadn't noticed it until it was too late.

With eight rowdy boys who oftentimes transformed into eight rowdy young dragons, accidents weren't uncommon. Perry had kissed better gashes made by clumsy claws and accompanied the children on visits to Everard's office to heal varying degrees of burns. From time to time, the boys did get nippy and sometimes that meant scales were shed, but the longer Perry looked at the scale, the more a feeling of wrongness prickled in the back of his mind.

The scale was too...

Too something.

Too thin, too small, too abnormal.

Young dragons had thick scales to help protect them from

themselves, and as a dragon grew older and larger, those scales tended to thin somewhat, but never as much as this. The scale in front of him looked flimsy, and would do little to ward off claws, teeth, or flame.

It was almost like…

No.

No, he refused to entertain the notion. That couldn't be it.

But what other explanation could there be?

Heart in his throat, Perry eyed the window for signs of danger and found none. When he was sure no harm would come to him, he stepped forward, locked it, then stooped to pick up the scale. It fit neatly on his palm and was so thin, it had started to curl slightly at the edges. When he tested it with his finger, it flattened under the pressure, then popped back into its original shape. Flimsy, just like he'd thought.

Such a scale couldn't belong to any of the children, nor had it been shed from an adult dragon.

There was only one time Perry had ever seen scales quite like these.

"Heaven help us," he uttered, then clutched the scale to his chest and hurried from the room to make a phone call.

2 2

PEREGRINE

1509

Heaven could not save Peregrine—not now, and perhaps not ever —for hell had risen up to claim him, and from it, there was no escape. Consciousness meant pain, but the endless black of the oblivion he fell into when he shut his eyes was worse, and Peregrine feared it with all his heart. If he gave in to it, he knew that he would never come back out. He would die and so, too, would the eggs. For them, he had to push through.

In moments of lucidity, Peregrine sought his dragon. More often than not, he'd find Sebastian at the bedside or slumped over with exhaustion in a nearby chair, but sometimes he was missing, and those times struck fear in Peregrine's heart worse than the deep dark that waited for him when he closed his eyes.

"Sebastian?" he asked in a feeble voice upon waking to an eerily quiet room. "Sebastian, my lord? Where are you?"

There was no response. Not even the servants came to tend to him. Perhaps they'd pieced together what he already knew—that death was coming, and there was nothing to be done. It would be a small but sad mercy to die alone. At least then, no one would see what a terrible omega he'd turned out to be.

If only he'd thought to run away and sail the seas with Lus. It would be a lonely life, and one fraught with peril, but at least then he'd never have been given a taste of what he wanted only to have it snatched away so soon.

Peregrine blinked tears from his eyes. When they formed again, he did the same, then gave in and let himself quietly cry. Pain pulsed inside of him where he thought the eggs should be. Would they make it? If he could lay them and make Sebastian happy, at least he'd die knowing he'd served his purpose. It was more than most members of the Pedigree could say.

While he despaired, the door opened, and in stepped a familiar face. It was Everard, the doctor.

"Oh, you're awake," Everard said. "What an unexpected surprise. You're a fighter, aren't you, Parakeet?"

Parakeet? Peregrine blinked and tried to sit up, but the pain that ripped through him when he tried stopped him from moving at all. He hissed through his teeth to mitigate the worst of it and settled for shaking his head. "No, my lord. I am but an omega."

"Nonsense." Everard came to the bedside. "You are an omega, yes, but the fact that you live and draw breath proves your mettle. Although I do so hope we stop meeting like this. I'd much prefer to become acquainted at a time when you're not covered in your own blood."

Peregrine's eyelids drooped of their own accord, and he had to fight to keep them open.

Was there that much blood?

It occurred to him that, apart from the pain churning inside of him, he couldn't feel much of anything. The sheets could be soaked and he wouldn't be any the wiser. If only that same numbness would dull the pain inside of him.

"Am I to die?" Peregrine lifted his head to look at Everard. "Please, I beg your honesty. I must know."

Everard's lips tightened. "Should I do nothing you surely will, but there's hope for you yet, Partridge. Now, lie still. I'll do my best to right the wrong inside of you."

"The wrong inside of me?" Pain be damned, Peregrine propped himself up on his elbows to better look down his body. The pain was so intense he saw white, and when it receded, he'd fallen back onto the bed. Everard, eyes wide, leaned over him. Both of his hands clasped Peregrine's shoulders, holding him down.

"Easy, now!" Everard smoothed a hand over Peregrine's forehead to push back his sweat-soaked hair. "Struggling will only make it worse. You need rest."

"But... but the eggs," Peregrine panted. "The eggs are yet to be laid. I can't rest. I have to push them out before what's wrong with me makes wrong of them, too."

A look of pity saddened Everard's face. "There are no eggs, Peacock. There's nothing in you at all."

Peregrine's heart stopped, and his breath caught in his throat. "That... that can't be true."

"It is."

"But my lord dragon claimed my heat. It ended early. I conceived."

"And I am not doubting you did." Everard reached for the bedside table and from it, drew a damp rag he used to dab the sweat from Peregrine's brow. "Nature is not always kind—not to dragon, and not to man."

"No." Peregrine squeezed his eyes shut, wanting—needing—to be anywhere but here, but the darkness wouldn't take him. "No, you're not making any sense. I conceived. Sebastian took my heat and I conceived! If not eggs, then there must be a child. Where is the child?"

The rag parted from his forehead and sloshed into the basin of water it had been plucked from. There was a long, terrible pause during which Peregrine opened his eyes in time to see Everard

197

take his hand. "You've miscarried, Pigeon," Everard confessed. "The babe is no more."

It was a lie.

It had to be a lie.

Peregrine slid a hand down his stomach to feel where the tiny bump should be, but there was nothing, and when he pulled his hand back, it came back crimson with sticky blood.

No one in the Pedigree spoke of miscarriages.

No one had prepared him for this awful possibility.

This was worse than if he'd not conceived at all—a failure at the highest level—a sign from the divine that a Disgrace like him truly had no right to be at a dragon's side. The future he'd envisioned—the one where Sebastian would keep him and somehow save him from egg madness—shattered like glass. He'd lost his child, and now he would lose his dragon's love.

It was too much.

The pain in his heart was worse than the pain that throbbed inside of him, and it ached so unbearably he longed to have claws so he could rip his chest open, tear out the damned thing, and throw it away.

"I'm sorry, Parrot," Everard said, and just like that, all of the hurt inside of Peregrine ignited into unholy rage. He sprang up from the bed, grabbed Everard by the front of his tunic, and drew their faces together.

"*Peregrine*," he snarled through clenched teeth. "My name is *Peregrine* and you shall never, ever call me anything but that ever again."

Everard's eyes flew open. No dragon would struggle to subdue an omega, especially one in such poor condition, but the terror on his face was quite real. It was the most powerful Peregrine had ever felt in his life, but also the most helpless, because no matter how many dragons he scared into speechlessness, nothing would bring back what he had lost.

The pain in his heart and the pain down below resurfaced, this time worse than ever, but the darkness refused to take him. It was a wretched thing, to have to suffer like this. To be broken in so many ways. Peregrine's grip weakened, and as uncomely as it was, he buried his face against Everard's chest and started to cry.

"*Everard*," boomed Sebastian from the doorway, and in moments Peregrine was no longer in bed, nor clutching his lord's brother. He was wrapped up safe in Sebastian's arms, and although the wrong inside of him hurt worse than ever, being so close to his lover put back the pieces of his broken heart. "What," Sebastian seethed at Everard, "do you think you're doing?"

"He attacked me!"

"He is ill and in need of healing."

"Which he would get if he were to be still." Everard adjusted his tunic, now stained with blood on its right breast. "Lay him down. It's no easy feat to stitch together a wound you can't see, and harder yet to do a second time around. I must concentrate."

"Be still, Perry," Sebastian whispered, and laid Peregrine on the bed. "Everard's magic is powerful, but in order for it to work, he needs your cooperation. Let him help you. All will be well."

Only Peregrine couldn't be sure of that, because as wonderful as it was to have Sebastian with him, his presence served as a reminder that other terrible things were yet to come. Soon enough he would have to tell Sebastian the truth—that there were no eggs, and that there would be no child—and Sebastian would look upon him with pity and send him away.

No dragon had use for an omega who couldn't bring a babe to term.

No matter how Sebastian claimed to love him, he would change his mind when he found out how badly Peregrine had failed. A clutch was the only goal of a coupling like theirs, and without a body willing to carry one, their love would fizzle, and it would die.

So while Everard undid the wounds that caused him pain, Peregrine wept.

He wept for the babe he'd never meet and for the lover he'd lose.

Because no matter how much magic Everard used, it would never be enough. Magic could end pain, but it was useless against suffering, and suffer Peregrine would until he returned to dust.

23

SEBASTIAN

1509

"You'll have to send him back," Everard said. "If you wish, I can take him. If that would be easier for you to bear."

Sebastian slumped in the throne he'd procured and placed in the palace's great hall. It had belonged to some prince or another, but that didn't particularly matter. It was uncomfortable as hellfire, but it was very shiny, so he supposed that was something. It was also quite large, which was the other reason he'd purchased it. The plump cushions made it nearly tolerable and the gold and inlaid jewels were soothing.

Nothing, however, could quell the storm raging inside of him. It had been a day since the loss of the babe, and Sebastian's despair had whipped itself into a frenzy. Unlike Peregrine, who was able to weep and mourn, such things were not Sebastian's nature. Rather, he was a lion whose very heart had been pricked by a thorn. The pain made him want to rip the entire world apart.

Despite his brother's silence, Everard pushed on. "I've already discussed it with him. I think he'd prefer it, to be honest."

In a flash, Sebastian was on his brother, pinning him to the ground and holding a wickedly sharp talon to Everard's neck. "Never," he snarled. "I would kill you myself with teeth and claws, bedamned what Father will think. Peregrine is mine, and I will slay any man or beast who attempts to steal him from me."

Everard blinked, for once no caustic jest leaping out of his cursed mouth.

Sebastian shook him, making Everard's head bounce on the floor. It was, much to Everard's good fortune, covered in a thick wool carpet. "Do you understand me, little brother?"

Still looking wary, but making no move to shove Sebastian off or defend himself, Everard shook his head back and forth. "No, I damned well do not understand. Also. That hurt. I need my brain. Unlike you, I make use of it often."

"*You will not take my omega.*"

"God, no. I wouldn't dream of it. I didn't wish to purloin him, brother. I was hoping to spare you the pain and trouble of sending him back to his cloister."

"Offer again and I will rip your spine out of your body and make a necklace of the bones."

"That's very specific," Everard said after another one of those blinking pauses.

"I've given it much thought."

"Clearly. But do be reasonable. I promise you I will never steal, borrow, or abscond with your omega. Neither will I harm him. But you can't keep him, don't you see? The council will not have it, and I don't wish to have you dragged all the way to Cathay to stand trial. Besides, it will annoy Geoffrey, and you know how he is when he's annoyed. Now, can you please get off me so we can discuss this like the rational beings I know we are capable of being? It will be a struggle, I'm sure, but I have faith in you."

Sebastian snarled at his brother, then sprang off of him. He didn't go back to the uncomfortable throne, however. He would have to make plans and it was easier for him to think while pacing. The mere thought of losing Peregrine made him want to howl with fury and pain. He'd already suffered one loss—he would not abide another. "There is nothing to discuss," he growled. "Peregrine is mine."

Everard stood nimbly and brushed at his tunic. "God's bones. Are these cat hairs?" He sneered in distaste.

"They're good mousers," Sebastian said absently. Inside, his mind was churning. If his brother would not listen to his word, then perhaps he could be persuaded by reason. "Peregrine's contracted time is not yet up. I see no reason why I can't keep him."

"Did you not listen to a bloody word I just said? It is not done. Why can't you be like Bertram? He sired his clutch with a perfect Pedigree omega and went on his way. You, meanwhile, are consorting with a Disgrace who may very well be barren. What are you thinking?"

Sebastian grabbed his brother by the front of his tunic and tried to shake some sense into him. "I'm thinking that I love him."

Everard's eyes sprang wide. "You love the omega?"

"He is mine."

"You keep saying that. It's very curious." Everard beetled his brow. "I wonder if... no, it cannot be the case. It would be unprecedented. As far as I know."

"Talk sense, man. What are you on about?" Sebastian released his brother's tunic and Everard staggered back a few steps before regaining his footing.

"Ah... nothing. But a mere stray thought." Everard looked away from Sebastian. "Theoretically, were you to keep this omega and live with him for several years and then he bears you a clutch, what would you do? You know he'll go mad if he doesn't have the eggs taken away before he bonds with them. You say you love him, yet you would put him through that. Are you saying you'll look into his extremely fetching eyes and tell him he has to go away for his own good, and for the good of the clutch? Are you truly capable of that, brother? Because I think you are not. Better to sever this now rather than later. Your love will fade. There will be other omegas."

The idea of bedding another omega made Sebastian feel sick. Unsteadily, he sat on his throne and then looked up to see Peregrine standing silently in the shadow cast by the hall's entryway. Sebastian's heart constricted within his chest. Lose Peregrine? Give him up? Impossible. "My love will not fade," he said, more for Peregrine's ears than Everard's. "There will be no one else. I will carry Peregrine in my heart until I am no more."

Everard groaned and clutched at his hair in frustration. "You must see reason, Sebastian. You are courting heartbreak not only for yourself, but for Peregrine as well. There is no happy conclusion to this business, I assure you." Then he added, "Probably. The best scenario in this situation is that Peregrine is, indeed, barren. If he produces no clutch, you may keep him with you until he dies, although there will be talk. With dragons, there's always talk."

"Dragons can talk until they have no breath or fire left. It will not change my mind."

"Or he could be fertile enough to bear you either a clutch or a human child. You're already aware of what a nightmare it would be should he fall gravid with eggs, but have you considered fathering a Disgrace? What on earth would you do with the child? Lord knows you couldn't keep it. The family would never live it down."

Sebastian stared hard at Peregrine and willed him to see the sincerity in his words. "Then I will be an Amethyst no more, and therefore cannot bring shame to our clan. I will take Peregrine and whatever offspring he gives me, and we will be our own clan. I'm young and strong enough to protect us all. I can hide. I can make a new hoard. I will leave everything behind, but not him. Never him. If he brings me no child, he will live with me as long as he can draw breath and his heart beats."

Everard strode over to stand right before Sebastian. "And what if he bears you a clutch? He will go mad. You must see that."

But Sebastian couldn't see it. While he could envision his lovely and sweet Peregrine with his eggs, or even caring for a human child, he could not see the man ever harming his own young. It was utterly impossible. It would not happen. "No," he told Everard curtly. "I don't see that at all. What I do see is the man I adore wandering around this misbegotten palace like he's already a ghost. I will not have it. I will do whatever it takes to keep him by my side. There is no depth I wouldn't sink to in order to protect him."

Everard threw up his arms in frustration. "I suppose it doesn't matter if the omega catches egg madness when you're mad already."

"Mayhap I am," Sebastian said, looking at Peregrine and not his pesky sibling. "It's of no consequence."

"Your mind—what little there is of it—is made up, then? There is to be no talking you out of this?" Everard sounded like he'd already given up. "Fine, then. I will keep your secret and I will endeavor to silence Al, although I can't promise much luck there. Unless he keeps traveling, which actually might be for the best. If you need me again, ever, you know how to contact me."

Sebastian shifted his attention back to Everard. "You would do that for me?"

Everard shrugged. "You're my brother and I'd hate to lose you. I might need to use you as a battering ram at some point."

That made Sebastian, despite everything, bark a laugh. "Enough, brother. At least for tonight. I have matters to attend to." He rose from the throne and strode past Everard and toward the lovely ghost that haunted the palace. Everard must have turned around and seen Peregrine, judging by the surprised intake of breath Sebastian heard. That, however, was secondary and unimportant. The only thing he could think of or see was Peregrine, because Peregrine was his world. They were bound, somehow, no matter how unlikely, and he'd see that they were never parted.

"My lord dragon," Peregrine said. His voice was thin and wispy, as if he were a specter in truth. He looked as if he wanted to say more, but was afraid to do so.

"My love," Sebastian said.

Peregrine started to cry silently. Tears more precious than any diamond fell down his cheeks. Softly, carefully, Sebastian touched Peregrine's face and captured one of the tears. "Don't cry."

"I can't help it," Peregrine sniffed. "I know feeling isn't any part of my purpose, but I feel everything. I feel too much. Everything hurts, Sebastian. Not just my body, but my very being. But I'm not supposed to feel, and so I've no idea what to do. My only purpose in life is to please a dragon. To please you. And I failed." At this, Peregrine's crying became sobs as great and frightening as a dragon's roar.

Weeping omegas were not something Sebastian had ever prepared to deal with, but somehow that didn't matter. The man before him wasn't just any omega. He was Peregrine. He held Sebastian's heart. So he scooped Peregrine up into his arms, noting he felt lighter than he ever had, and carried his love back to their bedroom.

Sebastian didn't know what to say to help Peregrine, so he laid him down on the bed and then stretched out beside him and took Peregrine's hand into his own much larger one. The small hand enveloped in his fluttered, much like a captured bird might, so Sebastian reminded himself to be gentle, gentle, gentle.

He held Peregrine's hand like it was the most prized possession in his hoard.

His dragon wasn't much of a talker, but he agreed with Sebastian. *Mine. Take. Keep. Forever.*

"Sebastian," Peregrine said quietly.

"Yes, love?"

"You said you loved me. It was to your brother, but I did hear the words."

"Aye. I did say that."

Peregrine turned so he lay on his side, facing Sebastian. "You can't."

"I can," Sebastian assured him. "I can do anything I wish."

"You shouldn't." Peregrine sniffled. "It isn't right. You are worth so much more than I can offer."

"I don't care."

"But you should."

Sebastian shrugged. "I am not easily swayed. You should accustom yourself to it. I don't imagine that will ever change."

Peregrine let out a shaky laugh. "No, I don't suppose it will."

"I love you," Sebastian said, "with all of my heart. And don't tell me what I should or shouldn't do, Perry. I am a dragon. I live as I wish."

"And what of the council?"

Sebastian shrugged again. He would keep Peregrine safe. He would do so for the rest of his life. The council would have no say in the matter. He had more than sufficient income to father a clutch and if it came to it, he'd protect his children and his mate until the very end. "The council does not factor into my decision. I will always keep you safe, Peregrine. You and any children you might bear for me, be they dragon or human, or be there no offspring at all."

Despite his tears, Peregrine managed a shaky smile. "And if I bear a Disgrace?"

"I will love him, because he comes from you."

More tears streamed down Peregrine's cheeks, and Sebastian hastened to wipe them away.

"We are taught," Sebastian murmured as he pushed Peregrine onto his back and climbed atop him, straddling his narrow hips and lowering his face so they were lip to lip, "from our earliest days as whelps that Disgraces are unlucky creatures, but I do not agree. For you are a Disgrace, and I have never felt more lucky in my entire life than I do now here, with you."

Peregrine whimpered pitifully and drew a shaky breath. Hesitantly, he wrapped his arms around Sebastian's neck and slid just the tips of his fingers into the hair of his nape. It was gentle affection, but it was affection nonetheless, and it bolstered Sebastian's spirits.

The pain of losing the babe was severe, for Peregrine even more so than him, but as vulnerable as it now was, there was still love in their hearts for each other. It was buried by grief, but it had not died, and no matter what it took, Sebastian would excavate it.

Peregrine was his, and he would not let anything pull them apart.

Heart full to brimming with love for his omega, Sebastian pressed their lips together in a sweet kiss. It was a promise, and it was one Peregrine earnestly returned.

How strange yet wonderful it was how something so innocent could leave Sebastian breathless.

Peregrine.

His Peregrine.

No matter what happened, he would spend the rest of his life by Peregrine's side. It was as sure a thing as the rise and fall of the sun.

When the kiss broke, Sebastian came to lie next to Peregrine and took his hand once more. "Do you think you might love me back?" he asked after some time.

Tension ran all through Peregrine's arm, and he did not reply.

"I didn't mean to demand your love," Sebastian hastened to add. "There is much weighing on you, I know. There is much weighing on me as well. It seems selfish to ask for your heart when it has been so recently broken, but I am a dragon, and selfishness is my nature, so it behooved me to ask. I understand if you are not able to give me a response. I do hope that it does come one day, however."

Peregrine sucked in a tremulous breath, like he was once more on the verge of tears. "Sebastian..." he whispered, then was quiet.

"I am not a dragon of many words," Sebastian admitted into the silence that followed. "And I often do not know how to convey the truth in my heart. It comes out as grunts and snarls and smoke, and sometimes in teeth and claws. But as inadequate as I am, I do have words for this. I am gutted. Not because there will be no eggs, but because of the loss we have suffered. And in truth, the only reason I have not gone mad is because of you." Sebastian paused to reflect on it. "Because the love I have for you makes me feel like this isn't the end. So even if you cannot love me, please tell me that this is not over. That we are not over. Because if that is the case, I must learn to accept it now, or surely I will succumb and madness will claim me."

Peregrine sobbed, his hand escaping Sebastian's so he could cup it over his mouth. Fat tears rolled down his cheeks. "You," he warbled, "are the reason I have not broken entirely. I love you, Sebastian. I love you with every beat of my heart, no matter how foolish that may be."

Grief could not be brushed aside by a declaration of love, but it could be soothed by it. Such was the case for Sebastian, whose heart mourned for what it had lost, but rejoiced for what it had gained.

Tears in his eyes, he pulled Peregrine into his arms and kissed him fiercely. Peregrine whimpered, then locked his arms around Sebastian's neck and kissed him back.

It was perfect in a way Sebastian had never known perfect could be. Goose bumps rose on his arms, and a shiver worked its way up his spine.

Mate, whispered his dragon. *Ours.*

And Sebastian, even without absolute proof, agreed. He and

his dragon both knew it in their sinews and muscles, scales and bones.

Peregrine was their mate.

All that was left was for him to prove it, for once he did, no man—dragon or otherwise—would dare speak of parting him from Peregrine again.

24

SEBASTIAN

Present Day

"Your brother's mate is here to see you, sir," Stanford, the butler, intoned gravely.

Without looking up from the papers on his desk, Sebastian said, "Which one?"

"He specifically means me." This was proclaimed, rather than said, and spoken in a Russian accent. It had to be Misha. And indeed, when Sebastian looked up, that was who he saw.

Misha, Reynard's mate, was of the Pedigree, but the difference between him and Perry could not be more stark. While Perry favored clothing that drew the eye and enhanced all of his best features, Misha preferred the kind of fashion most commonly found on the street. Such was the problem with the modern iteration of the Pedigree—or at least the Diamond cloisters, in which Misha had been raised. They were entirely too informal. A dragon's mate was a living jewel deserving of finery, not this common dross. Alas, Sebastian had no say over any omega—not even his own—and so he kept the comment to himself.

Misha did not dress to please him, after all, and as unfortunate as it was, the omega was entitled to wear whatever he liked.

Today, what he liked was a baggy black hoodie with cat ears on its hood and tight-fitting skinny jeans that conformed to his slender legs. A shock of blond hair swept over his brow, unkempt, and the look on his face suggested he didn't give a damn what Sebastian thought about it.

It was, perhaps, the part of his look that Sebastian most enjoyed.

"Where is Reynard?" Sebastian asked. "Has something happened? I see no other reason you would be here on your own."

"Calm down, *drakon*. Reynard is well. He is with the boys." Misha slid his phone out of his pocket to check something, then returned it and looked Sebastian in the eyes. "I am not here because of him. I am here because of you."

Sebastian prickled. "Go on."

"Your security system." Misha gestured into the air. "Substandard at best."

"My security is not substandard."

"Yes, it is. Unless you have an explanation for what happened last night?"

The hair on the back of Sebastian's neck stood on end, and he eyed the scale that Perry had brought him in a panic well into the midnight hours. While small, it was too thin and flimsy to belong to a juvenile dragon, which meant there was only one explanation as to its origins: it had been plucked from an adult dragon in the midst of his transformation—a feat very few were able to accomplish without losing their lives in the process. There was only one dragon Sebastian knew who had been tortured in such a way, and the scale's very familiar purple hue confirmed his suspicions.

So Misha knew, then.

Sebastian took a deep breath and rolled one shoulder, then the other, like he was warming himself up for a fight. "Perry called you, then."

"Da."

He picked up the scale, slotting it between his index and middle finger to show it to Misha. "Will you confirm?"

"Da, it is Reynard's. He has told me the man who stole our eggs tortured him by plucking his scales one by one. And now one of those scales, taken from him six years ago, shows up in your lair below an open window. Do you think I am dumb, *drakon?*"

"No."

"Surprising. I suppose there is some sense in that head of yours. Not much, but some." Misha took the scale and twisted it between his fingers. "The man who took my eggs was never captured, and now here is my mate's scale in your lair not long at all after Finch was attacked and drugged. Prior to my arrival in the United States, I was targeted as well—stalked and harassed by someone who knew enough about the world of *drakons* to find my personal information and track down my cloister. I did not know what to think back then, as I do not exist outside the draconian world, but I do now. This person, this stalker, only discovered me after I meddled in Reynard's affairs." Misha tossed the scale onto Sebastian's desk. "Someone is hunting the mates and children of the Drakes, and that someone has now set his sights on your family."

Sebastian threw his hands down onto his desk and sprang to his feet, snarling at Misha, but the omega did not back down. "And you are here to taunt me, then?"

"No." Misha crossed his arms. "I am here to save your ass. Now, come. There is work to be done."

A bit of smoke escaped Sebastian's nostrils, but after some consideration, he grunted and came out from behind his desk. Misha was abrasive, but he did not mean harm. If his help could keep Perry and the children safe, then Sebastian would accept it gladly. "Very well," he said. "Do as you wish."

Misha's eyes sparkled with excitement, and he rubbed his hands together with glee. "Finally. Another *drakon* with common sense. I will begin with a full investigation of your lair. While I am at work, I have a task for you. You must arrange to have the children sent away. The farther the better. And soon. This person, whoever he is, is taunting you. He left the scale as a warning that he is in control, and he could strike at any time. The work that must be done to make this place safe will not be accomplished overnight. Therefore, if you care for your boys, they must go."

"How far?"

Misha shrugged. "California should suffice."

"You mean for me to entrust them to Geoff?"

"Da. He is smart, our hunter, and he will not travel so far and risk too much when there are plenty of *drakons* here for him to terrorize."

Sebastian did not like it one bit, and knew Perry would like it even less, but Misha was right. Geoff and Ian together were a fearsome force, and no one in their right mind would fly out of Aurora to attack a lair which two dragons called home. Especially not with so many vulnerable Drakes here.

"I will call Geoff and make arrangements," Sebastian said. "How long will it take you to evaluate? Bertram recently—"

Misha held out a hand. "Bertram is an idiot and knows nothing. I will be as quick as I can, but it will take time. Two hours? Three?"

"Fine. When you are done, come find me here."

"And you." Misha wagged a finger at him. "When you have finished with Geoffrey, you will speak with your mate. You will not hide this from him. If you try, I will tell him myself, and leave you to deal with the consequences."

Irritation throbbed in Sebastian's temples, and he clenched his fists. "I was planning on it."

"Good. Good." Misha waved him away. "Then off I go. I will see you soon, *drakon*, and we will discuss what it will take to make this place secure. Good luck with California."

Sebastian grumbled in response, plopped into his desk chair, and got to work. There was much to be done, and if Misha was to be believed, scant time to do it in.

"We must send the children away," Sebastian said after Perry sat in one of the office's leather armchairs. "It's not safe. Geoff is willing to take them in."

Perry's lips pinched in at the corners and his eyes glossed over with tears. "For how long?"

"For however long it takes. Misha is here, assessing our security. He will tell us. But he says it is not something that can be done overnight."

"I see." Perry, who sat cross-legged, dropped one of his legs to trace a circle on the floor with his toe. "But what of the older boys? Are they not enough?"

"They have given up enough of their time, Perry. We can't ask them to put their lives on pause to protect their brothers forever."

"I just..." Perry swallowed. "I don't want them to go, Seb. I am not allowed outside the house to visit our friends and family, and now I'm to be without my boys as well?"

"It is for their safety."

"I know." Perry hung his head and looked very miserable indeed. "I understand that they must go, but... what if this persists? What if we never catch who is responsible?"

"We will."

It looked like Perry had something to say to that, but whatever it was didn't make it past his lips. Instead, he wrapped his arms around himself dejectedly and sighed.

"The boys will leave tomorrow," Sebastian said when his mate was silent. "And we will sleep in the hoard room at night."

Perry opened his mouth to speak, but was stopped when the door opened. He whipped his head around and Sebastian leapt up from his desk, ready to set fire to any threat that walked through the door, but it was only Misha.

"My investigation did not take long," he said. "First, a compliment. I must applaud you for how well you have protected yourself against *drakons*, but any human thief with half a brain cell would have no issue getting inside. Fixing this will take time. A month. Perhaps two. During this time, you must leave. There will be too many people in and out to guarantee your safety, which will give our *friend* the perfect opportunity to strike. Do you have somewhere you can go? Somewhere no one will think to find you, where you might be safe?"

Sebastian thought on it a moment, then nodded.

"Good. Prepare to leave. We must find a crew to start renovations as quickly as we can, and you must be gone before they arrive." Misha clucked his tongue. "Oh, and do be mindful not to tell the staff. No one must know anything. *No one.* Information travels. You must stop it before it begins."

Sebastian thought back on what had happened with Finch, who'd been attacked by who he assumed was a member of the staff, and nodded. "Agreed."

"Will we be able to return home after?" Perry asked, climbing carefully out of his chair with one hand on his belly so he could face Misha when he spoke. "Will the boys?"

"You, yes. The boys..." Misha shrugged. "We shall see."

Perry sighed, and Sebastian knew that he was not happy, but it could not be helped. This was a necessary pain. Danger was at their doorstep, and if they did nothing, they would suffer from more than simple discomfort, and Sebastian would not allow that to happen. No matter how painful, they would see this through, and by doing it, they would keep their family safe.

PERRY

Present Day

In a flurry of luggage and laughter, the boys were gone. Perry smiled with all his heart and waved high over his head until the fleet of stylish black Town Cars whisked them away, but when the last car disappeared beyond the walls of the estate, it took Perry's joy with it. Depleted, he dropped his arm and slumped against Sebastian, who stood all too rigidly at his side. Through their mate bond, Perry picked up on all the emotions Sebastian would not let surface—he was sad to see the boys go, too, and anxious over what was still to come.

"It won't be forever," Perry assured him, taking Sebastian's hand and slotting their fingers together. "We have weathered storms before, Sebastian, and we shall weather this one, too."

"We shall."

"There's a 'but' hiding in that sentence."

Sebastian released Perry's hand to squeeze the cheek of Perry's ass. "There is only one butt I concern myself with, and I can assure you, I would never hide it."

"Scoundrel." With a weary smile, Perry lifted onto his toes to kiss Sebastian's shoulder. "I would not hide it, either, were it not for the well-being of the children. And the staff, I suppose, although I dare say there are some who would not find it much of a hardship were I to parade about in the nude. I've seen how they look at us, you know." With tremendous elegance, Perry slipped around to stand in front of his mate and placed one hand on his chest. Chin tilted up to look Sebastian in the eyes, he channeled what little happiness he could muster and infused it alongside a tremendous deal of flirtatious playfulness into their mate bond. "The flashes of white when their eyes go wide upon discovering us tucked away in a corner. The small gasps and the delicate clicks of softly latched doors when they find us pursuing our passions in... unusual places. And have you seen the way some of them look at me now? How their eyes wander to my bump to see for themselves how deeply you've claimed me? For those souls, transparency would be a delight."

"And those souls," Sebastian growled, scooping Perry into his arms in one swift movement, "had best keep their hands to themselves, lest they lose them. I do not share treasure. Ever. You, Perry, are mine."

"Yours forever," he swore, and meant it to the very core of his being. "However you may need me, and wherever we shall go. Which, come to think of it, is the question of the hour, isn't it? Where shall we go, my lord? If we must leave here, where shall we make our home?"

"I cannot say."

"Have you not made a decision? The workers arrive tomorrow."

"No. Misha has ordered me not to speak it aloud for fear unwelcome ears may be listening."

"He did, yes, but I thought at the very least, you'd be able to tell me. I suppose I see reason in it, though. You never know who might be listening." Perry trailed a finger suggestively down Sebastian's chest. "I suppose, then, it will have to remain a mystery. If only I weren't so perpetually curious. However shall I distract myself? There's only so much to pack..."

Excitement lit Sebastian's eyes aflame, chasing away his melancholy, and while it did little to improve Perry's own mood, it was a very welcome change indeed. Without a word, Sebastian turned on his heel and carried him into the house, and from there down the long corridors leading to their hoard. A distraction was found between the sheets of their hoard bed, where sparkling treasures dimmed in comparison to the dragon who owned them.

It was noon by the time they stopped.

By then, the sheets and blankets both had been kicked to the foot of the bed, golden trinkets winking from their folds like baubles on a Christmas tree. Both he and Sebastian were nude, as they so often were when they were in bed together, although Perry was saved from total nudity by all of his favorite finery. Beautiful golden bangles climbed the length of his arms and a diamond-studded golden anklet adorned his ankle. The body chains he liked to wear did not agree with his pregnant belly, so Sebastian had crowned him with a sapphire circlet and clasped necklace after necklace around his neck until Perry was so weighed down with riches that sitting upright proved to be a challenge.

Now that he and Sebastian had finished making love, he removed each of the necklaces carefully, pooling them on Sebastian's chest.

"We should eat," Perry said as he placed another necklace on his mate. "We shan't have any strength for the journey ahead should we lounge about in bed all day."

"Is that so?" Sebastian rolled onto his hands and knees, a sea of jewelry sliding from his chest in the process. It clinked prettily as it landed on the bed, then again as Sebastian rolled Perry onto his stomach and crawled into position between his legs. Perry, pleased with what was happening, allowed Sebastian to lift him by the hips until he was elevated enough he could get his knees beneath him. Which he did. It gave Sebastian the freedom to part his legs and trail kisses up the inside of his thigh. "Must we get out of bed to eat?"

"Mm, no, I suppose not." A shiver of pleasure worked itself up Perry's spine. "You do know I love it when you touch me there. How could I ever tell you no?"

Sebastian growled in appreciation and kissed his way to the spot Perry was talking about—the mate mark on his cheek, their private proof that Sebastian had claimed him forever—then beyond it to places far more intimate. Perry gasped and moaned and writhed, but Sebastian was insistent, and while he'd never been much for words, his tongue was skilled in things unspoken. Delights only his mate would know.

"Oh, Sebastian," Perry cried. "*Sebastian.*"

It was near one by the time they stopped.

Lunch would be served cold, but it was not without its merits. Perry felt much improved, and the sly little looks Sebastian shot him across the dinner table promised this was only the beginning.

It was agreed, sometime between a hurried blowjob behind one of the bookcases in the library and their retreat into their hoard and the bed therein, that they would leave in the morning before the workers arrived. Perry escaped distraction long enough that evening to check in with a harried Geoffrey and the children, then called it a night. Early the next morning, he collected the last few golden trinkets he simply couldn't bear to part with and tiptoed across the hoard room to stow them in his travel bag. In it was enough clothing to see him through the week, several gold pieces he'd already packed for fear he'd forget them, and a few of his favorite personal care items. Presumably, Sebastian would take him to one of the other American proper-ties he owned, where Perry would already have a store of everyday essentials and loose, billowy clothing even his pregnant self could wear, but it wasn't a sure thing, so packing felt necessary.

But no matter how much gold Perry stowed away, he couldn't shake the feeling he was forgetting something.

Whatever could it be?

Before he could figure it out, Sebastian sighed in his sleep and rolled over, groping the spot in their bed where Perry had last been. "Peregrine... where are you, my Peregrine?"

"I'm here, my love. I'm never far."

Sebastian grumbled incomprehensibly and rolled over, dragging the blankets with him. Perry waited for a moment to see if he'd stir, and when he didn't, went about his business. If he left without figuring out what it was that was bothering him, he'd regret it the entire time they were gone, and he had precious few hours to figure it out.

It couldn't be clothing, which could be easily purchased no matter where they went, or jewelry, as he'd spirited away all of his favorites already. Could it have something to do with the children? It had been eight years since he'd last had an empty nest, and he'd grown used to packing for all the unexpected disasters that came hand in hand with having offspring.

But still, it didn't feel right.

Perhaps it wasn't about packing for disasters so much as it was the forces that caused them. Without the children, what was he to do for the next few months? Perry prodded at the jewelry in his bag as he considered it. Sex was wonderful, but he couldn't depend on Sebastian to occupy his every waking hour. Besides, Perry had a feeling that with everything going on, he would be called away for business, and how long he'd be gone was anyone's guess. If that did happen, Perry would have no one.

Unless...

He zipped his travel bag in a hurry and crept across the hoard room, hoping not to wake Sebastian, but it was too late. Sebastian was awake, and when Perry sneaked by the bed, he sat up. "Where are you off to, Perry?"

"To pack," Perry told him. "There are a few more things I must see to before we leave."

"Come to bed first."

Perry eyed Sebastian's erection, which was tenting the bedding. As tempting as it was, he shook his head. "I'm afraid what I must see to will take some time. I'll make it up to you this evening, after we've arrived."

Sebastian grumbled, but didn't otherwise object. It was a good thing, as the longer Perry spent looking at what fun he could be having, the weaker his will became.

"I'll meet you in the garage in a few hours, Sebastian," he said, turning away to block out temptation. "And please, feel free to take your time. I'm not sure exactly how long I'll be, but I can assure you it won't be quick."

Sebastian Drake's primary garage was modest in comparison to the mammoth constructs owned by some of his brothers—Geoffrey in particular—but there had once been a time in Perry's life where he would have considered such a place immense. From one wall to another it could fit seven cars with enough room between them that even Sebastian could walk between them with their doors open, and it was wide enough to fit five such rows with enough room to drive between them. In years past it had homed its fair share of luxury sports cars, but these days they were outranked by safe, sensible, and roomy models purchased after the laying of their clutch. It was, after all, impractical to fit eight nestlers into a Jaguar. And eight children? It simply could not be done.

Luckily, the Jaguar had been taken off their hands by Alistair and the older children had stepped in to relieve them of one vehicle each, leaving plenty of room for new purchases. One of them—a boxy black van with seating for twelve—was parked in a space near the front of the garage, near the leftmost door. Perry made a beeline for it. There was something he needed to see.

"Shall I see to it that she's detailed before your excursion today?" inquired Pritchard, their live-in mechanic and automotive overseer, as Perry studied the van's backside. Perry turned his head to look at her, unaware that she'd noticed him enter, but glad to have her on hand. There was no one better suited to do what he needed done.

"Pritchard," he said with a smile. "You look positively radiant. Have things been going well with Hastings?"

Pritchard's cheeks colored, "Quite well, sir. Thank you."

"I'm glad to hear it." Perry dimpled. "Both of you work so hard, and I couldn't be happier that you've found each other. The more love these walls keep safe, the better."

Pritchard, seemingly flattered, swept a loose lock of hair behind her ear, which was quite charming, but slightly less so when she dropped her hand to reveal she'd accidentally streaked grease across her forehead. Perry stole a look at her hands, which were black from dirty things he couldn't name, then lifted his chin to look her in the eyes and smiled more brightly than ever. "In answer to your earlier question, detailing isn't quite what I had in mind. Close to the opposite, in fact."

"The opposite, sir?"

"Yes. But before I tell you what it is I mean, let me refresh my memory with a look at the vehicle's interior. So much hinges on the space available, you see." Perry took a small step forward and pressed the button on the handle of the van's sliding back door. It disengaged from its setting and slid open all on its own. It was, in Perry's opinion, a marvel of the modern age that defied explanation and, much like when he'd first seen a light bulb flicker to life, convinced him that man was more magical than he let on.

The interior of the van was quite large indeed. It was filled with rows of seats with scorch marks on their backs—an unfortunate rite of passage for any vehicle in which children who could summon flame were ferried for any amount of time. Perry stuck his head inside to get a good look, then stepped back. "It is quite large in there, isn't it?"

"Quite, sir. She's the largest vehicle in the fleet."

"Excellent." Perry pressed the button and delighted in watching the door slide shut. Would technology never cease to be thrilling? He sincerely hoped not. "Tell me, Pritchard… would it be possible to make some modifications to the van's interior?"

"Modifications, sir?"

"Small ones. Nothing permanent." Perry folded his hands politely behind his back and looked up at the Attendant. She was quite beautiful. Silver streamed through her long brown hair, which she kept pinned in a messy bun stuck through with a ballpoint pen. Age and exposure had leathered her skin somewhat, but if anything, it added to her charm. She reminded Perry quite a lot of Lus, who had worked hard all his life, fallen in love with a sweet young thing who'd made him happy, and raised a family any good man would be proud of. "Would you be willing to discuss the specifics with me over a coffee break?" He laid a hand delicately on his stomach. "I won't be drinking, of course, but I am a little peckish. Do you enjoy fruit tarts? I do, and I am craving one in the worst way."

Pritchard's gaze dipped to his belly and stayed there for a thoughtful second. "Of course, sir. I'd be happy to indulge you."

"Oh, darling, you mustn't let Sebastian hear you say that." Perry twittered with laughter. "He is ever so possessive these days, which I suppose is the way it ought to be, considering the circumstances. Now, come. The sitting room isn't all that far. On the way I'll speak with a member of the staff and have our refreshments delivered. Do you need to stop to freshen up before we sit?"

Pritchard tugged free a grease-streaked rag previously tucked into her belt and held it up in demonstration. "No, sir, but thank you. That's awfully kind, but I already have all I need."

Perry nodded. "Well, I'll have moist towelettes brought in as well, just in case."

The fruit tarts were delicious, and the company even more so. While their conversation was disappointingly brief, it wasn't for lack of things to talk about—Pritchard was absolutely charming, and if it weren't for the pressing nature of that morning's activities, Perry would have loved to talk with her for hours. Perhaps one day, once the lair was safe and the children were otherwise occupied, he'd do so, but for now it was of utmost importance that he and Sebastian leave before the construction crews arrived later this morning.

In any case, once her coffee was drained, Pritchard excused herself to see to Perry's requests. There would be just enough time, she assured him, to make sure everything was done before Sebastian arrived. Perry saw her as far as the sitting room door, thanked her sweetly, and let her go on her way. There were other matters he needed to tend to and a cold-blooded ball he needed to get in the air. It was a blessing, he thought as he returned to his near-empty plate, that Cook had been so thoughtful as to garnish his breakfast with fresh fruit. The strawberries would make his next chore much easier to accomplish, for Perry had long ago learned that the best way to convince a reptile to do anything was through his stomach.

So, plate of fruit in hand, off Perry went. There was one last thing he needed to pack, and it would require a little finagling and a fair amount of bribery to get it stowed away.

"Must we take this vehicle?" Sebastian eyed the van with distaste, arms crossed over his chest. He'd dressed in simple clothing today —a white button-down tucked into belted black slacks, the sleeves of the shirt rolled to his elbows. Perry thought he looked quite fetching this way, but then again, he found Sebastian to be fetching no matter how much or how little clothing he saw fit to wear. "It's excessive."

"It's not excessive in the least," Perry countered. "In fact, I'd call it just right."

"The children are gone. We have no one to ferry."

"You are only partially correct." Perry stepped forward and pushed the button on the door handle. The door slid open slowly, revealing an inch at a time what waited inside.

"You see," Perry explained as the door came to the end of its track, "we do have someone to ferry."

"*Peregrine.*"

"Please, Sebastian?" Perry clasped his hands together. "The children are gone and you are to uproot me from all the familiar comforts of my lair. Will you have me stay wherever it is we're going without a friend?"

Sebastian sighed heavily and dropped his arms from his chest. "You will have me for company."

"And what of the times when you must step away to tend to business?"

"They will be few and far between." Sebastian stole another look into the van and sighed again. "I have told Bertram that until the threat to my family has been neutralized, I will not be available to him, and there is no one else who would call upon my services."

"What of your father?"

"Father?" Sebastian shook his head. "Father is too busy caring for his expectant mate."

"I wouldn't be so sure."

The easy, if somewhat vexed, expression on Sebastian's face darkened. "You speak as though there's something I should know."

"No. Not at all. Your father and I are not in close contact and I haven't heard from him since I last paid Walter a visit. I know nothing. I said what I did off intuition alone." Perry met Sebastian's piercing gaze and held it. There had been a time where such a cold look would have frozen him to the core, but he was the mate of a dragon now, and no one loved a beast without learning to tolerate its claw. "But you must also know that my intuition is often right. I don't know how I know these things—only that I do."

"You worry me, Perry."

"Darling, I worry me, too." Perry smiled and stepped forward, lifting up onto his toes to better cup Sebastian's cheek. "But all will be well. It always is. Even though we sometimes suffer, we will recover. And perhaps, if you are busy, it will be for the best— you'll be less inclined to worry over me when you have work to focus on. But, should you need to leave..." He pouted his bottom lip. "May I please have this one small concession? Please?"

"You absolute vixen," Sebastian grumbled as he drew Perry into his arms. "I can't tell if you're being honest over this intuition of yours, or if it's all a tangled web meant to ensnare me into doing your bidding."

Perry hid his smirk against Sebastian's chest. "I'm afraid that's my secret to keep, my love."

A rumble sounded behind Sebastian's ribs, and very suddenly Perry's feet left the ground. The dragon had scooped him up as though he weighed nothing, and now moved to pin him against the side of the van.

"What will I have to do," Sebastian whispered against his lips as the kiss of cool metal chilled his back, "to coax the truth out of you?"

A thrill shot through Perry, and he wrapped his legs around

Sebastian's waist. "Whatever it is," he whispered back, "you'll need to work long and hard at it, indeed."

Someone nearby cleared their throat, causing Sebastian to growl in frustration and Perry to peek over his shoulder, where he found Pritchard standing a few feet away. Next to her was a small silver hand truck onto which had been loaded a wooden crate, its top missing, filled to the brim with assorted greens. Perry had been taught to identify jewels, amongst other luxuries, so not all of them were familiar, but he did recognize a few—romaine, collard greens, kale, and arugula.

"Excuse me, sirs," Pritchard said. "The kitchen has just had this delivered—would you like me to load it into the back?"

Sebastian set Perry on his feet and turned to face her. "Is there not enough in the van already? It's everywhere, Pritchard. All over the goddamn floor. You've turned my van into a salad bowl. Tell me why we need more."

"The Attendants were insistent," she replied with a simple shrug, not in the least bit intimidated. "Shall I load it?"

A bit of smoke escaped Sebastian, but it was all for show. Perry was certain of it. Of all the wonderfully heroic things at which Sebastian was skilled, theatrics topped the list. At least when he was grumpy. It was unabashedly adorable.

"Yes, thank you, Pritchard," Perry replied while Sebastian smoldered. "We'll be in need of all the greens we can get at this mysterious destination of ours. Isn't that right, Sebastian?"

Sebastian glanced menacingly over his shoulder at Perry. Smoke continued to curl from his nostrils, which Perry found to be absolutely precious. "Of course, beloved," he said flatly. "Nothing would bring me greater joy."

It was settled, then.

What Perry wanted would be his.

Had Perry not been pregnant, he would have bounced up and wrapped his arms around Sebastian's neck to pepper his face with kisses, but with the babe in such a delicate state, Perry settled for beaming at Sebastian instead.

The smoke stopped pouring from Sebastian's nostrils, and after a moment, he smiled back.

"Do you hear that, Pake?" Perry asked as he spun around to look into the back of the van, where all the seats had been stripped out and one very large, very old tortoise had been loaded into the cabin. He sat on a nest of greens that closely resembled the ones in the crate, which he was in the process of eating. An empty plate was tucked into a nearby corner, empty save for a strawberry-red streak. "Sebastian says you can accompany us. How much fun we'll have. You do so adore to travel, and it's been so long since we last went anywhere."

Pake lifted his head to regard Perry. Assorted greens hung out of his closed mouth. After a moment's consideration, he began to chew, and the greens slowly disappeared.

"Look, Sebastian," Perry cooed. "Pake is glad to hear that he's welcome to come, too."

Sebastian sighed. "I'll load the crate. Perry, you get settled in the front seat. It's time to go."

Perry reached into the back and stroked Pake's smooth, cool skin, then sat in the front and prepared himself for the journey. It was a dark time, yes, but with his mate and a friend with whom he could share the burden, he'd survive. There were still happy days ahead. He knew it. All he had to do was wait and one day, they'd be his.

In the interest of security, Sebastian ordered their chauffeur to take a long and relaxing vacation and drove the van himself. Traffic in Aurora was always thick, so leaving the city took some time, and from there, Sebastian took scenic back roads through the country where theirs was often the only vehicle to be seen. Perry hadn't a clue whether Sebastian knew where he was going, or if he was driving at random to flush out any potential pursuers, but, whatever the case, they emerged onto the interstate several hours later and drove for several hours more before Perry recognized a road sign.

"Are you taking us to Gardenia Cottage, Sebastian?" he asked, twisting around in his seat to face his dragon. "Are you quite sure?"

"Extremely."

"It's been ages since we've been to visit."

"I'm aware."

Excitement brought a flush of warmth to Perry's cheeks. "Is April too early for the gardens to have flowered? It's been so long I can't recall. But I suppose, with warmer weather here to stay, that we'll be in residence long enough to see them flourish, even should we arrive before the first bloom. I simply cannot wait! Have the staff been made aware of our visit, or will they be in for a surprise?"

"They are not aware."

"Poor dears." Perry fidgeted with his seat belt, which had locked when he'd turned so hastily toward Sebastian. "Well, I suppose it can't be helped. We'll be gentle with them. I wouldn't want any of them to feel ashamed over any potential shortcomings with the property's upkeep. They are, after all, a skeleton staff meant to keep the house in order, but not necessarily in pristine condition."

Sebastian grunted in acknowledgment, which was as sure a sign as any that he agreed.

"Oh, Gardenia Cottage," Perry sighed. "I hadn't realized how much I missed it until now. When is the last time we stayed, Sebastian? A decade ago? Longer?"

"It was years before the whelps were born." Sebastian took the upcoming exit and followed the road away from the small hub of civilization clustered at the highway's edge. "Fifteen years total, if I were to guess."

"Fifteen years." Perry shook his head. In terms of a dragon's lifespan, fifteen years was barely any time at all, but Perry had been raised to believe he'd never see life past thirty, and even five hundred years later, fifteen years was a small eternity. "We must find time to come here more often once all is said and done and life returns to normal."

Pake stuck his head between their seats to lay his chin on Perry's armrest. Pleased, Perry took to stroking his head.

"We shall find time to bring the children before they are grown," said Sebastian as they drove by dense, rich evergreen forests. "Perhaps for their next birthday. We must also find time to visit the palace near Beirut as well."

"After the babe is born," Perry said as he placed a hand on his stomach. "I would like very much to bring her."

Sebastian nodded, and from there it was a quiet drive to their old, much beloved, home.

Gardenia Cottage was tucked into a clearing in a peaceful part of the forest not all that far from a large freshwater lake. It was a newer construct—only two hundred years old—and had been built in true English style. Perry, homesick for England, had begged for it, and Sebastian, ever the gentleman, had made it happen. At one time, it had been Perry's fondest possession, and as Sebastian pulled up the long driveway, he remembered why that was.

Gardenia Cottage was surrounded by gorgeous dry-stone walls behind which were neatly manicured lawns, nary a weed in sight. There were lush gardens both in front of and behind the house, and in the spring and summertime, they bloomed in all shades of purple. Perry was fondest of the lilac trees, as they were the most constant of the flowering plants, and, in his opinion, some of the most beautiful. Time would tell if he'd get to see them at their peak magnificence this year. It both would and would not be a pleasure for entirely separate reasons.

The cottage itself was made of stone and was an impressive size. It boasted a modest fifteen bedrooms and its own tiny hoard, where Sebastian's lesser treasures were stored. There was a large kitchen, a dining room, several sitting rooms, and an atrium designed for Pake, although it would work in a pinch for a family with a small number of whelps. It was into that last room that Perry ushered his beloved tortoise, prompting him to follow with a selection of fruit proffered to him by one of Gardenia Cottage's befuddled Attendants. The staff's confusion was understandable— it wasn't often a dragon arrived at one of his seldom-visited properties with a mate and a tortoise in tow.

In any case, adjustments were made. Sheets were changed in a hurry, Cook launched into action, and a few of the braver Attendants even came to visit Perry and Pake in the atrium, where Perry taught them everything they'd need to know should they need to care for his tortoise in his absence. Sebastian, meanwhile, hovered nearby, nose buried in his phone and lips twisted into a menacing scowl that could only mean one thing.

It came as no surprise when he approached and broke the news to Perry. "I must travel on the morrow."

Perry looked up at him from where he lounged on the grassy atrium floor, Pake at his side. "Your father?"

"Indeed."

"I'm very seldom wrong, aren't I?"

"Troublingly so."

"Well," Perry smiled, doing everything in his power to make it as charming as possible, "I can't say that I'm surprised. I will be here, of course, and you needn't worry—Pake will keep me company. Do you have any clue how long you'll be gone?"

"No."

"Business as usual, then." Perry distracted himself from sighing by tracing the ridges of Pake's shell. "I have faith you'll have it done quickly and come home to me before long."

Without hesitation, Sebastian dropped to his knees there in the atrium and leaned in to touch his forehead to Perry's. It was so unexpectedly intimate that Perry inwardly gasped and closed his eyes, lost to the love between them.

"I vow it," Sebastian swore. "I will come home to you."

"I love you more than anything, Sebastian Drake," Perry whispered. "More than gold, more than jewels, more than life itself. I don't care how long it takes—I will wait."

With tremendous care, Sebastian lowered Perry into the grass and kissed him with the sincerity of a love five hundred years in the making, and Perry returned the kiss with enough love to see them through five hundred more.

Sebastian left the following day, and in his absence, Perry spent his time divided between getting to better know the staff and relaxing in the sunshine with Pake. It was, if he was honest, difficult to transition from being a father of eight mischievous boys to an empty nester with no idea of when that might change, but he warded off loneliness by devouring good books and making himself useful. And, of course, by charming whichever member of the staff happened to be nearby so he could use their phone and call the boys in California. Under Misha's orders, the use of phones and other electronics had been banned for fear that Raven would be able to track them down, and the one phone they were allowed to use—given to them by Misha himself—had been taken by Sebastian on his trip, but the staff at Gardenia Cottage was under no such edict, and it had become somewhat of a game to see whose phone he would borrow on any given day.

One week into his new routine, a letter arrived from Sebastian. The job was taking longer than expected and Bertram had been called in to help. With some luck, it would be over before the week's end, but he could make no promises. Judging by the somewhat terse language used, Sebastian was not happy that Bertram was there, and Perry predicted that would make the job all the more complex.

He was right.

Two weeks after arriving at the cottage, another letter appeared. The job was not yet done. Bertram was proving difficult to work with, and they were butting heads on the best way to manage the situation—whatever that might be. Perry hadn't the foggiest. But it was ever so strange for Bertram, who strove to be so much like their father, to butt heads with Sebastian on a mission of their father's design.

One month after arriving at the cottage, while taking the morning off to elevate his swollen feet, a third letter arrived. The job was done, but there were loose ends to wrap up that would necessitate Sebastian to stay away for a little while longer. It wasn't welcome news, but Perry took it in stride. He was seven months pregnant now—more pregnant than he'd ever been—and the babe kicked and fluttered. She'd yet to go still. Like him, it seemed she would wait for Sebastian to come home, and as long as that was the case, Perry wouldn't rush him. He wrote back to Sebastian with all his love, then spent the rest of the day with Pake in the atrium, where they basked in the sunlight and ate fresh, delicious food brought to them by the Attendants.

It was, in a word, bliss.

Only two months remained until they'd welcome their first dragonet into the world, and even should things go wrong and Perry deliver prematurely, at this point in her development, there was a chance she would live. Drenched in sunlight and relaxed as could be next to his oldest friend, Perry ran his hand over his belly and allowed himself to dream of holding her. How sweet it would be to kiss the top of her head and hold her tiny hand in his. And maybe after her there would be others—precious children with their father's dark features and Perry's beaming smile.

He wanted them.

All of them.

And for the first time, a world where it was possible was within his reach.

Two more months.

Just two more.

Which was no time at all for a dragon, but an eternity in the same breath.

Sebastian returned home a month later, a week after Perry entered his eighth month of pregnancy. For such a small omega, Perry had ballooned, and while the baby weight was cumbersome and made it difficult to get around, he had never been so happy. Which was why, after hearing from one of the Attendants that Sebastian's vehicle had been spotted on its way down the driveway, Perry left the comforts of the atrium to greet him at the door.

Smyth, the Attendant who'd taken on doorman duties since their arrival, bowed his head politely at Perry and stepped forward to open the door. On the other side stood Sebastian, whose expression went from stoic to wide-eyed after laying eyes on his mate.

"Perry," he uttered, then rushed forward and came to an abrupt stop an arm's reach away. Hesitation played across his face. To Perry, it looked very much like he was a child confronted by something small and sweet and delicate—something that could easily be destroyed by a single careless act. "You..."

"I've gotten quite big, haven't I?" Perry grinned and reached forward, taking Sebastian's hand and placing it on his belly. "She's doing well, Sebastian. She grows more every day. I truly think we've done it—after all these years, the curse has been broken. We'll have a child to call our own. Our very first."

Sebastian's nostrils flared, and after a long moment, he took his hand away and tugged Perry into his arms, lifting him up so they were face to face. Joy shone in his eyes. "My love. Oh, my love. We've done it. She will be ours, I swear."

Perry nodded, then looped his arms around Sebastian's neck and laughed until tears streamed down his cheeks. It was a dream come to life, and with his dragon home, it was only getting better.

"The construction has been completed," said Sebastian one morning as they lay in bed naked, Perry dripping with gold and satisfied from that morning's lovemaking. Sebastian held his phone aloft and was looking at its screen. "Misha says we can come home."

"Do you think it wise to move now?" Perry asked, propping his chin on Sebastian's shoulder. "There are only a few weeks until my due date—we could stay here where it's peaceful and quiet. Why return to somewhere we've been threatened? I do quite like it here, and I would be fine with staying until the threat has been contained."

"I would stay as well, but Everard will not travel."

"Why not? He's done so before—and over greater distances, might I remind you."

"Remind me not. I know. He is choosing to be cautious. Father saw fit to send him along on our latest mission, as there were some," Sebastian set his lips, "*unsavory* moments in which his skills proved useful. However, he has become aware that something is afoot, and he won't leave Harrison or his whelp again. Not for love or money."

"Mm. Sensible." Perry sighed. "Would it be a travesty were we to invite them to stay?"

Sebastian set his phone down and narrowed his eyes.

"I'll take that as a yes."

"How very perceptive of you."

"My intuition is next to none." Perry kissed Sebastian's cheek, then moved as gracefully as he could to put some distance between them. Loose gold coins tumbled from his body and became lost between the sheets. "When are we to leave, then?" he asked as he struggled to sit up. Sebastian moved to help him, bracing him from behind. "I imagine the sooner, the better with my due date so close at hand."

"Today, if we're able."

"Today?" Perry, surprised, peered over his shoulder at his mate. "When I meant soon, I'd thought perhaps tomorrow—I hadn't realized we were in such a rush."

"Misha is insistent."

"Why?"

"The longer our lair sits empty, the more vulnerable it becomes. In addition, Everard has availability this evening. It has been too long since his last visit. I would sleep better knowing he has checked on you and the babe."

A creeping feeling that something wasn't quite as it seemed spread through the back of Perry's mind, prickling its way along his skull, but he pushed his doubts aside. Misha was an expert and Sebastian was right—as healthy as the babe seemed to be, having Everard there to assure them all was going well would do them both a world of good.

"When shall we leave, then?" Perry asked. "I only care for the jewelry I've brought and Pake, of course. The rest of my belongings can be shipped to us at a later date."

"We'll aim for noon," Sebastian said, and picked up his phone anew. "I'll notify Misha and get in touch with Everard. While I do, you should rest. I'll pack your belongings when I've finished."

With great effort, Perry climbed out of bed and onto his feet. "I'm pregnant, not paralyzed," he said as he picked what jewelry he could find out of the sheets. "I'm sure you have matters to tend to, my love. I'll be fine on my own."

What should have been a five-hour drive took seven, owing to a certain mischievous miss who thought it hilarious to kick Perry in the bladder, but at half-past seven, right as night was setting in, they arrived. It was strange to be back in Aurora after living in the country, and while Perry was glad to be back in his lair, a certain uneasiness persisted that he couldn't shake. The house hadn't changed much, as construction had been done on parts not often seen by the eye, but there was something different about it. Something cold. Like in their absence, the workers had stripped out what made the place a home and left behind an empty shell.

Upon arriving, Pritchard and a small team of core Attendants met them in the garage to help unload their belongings and coax Pake back into the atrium. Perry would have helped, but Pake seemed glad to be home, and trudged his way out of the van and into the house without having to be bribed. It was a good thing, as Perry was sore all over and in dire need of a bed. After Everard saw to him, he'd call it a night. Traveling while pregnant was nowhere near as fun as traveling while not, and he would be sure to remember it the next time Sebastian took his heat.

"I'm off to bed, darling," Perry told Sebastian as he waddled around expensive cars on his way across the garage. "Would you prefer I lie down in the bedroom, or in the hoard? Which will be most convenient to Everard?"

"The hoard. I'd rather you be safe. I will show him in when he arrives."

"Wonderful. Thank you." Perry reached Sebastian, who was standing by the door into the house watching as Pake led a group of Attendants down the hall, and gave his mate a chaste kiss. "Should I happen to fall asleep, don't feel poorly over waking me. I will be delighted to see Everard, and I would be quite cross were he to conduct the examination and leave before I had a chance to say hello."

"I will wake you," Sebastian vowed, and kissed Perry very sweetly before sending him on his way.

The hoard room was not all that far from the atrium, so Perry followed Pake for some way, then split off down the hall in the hopes he'd feel refreshed by the time Everard arrived. Before he reached the hoard room, however, something peculiar stopped him—a familiar voice. It belonged to Misha, and it was coming from behind a door that had been left ajar. "It took you long enough. I've been waiting. Where have you been?"

"Misha? What are you doing here?" The uncomfortable feeling that had plagued him since this morning returned in full force. "Why aren't you with Reynard? Have you been hiding all this time?"

"The details are irrelevant. There has been a new development and I must speak to you before it's too late."

"Too late? For what?"

"Come inside, *koshka*. All will be revealed, but not where someone might overhear. Privacy is essential. You must come here."

Perry glanced down the hall, which was empty, then at the door. It hadn't budged since he'd arrived, and it was open to such a small degree that he couldn't spot Misha through the crack. "Darling, I'm so terribly exhausted from today's trip. Is this why you called us home? So we could talk? I appreciate all the work you've done to keep us safe, but I'm not sure how much I'll retain of what you have to tell me. Pregnancy brain is every bit as real as egg brain, and I am deep in its throes."

"It is of no issue. Come." The door crept open another inch. "You can sit while we talk inside, but you must come. What I have to say must not be heard by your dragon."

239

The feeling of wrong intensified, and the hair on the back of Perry's neck stood on end. "Come again?"

"It is a sensitive topic, and must not be overheard."

"No, what was it you called Sebastian?"

"What is the matter, *koshka?* Sebastian is your dragon."

"No, he's not." Perry's heart began to race. "Misha never pronounces 'dragon' that way. Who are you?"

The door flew open, and all Perry had time to do before he was grabbed and dragged inside was scream. So scream he did, as loud as he could, in the hopes that it would be enough to save him.

26

PEREGRINE

1509

Peregrine screamed as pain twisted inside of him. It tore through his lower abdomen like a blade slicing him from the inside, then radiated as though his guts were being set on fire. No matter how much he struggled or clenched or cried, it never got any better. Worse, he knew it would continue. Over the last two weeks, he'd received treatments identical to these every other day while Everard chased the rot out of him. It was excruciating. But, if he was lucky, this would be the last of it, and he'd never have to feel this way again.

"Settle, Peregrine," Everard demanded, pushing his hand more firmly into the space below Peregrine's navel. "Magic is difficult enough—I need you to cooperate and stay as quiet and still as you can, or I can't guarantee my work."

"It *burns*."

"I would worry if it were to freeze. We are dragons, omega. Fire is in our blood, and that same fire that fuels us is now fixing you from the inside. Do not fight it."

Peregrine squeezed his eyes shut and clenched his teeth, but the pain continued, and it was torture.

"Much better." Everard moved his hand lower, closer to Peregrine's groin, and the pain intensified. Peregrine let loose with another cry, yanked a pillow from the bed, and pushed it over his face to muffle the sound.

"We're almost done," Everard said, but the pain did not lessen until he took his hand away. "There. Finished. I've flushed the new rot. You should expect to bleed, but not severely. If there is pain, you must tell either me or Sebastian right away."

Exhausted from the procedure, Peregrine pulled the pillow off his face, but otherwise stayed exactly where he was. It was too much to move. Too difficult. Too potentially painful. And while Everard had promised that he'd been made new, Peregrine wouldn't believe it. Not entirely. Not after the pain he'd just been through.

"Why isn't he moving?" Sebastian demanded from where he stood at the bedside, his face stoic, but his tense body language anything but. "You've hurt him, Everard. You must fix this at once."

"Hurt him?" Everard squawked. "Surely you're mistaken, brother. I haven't hurt him—I've healed him. There's a difference. My magic knits back together the things your claws have destroyed."

Sebastian growled in the same deep, fierce way he had when Peregrine had been injured. Peregrine cracked his eyes open a sliver just in time to see his dragon rush the doctor and grab him by the front of his tunic, hoisting him onto the tips of his toes.

"My claws were not what did him wrong, brother," he seethed, smoke escaping from his nostrils. "I would do nothing to harm him, *ever*. Do not pretend that this was my fault, or I will be forced to pretend that what happens to you was of your own doing. Now, out with you." With a push, he sent Everard stumbling back. "I must tend to my omega. Alone."

Everard grumbled something as he smoothed the front of his tunic, but he left without further complaint after Sebastian fixed him with a glare. Once he was gone, Sebastian came to sit on the bedside and gathered Peregrine in his arms like one might a child. Peregrine, of course, was too old for such comforts, but he sighed and relaxed against Sebastian all the same. He was so large, so strong, and so mighty that it was impossible not to feel safe when wrapped in his embrace.

"Are you well, Peregrine?" Sebastian asked. "Do you feel improved?"

Peregrine smiled as charmingly as he could. "I must admit, now that the doctor is gone, I do feel better."

Sebastian snorted with laughter and nosed his way into Peregrine's hair. "Strange how that works."

"Strange indeed." A beat of silence passed, during which Peregrine made himself comfortable on Sebastian's lap. Once he was settled, he looked into his dragon's eyes and asked, "How much longer will it be before I've recovered?"

"I know not."

"And the doctor?"

"He knows even less." Sebastian kissed the tip of his nose. "But fear not, for you are strong. I have faith you will shake this, Perry. The rot cannot persist forever. Once it clears from your body, you will be well, and we will begin our lives together in earnest."

"A pretty dream, my lord."

"It's no dream. You and I are destined for each other. I know it. The dragon inside of me tells me so."

How magical it was that a dragon who spoke so little knew all the right things to say. Peregrine cuddled close and let the joy of Sebastian's love ease the pain in his heart. All would be well. It seemed impossible, but he knew it to be true.

"Perry?" Sebastian asked after a while.

Peregrine looked up attentively and met his gaze. "Yes?"

"When you are well, and the rot has been cleared from your body, I wish to try again."

"Try for what, my lord?"

"For a clutch. For a child. For whatever you will give me." Sebastian laid his hand on Peregrine's lower abdomen, right where Everard's had been, only there was no pain when Sebastian touched him. Pleasant goose bumps raced up his arms instead, and tingling pleasure pooled in his groin. "I wish to take your heat, as often as you'll give it to me, come whatever may."

Peregrine blinked away tears. "You can't mean that."

"I do."

"But—"

"But nothing." Sebastian kissed his forehead. "You are what I want, and I will not back down. I meant what I said—if you will not bear my clutch, I shall have no clutch at all."

"You treat me as though I am not a Disgrace."

"I treat you as though you are my mate... and I believe, in my heart, that you are."

It all seemed so impossible, but Sebastian was not the kind of dragon who told tales. Overwhelmed by it all, Peregrine blinked tears from his eyes. "How will we know?" he asked. "Is it enough to believe it, or are there other signs? If we are mates, then... then if I do conceive, you need not send me away, but if not..."

"There are ways to tell." Sebastian brushed a tear off his cheek. "An omega mated by a dragon will bear a mark—I have memorized your body from head to toe, and should one appear, I'll know. I have heard tell of a bond that forms between mates, although I have no way to know if it is real, or a legend told to encourage starry-eyed whelps to dream. Through it, you should be able to feel the things I feel—both emotions and physical pain."

"And should you be able to feel mine in turn?"

"I believe so, yes."

"Then did you feel it?" Peregrine asked. "The pain as Everard scrubbed the rot from me?"

Sebastian frowned and shook his head, but it did not look like he'd given up hope. "I do not know how long a bond takes to form, or if they exist at all, but the dragon inside of me tells me you are mine, and so it shall be. For I love you. I love you deeply. I will find a way to keep you, no matter what it might take."

Peregrine closed his eyes and rested his head on Sebastian's shoulder. It seemed so much like a dream, to have won his dragon's love by being nothing but himself, but it was real. Sebastian knew he was a Disgrace, and still he wanted forever.

"I love you, my lord dragon," Peregrine whispered. "I will gladly be your treasure for as long as you shall have me, and I will give you my heat for as long as you should want it."

"Always, then," Sebastian said with a laugh, and kissed the top of Peregrine's head. "I cannot wait until you have recovered so we may try again. Our family will be beautiful. You shall be an excellent father."

"And you," Peregrine said, "will be an excellent mate."

Something changed in Sebastian then—a tightening of his muscles, an inward draw of breath, and a flaring of desire. Peregrine felt it in the air, in his heart, in his bones. It unspooled inside of him, heightening his own desire, and so it came as no surprise that when he lifted his head to look at Sebastian, Sebastian kissed him fiercely. Peregrine wrapped his arms around his neck and shifted his position to straddle Sebastian's lap, deepening their passion until they were both hard, panting, and desperate for more.

"When the bleeding has stopped," Sebastian uttered breathlessly, "you must tell me at once so I may ravage you."

"I will."

"Do you know the things you do to me? How enraptured I am by you?"

"No, I can't say I do..." Peregrine paused and considered it. "Although I cannot fathom that anyone could desire a lover with greater ferocity than I desire you."

Sebastian growled and kissed him again, pushing him down amongst their bedding while yanking aside Peregrine's hose. Peregrine gasped and kissed him harder, wanting nothing more than for Sebastian to claim him, but as aroused as he was, he knew better than to give in. "You must refrain, my lord."

"Refrain from what?" Sebastian wrapped his hand around Peregrine's dick. "From pleasuring you?"

"Everard says I will bleed to pass the rot. You mustn't come in contact with it. I cannot say I understand, but there is tissue trapped inside of me, and it must come out before I am to serve you lest we exacerbate the problem."

Sebastian chuckled and kissed Peregrine's neck. "There are other ways to please a man. Let me show you."

From there, it was nothing but pleasure—hands, then lips and a skillful tongue. Peregrine clenched fistfuls of Sebastian's hair and held him in place, and Sebastian rewarded him for his greed by redoubling his efforts. Not long after, Peregrine cried out and came into his mouth. Sebastian took it all.

"Should I pleasure you now, my lord?" he asked breathlessly as his orgasm ebbed. "I would be glad to."

"No." Sebastian kissed the underside of his jaw, then climbed out of bed and adjusted his codpiece. "We will wait for later, when you're well. For now, I must go. You tempt me enough that to stay would be impossible."

"Where shall you go?"

"About." Sebastian waved his hand. "I shan't be far. Not today. Not while there is a risk you are still unwell."

Peregrine smiled. "I'm sure this time Everard has fixed me."

"We shall see." Sebastian adjusted his doublet and belt, then smiled at Peregrine, who remained disheveled on the bed. "Should you feel even the slightest discomfort, you must let one of us know. I will not have you suffer. I love you so."

Sebastian could say it a thousand times and it would never grow old. Peregrine blushed and, true to his training, positioned himself in such a way that all of his best angles and features were on display. If he really was to be Sebastian's mate for all of time, he needed to look like the treasure he was. Beautiful always. A jewel amongst human beings.

"You are the most gorgeous creature I've ever laid eyes upon," Sebastian said in a low, husky voice, then shook his head and turned abruptly. "If I don't stop looking, I'll lose control. Find me when you're ready. I'll be waiting."

"I will, my lord. I vow it."

Sebastian left, and even though Peregrine was alone, he didn't feel lonely. Sebastian wasn't present, but he was there in Peregrine's heart, and would be forevermore. Brighter days were coming, and the future, while uncertain, was theirs to shape. And shape it they would. Peregrine would give his all to become Sebastian's mate.

Was it unlikely to happen? Of course. But it would never happen if he didn't try.

Peregrine did bleed, but it was over in a matter of hours. After the sheets had been changed he took a quick bath, then dressed in the finest clothes he owned and went to find Sebastian. It didn't take long. Sounds of conversation led him to the palace's foyer, where Sebastian and Everard were engaged in discussion near the front doors.

"Alistair must wait," Sebastian insisted. "I must know Peregrine is well before you leave."

"He is being insistent."

"Then I shall speak with him. He will listen to me."

"You're welcome to try, brother." Everard flapped a hand somewhat dismissively. "Alistair is bullheaded at best, and he is ever so set on… whatever it is. Some painting somewhere, or a mural, perhaps. Lord help us should it be a book. He's become near obsessed with the things. A waste of time, should you ask me. What could a man write that couldn't be taught through an apprenticeship or told on a cold night gathered together around the hearth? I cannot imagine what he'll fixate on next. One can only hope it will be something of value."

"What he's after doesn't matter. I will tell him to stay."

"Wonderful. While you're at it, perhaps you can convince him to forget this tour of his entirely. It's been nothing but trouble. Although, surprisingly, through no fault of his own."

Sebastian growled.

"What? I did not accuse you."

"Perhaps not out loud, but the intent was there all the same."

The conversation had begun to edge toward hostility, and while Peregrine had been taught not to involve himself with the affairs of dragons, his presence would likely put a cork in the erupting argument. As such, Peregrine gathered his courage and strolled across the foyer to stand at Sebastian's side, the billowing fabric of his clothing swirling around his ankles as he went.

"Lord dragon," he said to Everard upon arriving, then bowed to show his respect. "Imagine my delight upon finding you here. I'd thought you'd gone hours ago."

Everard gawked at him as though he'd never met an omega with a mind of his own. Which, come to think of it, he likely hadn't, but that was beside the point.

"You'll be pleased to know," Peregrine continued, "that I have bled, and now feel quite well. There is no more pain, not even so much as a cramp. With some luck, this will be the last time you'll need to visit. I have hopes my health will only improve from here."

Everard, mouth agape, turned his gaze on Sebastian. "Will you allow this, brother?"

"Allow what?"

"Your omega has derailed our conversation!"

Peregrine looped his arm into Sebastian's and leaned in toward him by a degree. To his delight, Sebastian didn't pull away or ask him to leave—he tucked Peregrine's arm closer to him and stood proudly at his side. "He may conduct himself as he wishes, for he is my mate."

Peregrine hadn't thought it possible for Everard to look any more like a fish, but his wide eyes really completed the look. "I beg your pardon?"

"Peregrine," Sebastian pronounced, "is my mate."

"Are you in need of medical attention, Sebastian? Did you hit your head when I wasn't looking?" Everard narrowed his eyes, thank goodness. Fish was not a good look. "Mates are so rare, they might as well not exist, and to find your mate in a Disgrace is—"

"*Silence,*" Sebastian boomed. "He is my mate."

"Sebastian, really. Where is the proof? You can certainly say what you like—no one can stop you from doing so—but saying something doesn't make it true."

Smoke poured from Sebastian's nostrils, and his skin grew hot to the touch. Peregrine looked up at him, afraid he'd misjudged and made things worse, but rather than attack, Sebastian stayed still and held Peregrine close. "You can talk down to me all you'd like, Everard," he said, "but I know it to be true. I feel it in my bones and to the very depth of my soul. Peregrine was made for me, and I will keep him forever."

Everard clicked his tongue. "Delusional, you and Al both. Until there is evidence, do you think anyone will believe you?"

"I don't care for the opinions of others."

Everard gave him a lengthy look. "Perhaps you should."

Sebastian snorted, expelling a cloud of smoke. "Are you quite done?"

"I should think so, unless you have other ludicrous notions to declare."

"I have none."

"Brilliant. Then I've officially said my piece. I'll be at the inn should you need me. If you wouldn't mind speaking to Alistair in the meantime, it would be appreciated."

Sebastian nodded. "I shall."

"Good." Everard turned his attention to Peregrine. "Should you experience further pain, be sure to speak up and let us know."

"I will," Peregrine said with a nod.

"Well, I shall take my leave, then. Farewell, brother." Everard bowed his head. "May your journey for a mate bond prove less eventful than this disaster of a trip."

That said, Everard left.

"Is he always like that?" Peregrine asked once he was gone.

Sebastian's expression stayed flat, but there was a twinkle in his eyes. "Sometimes he's much worse."

"Will he come to accept me one day?"

"He already has, my love. He would not act so much like himself if not."

"Oh." Peregrine chewed his bottom lip thoughtfully. "Well, was it right for me to have interrupted? I wasn't sure, but it seemed the best way to protect you from an otherwise avoidable argument."

Sebastian kissed the top of his head. "It was fine."

"I'm relieved. I wasn't sure. I came to tell you the bleeding had stopped and the tissue has been passed."

Sebastian paused. "In earnest? It wasn't something said to get Everard to leave?"

"Yes, my lord. I've stopped bleeding in earnest, and I am well. Better than I've been in ages."

"Well, then." Sebastian let go of Peregrine and scooped him into his arms. It was as much a thrill now as the first time he'd done it out on the streets of Ljouwert, causing Peregrine to gasp and lock his arms around Sebastian's neck as pleasure rushed through him. "I believe there's somewhere you and I should be."

The somewhere was the bedroom.

More specifically, between the sheets, where Sebastian claimed him repeatedly.

If this was how a dragon went about manifesting a mate bond, Peregrine could hardly wait.

A week passed, then two, during which Sebastian bred him every day. Peregrine did not know how long it would take before his body was recovered enough to go through another heat, but not knowing did not deter Sebastian, who lusted for Peregrine like he was at the peak of his cycle.

They made love in their bed, in the dining room, in the pool. The Attendants quickly learned to listen before they entered a room, and while Peregrine felt guilty for his indiscretion, it felt too good to stop. Better yet, the pain didn't return—Everard had finally chased the rot away. Everything was looking up, but still, the mate bond did not form, and though Peregrine routinely scoured his body, he never found a mark.

"Do not worry," Sebastian told him a month into his recovery. "Mark or not, you are mine. I feel it in my soul."

But Peregrine kept searching anyway, hopeful that he'd find it on some forgotten part of him, like the back of his arm, or the crease of his knee.

Three months following his recovery, in the early afternoon following a dip into the pool that hadn't stayed innocent for long, Sebastian threw Peregrine onto the bed belly down and kissed his way from his ankle all the way up to his inner thigh. Peregrine, aroused beyond belief, adjusted his position to get his knees beneath him and lifted himself up so Sebastian could touch him wherever he pleased.

But all at once, Sebastian stopped, and neither touched Peregrine, nor spoke.

"My lord?" asked Peregrine. "Is there something the matter?"

Sebastian was eerily silent.

"My lord?" Peregrine looked over his shoulder to see what was the matter and spotted Sebastian behind him, a look of awe on his typically emotionless face.

"Perry," Sebastian uttered. "It's there. I see it."

Sebastian traced a thumb along a spot near the inside of Peregrine's cheek, and Peregrine's heart started to race. It couldn't be, could it? But why else would Sebastian stop?

"What is it that you see?" he asked urgently. "You must tell me. I have to know."

"It's a mark," Sebastian breathed, then growled in triumph. "You are my mate. You bear my mark, and you will be mine forevermore."

27

SEBASTIAN

1509

Sebastian tried to remember everything he'd been told about marks and mate bonds, but came up with very little. They were rare to the point of being nearly legendary, and therefore not talked about very often. And while it had always been possible that, theoretically, Sebastian might find a mate, it was also theoretically possible he'd be struck by lightning and that had yet to happen.

But there it was.

A strawberry-shaped mark on Peregrine's skin that hadn't been there before.

A physical manifestation of their bond.

Sebastian was nearly paralyzed by the implications of it. Peregrine would not be his until the end of his short human life, but forever. For always. It was a heady notion. He traced his thumb over the mark and felt equal satisfaction radiating from his dragon.

Mine. Ours. Forever.

Mate. Mate. Mate.

"I am branded with your mark, then?" asked Peregrine, who craned his neck in an attempt to see. "It's true? You do not jest?"

"Aye."

Peregrine's lips twitched into a tentative smile. "And where is your brand, my lord, to show you belong to me?"

"I've never heard of a mate mark appearing on a dragon. Granted, I know very little about mating at all. Perhaps we are also changed, but in a way that's not so readily seen."

Peregrine's smile turned into a pout. "How unfair. I want everyone to know you are mine, and mine alone."

Sebastian rolled the two of them so they lay side to side and face to face, looking Peregrine in the eyes. "You and I know it, love, and it will be evident to anyone who observes us. I have not and will never love another in the way that I love you. I could live a dozen lifetimes and still, that would hold true."

A hint of something stirred in Sebastian's soul. It was a quiet kind of happiness—one he'd never felt before.

"Strange," he muttered, and focused in on the feeling. The more he concentrated on it, the clearer it became, until there was no hiding what it was and, more importantly, where it had come from.

Peregrine.

It had come from Peregrine.

"Sebastian?" Peregrine asked. He laid a hand on Sebastian's arm. "What's wrong?"

"The bond. I feel it."

"How?"

"Close your eyes," Sebastian said, "and try to see if you feel something inside. A tether, perhaps."

Peregrine did not look all that certain, but he closed his eyes and was quiet for a while. Sebastian was not sure what to do, or if he could help, but he reasoned that he had felt Peregrine's pleasure, and so he endeavored to feel pleasure so Peregrine could enjoy it in the same way.

To focus, Sebastian closed his eyes as well and thought of how beautiful Peregrine was. Of how strong and weak, brave and fearful, devoted and cherished Peregrine made him feel. He recalled memories of sweet kisses shared and the caress of Peregrine's body against his own and rejoiced that this would be their forever, and that he would never be alone again.

Peregrine gasped, and then there came a tug centralized in Sebastian's heart. Slowly, it became surer, braver, more solid, until there was no way to deny it.

It was the bond, and it tied them together. Through it, Sebastian knew the depths of Peregrine's emotions, and in turn, Peregrine knew his.

Peregrine's breath caught in his throat. "Can you feel that?" he asked, his voice soft and filled with wonder.

"I do. I feel you in my heart."

"I feel the way you love me," Peregrine whispered, his voice thick with emotion. "I feel it deep inside of me. I feel how true it is. Sebastian..." He laughed and tangled his fingers in Sebastian's hair. "My dragon, I love you. I love you so much. I never imagined... never thought..."

Something indefinable shifted between them. The aching, delicate perfection of their growing bond flooded with desire and need. It was more powerful than anything—claws or fists or magic—and it took possession of Sebastian from the inside out.

"What is this?" he asked Peregrine in a low voice, barely able to hold himself back from indulging in the love and want flowing through him. "This feeling... it's inside of me, but it belongs to you."

"It... it can't be." Peregrine shivered and curled up against Sebastian, his hands still in his hair. "It's far too soon..."

An inkling of understanding worked its way through the haze of need, and Sebastian groaned, his hard cock already aching. He needed to be inside his mate or he would go mad. This wasn't like their normal lovemaking, which was passionate and tender and often athletic. This was more like...

"Inside me," Peregrine moaned. "I need it. Need you."

"We need the oil."

With a strength Sebastian didn't expect, Peregrine pushed him so he lay on his back. "I'm sorry, my dragon," he uttered as he straddled Sebastian's hips, "but I must."

That said, he grabbed Sebastian's cock and sank down onto it, moaning.

He was wet.

So wet.

Had he found the oil, then, or—

Peregrine became a wild thing, riding Sebastian hard. The fucking between them had always been good, right from the first, but this was new and different, for everything Peregrine felt now echoed inside of Sebastian and took his own pleasure to heights unknown.

"Take me," Sebastian urged as Peregrine worked himself in a near frenzy. "Use me, Perry. I am yours."

Which was precisely what Peregrine did. He rode relentlessly, tirelessly, as though their bond afforded him stamina he'd never had before. While he worked, Sebastian ran his hands up Peregrine's thighs and hips, greedy for more, but not willing to take until Peregrine had gotten everything from him that he needed. When his mate finally did begin to flag, Sebastian rolled them so that he covered Peregrine's lithe body.

"Is it heat?" Sebastian asked in a rumble as he nosed beneath Peregrine's jaw, scenting his skin. It was faintly sweet. "Tell me it is. Tell me I can knot you and we can try again."

"I think it is." Peregrine drew in a shaky breath and threw his head back upon the pillows. His brow was glossed with sweat, and his curls were damp and limp. "It seems impossible—far too soon —yet... yet I burn, Sebastian. I burn for you. I need your knot. Your seed."

A thrill ran through Sebastian and into their mate bond, where he felt it thrill Peregrine as well. He would put a new child in Peregrine—a baby or a clutch, it mattered not—and they would have the family they wanted. Their broken hearts would never heal, but eventually, they would mend.

"Are you sure?" he asked Peregrine one last time. "If I do this, there is no going back."

"I've never been more sure in my life."

"Then I will make you mine, and you shall give us a child."

Peregrine moaned, and so Sebastian began to rut in earnest. The bed shook beneath them, threatening to collapse, but thankfully it held. Peregrine, as exhausted as he was, proved insatiable, and he rolled his head from side to side while his hips met each of Sebastian's frantic thrusts. "More. I need more. Lord, I need…"

Then Peregrine did something, and Sebastian's whole body went stiff with pleasure. It was like Peregrine was stroking their bond as though it were Sebastian's cock.

Pleasure echoed through him, his and Peregrine's both, intertwined and indivisible, so incredible there was nothing Sebastian could do to hold on. With a roar, he came, flooding his mate with his seed and knotting them together. Peregrine cried out and clung tightly to him, and through the bond, Sebastian felt him come as well.

It was pleasure unparalleled.

A delight like no other.

If this was to be the rest of their lives, Sebastian might not leave their bedroom again.

Sebastian rocked his knot inside Peregrine, binding them closer together, until his omega cried out again and came to a second climax. Sebastian held him close, like the treasure he was, until his knot finally slipped free. "Are you sated now, my love?" he asked, already knowing the answer.

Peregrine's eyes snapped open, and all the hunger Sebastian felt through their bond burned in them. "No. I need more."

257

Sebastian obliged him. He obliged them both, as he, too, became caught up in his mate's heat. They mated, then slept entwined, then mated again, over and over, until the crazed need abated. Peregrine, exhausted, fell to sleep soundly beside him.

The heat had passed, and in its wake, it was as if it had never happened. Sebastian had no true idea of how much time had passed, but it had surely been less than a week. Which meant...

Well, time would tell.

28

SEBASTIAN

Present Day

With the Attendants there to unload the van and unpack their belongings, Sebastian made his way to his study to await his brother's arrival. He'd rather be with Perry, but he knew what that would inevitably lead to and his mate needed rest, not Sebastian's cock inside him. There were a few matters which demanded his attention but Sebastian, for the moment, ignored them. He was in no proper headspace to deal with his finances or the squabbles that had occurred among the staff while he'd been gone. All of that would be dealt with, but later, after he and Perry were assured their babe was healthy and safe.

Sebastian dropped into his chair and let his thoughts wander. The babe would be coming soon, and he wasn't exactly sure what he'd do with a daughter. He'd had precious little experience with women. He'd had sex with a few in his youth—enough to know that it wasn't his cup of tea. But raising one seemed such a foreign concept that he wasn't sure where to begin.

Boys were easy.

Sebastian had been one once, many years ago, and while he'd started off life as a dragon and not a small, defenseless human, he figured it couldn't be all that different. But a girl? It hardly seemed the same. She would value different things and experience the world in different ways. Teaching her to stand up for herself would require a skill set Sebastian had yet to refine.

But he would do it.

He would do it for her.

And no matter who she grew up to be, he would encourage her every step of the way.

A scream splintered Sebastian's musings and he bolted upright. It had come from Perry. A heartbeat later, fear arrowed through their mate bond, sending Sebastian sprinting out of the room in a panic.

He had no clue what had happened, but he feared the worst.

Heart set to shatter, Sebastian flew down the hall toward the hoard, where he'd told Perry to rest until Everard's arrival. On his way, a pane of glass shattered somewhere unseen. An alarm began blaring, and Sebastian, enraged, began to change. Scales plunged down his neck and over his shoulders, his teeth sharpened, and deadly talons took the place of his fingernails.

So it wasn't trouble with the babe, then.

It was an intruder.

The omega.

Raven.

He'd found a way in despite Misha's best efforts and laid his hands on Perry, just like he had five hundred years ago.

Sebastian's ears told him that the shattered glass had come from down a hallway that led away from the hoard, but his bond with Perry led him onward, and he did not stray from his course to investigate. Raven was crafty, and if he'd managed to sneak inside beneath all their noses, then surely he could have arranged for distractions to lead Sebastian off the trail. But Sebastian didn't care for his windows—he cared for Perry, and so on he went.

If even a hair on Perry's head had come to harm, he would gut the omega, Bertram be damned.

To his consternation, the tug on his mate bond did not lead him to the hoard, but past it, to the atrium. Its door was ajar and there was movement from within. Anger spiked inside of Perry and echoed into Sebastian's soul, and Sebastian ran harder yet, bursting through the atrium door, claws out and ready to attack.

What he saw beyond the atrium doors stopped him in his tracks.

Raven, his pale skin near spectral in the moonlight, stood behind Perry, using him as a shield. He pressed a hunting knife to Perry's throat.

"Come one step closer," Raven warned, sounding eerily like Bertram, "and I'll kill him. You'll stay where you are if you don't want your pretty omega to die."

Sebastian snarled, but he did not move. He knew that if he did, Raven would follow through on his threat, and not even all the magic in the world could bring Perry back from the dead.

"What do you want?" he growled. "Gold? Jewels? Whatever it is, it's yours as long as you let him go."

Raven laughed, the sound so unhinged that Sebastian shuddered. "What I want," he cooed, smirking at Sebastian from over Perry's shoulder, "is your baby. So I'll be taking your omega. He'll be better off with me, anyway, away from the meat market you dragons have brainwashed us all into thinking is normal." The blade dug slightly into Perry's neck, causing him to wince. Through their bond, Sebastian felt its bite all too well. "So if you know what's good for you, you'll turn around and go on your way. No need for formality—I'll show myself out."

Sebastian glanced between Raven, whose expression was crazed and dangerous, to Perry, who was doing his best not to look any one way at all. Fear shivered through their bond, so Sebastian did his best to counter it by thinking calm, reassuring thoughts.

He would find a way to save Perry and their child. This mad omega would not win.

"If I go," Sebastian said in as even a voice as he could manage with a mouthful of pointed teeth, "you must swear he won't come to harm."

"You can bet your life on it." Raven paused thoughtfully. "Or his. Probably his."

"And the babe?"

"I would never."

As they spoke, the door behind Raven leading from the atrium into the hallway connecting with the garage was nudged open, and in toddled Pake.

An idea came to Sebastian then.

It was a long shot, but it was all he had, and he would regret it forever if he didn't try.

"If he is to leave me forever," Sebastian said as his transformation regressed, "then will you allow us one last moment? If you do, I shall leave and allow you safe passage out of my lair."

Raven's eyes narrowed. "This is a trick, isn't it? You're trying to trick me." He clenched his jaw and sneered at Sebastian, holding the knife ever steady to Perry's neck. "He's staying with me, and if you know what's good for you, you'll stay right where you are, too. Say whatever it is you need to say, but don't come any closer or I'll kill him."

"I won't come closer." Sebastian held out his talonless hands. "What I need to say can be said from here. Perry?" Sebastian locked eyes with his mate, and while he could see that Perry was afraid, he was proud of how steadfast his mate was acting despite the harrowing circumstances. It was far from the first time Perry had been targeted by an enemy, but Sebastian did hope that it would be the last. "Do you remember long ago, when we first met, on the morning before we left Ljouwert? How I bathed you and showed you dragon fire for the first time? Do you remember what I said to you then?"

A spark of curiosity lit Perry's eyes. "No."

All hinged on this moment. Sebastian composed himself, ignoring his hammering heart to focus on the task at hand. If Raven were to interpret his gestures as hostile, it could all be over in an instant, but Sebastian had hope that wouldn't be the case. Very slowly, so as not to spook the omega holding Perry captive, Sebastian summoned balls of flame into existence in the air above them, each one made to burn as bright as he could get it. Compared to the rest of his brothers, Sebastian's magic was crude at best, but he didn't need much to get the job done. All he needed was to make the fire bright enough that it cast its orange glow onto the grass beneath it, and with night having arrived, it was easy enough to do.

"What are you doing?" Raven's face tightened with anger. "If any of it gets close to me, I'll slit his throat."

"It won't," Sebastian said. "It's only meant to help Peregrine remember."

Sebastian held the flame in place, where it danced and flickered in the air, casting color all around them. From across the room, Pake perked up and began to trudge toward the light.

"I recall the bath," Perry admitted in a small voice, "but not what you said. What was it, Sebastian? Tell me."

Pake reached the first of the orange patches of light. Sebastian snuffed out the fire it belonged to, and on Pake moved to the next, coming closer to Raven and Perry.

"I told you that the fire yields to me, and that one day, I hoped you might, too." Sebastian snuffed out another ball of light, tempting Pake to come closer. "You told me that you did yield to me, but I explained that it wasn't in the way I wanted. You were no more than water back then, meekly pushed aside when introduced to any kind of resistance. What I wanted was to see you independent. Like a flickering flame. Do you remember now?"

Recognition flashed through Perry's eyes. "I do."

"You've grown so much since that day." Sebastian extinguished a third ball of light. Pake had come so close now that he'd arrived nearly behind Raven, where the patterns on the ground cast by the fire were reminiscent of stained glass. "When I met you, you were a proper Pedigree omega who aspired to nothing more than to serve his purpose, but now you are the mate of a dragon. A treasure worthy of any hoard. A brave warrior in your own right. My heart, my soul, and my voice of reason. Not just my equal, but my superior. Without you, I would be empty. You are the stars in my night sky, and without you, I am lost to darkness."

Tears streamed silently down Perry's cheeks. "But how can I be starlight when, without you, I'd never shine?"

"Nonsense." Sebastian smiled and extinguished one last light. "You have always shone, Perry. I was simply the dragon lucky enough to have noticed."

"Are we done here?" Raven demanded. "You've had your moment. Get rid of the fire and let us leave."

"As you wish."

Sebastian willed the flames out of existence, plunging the atrium in darkness. With their eyes having adjusted to the light, it was hard to see much of anything, but Sebastian knew better than to fly forward and attack in a rage. In just a little longer, he would end the omega once and for all, but not until Raven's guard was down.

"Goodbye, Perry," Sebastian said to the only man he'd ever loved. The one who had given him everything when he'd been least expecting it. The one with whom he shared eternity. "I have vowed to keep you safe, and if this is the only way I can do it, then so be it."

Through the mate bond, Sebastian told Perry all the things he couldn't say with words—that this was not the end, that he wasn't giving up, and that all would be well. He only hoped his emotions translated.

"Raven," he said. "You may go. I won't follow you. You've won."

There came the frenzied sound of shuffling feet, as if Raven was reeling back. "How do you know who I am?" he demanded. "Did Bertram tell you? I'll—"

Raven gasped, cutting himself short. At the same time, there came the clatter of something solid and metallic striking the ground, then a large thud and a sickening snap—the crunch of a broken bone. Pain be damned, Sebastian sped through his transformation to bring out his teeth and talons, and as he did, he willed fire back into the sky. In its light, he saw that his plan had worked—Pake, who'd once loved to play in the patterns cast by their stained-glass windows, had chased the orange patches in the grass until he was standing right behind Raven, and Raven, unaware that the boulder of a tortoise was there, had crashed into him while hurrying away from Sebastian and tripped, falling hard. He'd dropped the knife in his surprise, but had grabbed onto Perry and brought him tumbling down with him. They'd landed on their sides, but Raven had twisted them so Perry had landed partially on his stomach.

Sebastian saw red.

Kill, his dragon urged. *Maim. Destroy. Devour.*

It was not a bad idea.

Sebastian tore across the atrium, leaping over Pake's shell to land on his knees on top of Raven, whose arm was twisted at an unnatural angle. Without hesitation, he raked his claws down Raven's side, leaving deep gashes in their wake that gushed fountains of blood. Raven let out a bloodcurdling scream and writhed, but without his weapon, he was weak, and Sebastian would rend him limb from limb until there was nothing left.

Before he could attack again, something painful struck Sebastian in the head. Howling with pain and fury, he turned his head to look at what it was and there was Bertram. He was wielding a Glock, the butt of which he'd slammed into Sebastian's skull.

"Stop now," Bertram growled, "or I'll shoot you, and I'll keep on shooting until you die. Do you understand me, brother?"

"What the bloody hell is going on?" a querulous voice asked

loudly. It was Everard. "Sebastian, why are you half dragon? Bertram, put down that gun. You will not shoot our brother. What on earth is the matter with you?"

Bertram ignored Everard and kept his gun trained on Sebastian. "Step away from the omega right now," he snarled.

Sebastian's head spun. Alarms were blaring. His brothers were shouting. The smell of blood spiced the air, and through it all, distress warbled through the mate bond, and with it, pain.

It was Perry.

Sebastian shoved himself off Raven and crawled on his hands and knees to be next to his mate. Everard and Bertram were squabbling, but it didn't matter. Nothing did. Because Perry's fair skin had gone ghostly white, and he clutched his round stomach as though in agony. Sebastian attempted to reach out to him through the bond, but Perry shut it down, and like an elastic stretched too far, the sudden severing snapped back and struck Sebastian in the heart.

"Perry?" Talons gone, he caressed Perry's cheek. "Open the bond back up to me."

"I can't." Perry winced, opening his mouth in a silent scream. "It *hurts*. Sebastian… the baby… she's coming."

Sebastian reared back to bark orders at Everard, but Bertram had pressed the gun to his back and forced their brother onto his knees next to Raven. Everard's hands were on him, and slowly but surely, Raven's wounds stitched themselves shut.

Bertram kept the gun pressed against Everard's back, but looked into Sebastian's eyes. "We are equal now, I suppose. Take your mate and do for him what you can. Everard stays here until Raven is healed."

Sebastian wanted to argue, but Bertram truly had gone insane, and there would be no reasoning with him. Without a word, he scooped Perry into his arms and headed for the door that led from the atrium to their hoard.

Behind him, he heard Everard pleading with Bertram. "Lower

the weapon, brother. I am healing him and have no intention of stopping."

"Finish the job and I'll lower the gun."

"Is this who you are now? Forever Frederich? I am doing my job. This is well outside of enough!"

Sebastian stepped through the door and hurried down the hall. While he feared for Everard, he knew he would not come to harm by Bertram's hands—he was too useful, and he'd saved their lives more than once after a job had gone wrong. Not even his lashing tongue would make Bertram forget it.

Bertram, however, would not be saved by prior good deeds.

They were well beyond that now.

He would answer for what he had done, but later, after Perry and the babe were safe.

"Sebastian?" came a voice from down the hallway. Sebastian looked up to see a familiar mop of brown hair, round glasses, and an eager expression. Harrison was on his way toward the atrium, his pet lizard on his shoulder. It was dressed for a day at the beach. "What's going on? Is Ev okay? I felt something through our mate bond that worried me, so I'm trying to find him. I wasn't supposed to come, but I followed him here because it's been a long time since anyone has seen Perry, and some of us were starting to get worried." Harrison seemed to come to the realization that Perry was in Sebastian's arms. He stopped abruptly and stared. "Is Perry okay? And why are there so many alarms going off? Is it the Topaz clan again? I thought Ian was working to dismantle the rebel groups."

"Everard will be fine, but if you go in the atrium, you might not be." Sebastian nodded in the direction of his hoard. "There's no time to explain. Come with me quickly. Perry is pregnant and has suffered trauma that has triggered his labor. I need your help."

Perry groaned in pain, and Sebastian, heartbroken, took off at a sprint down the hall. Behind him, Harrison squeaked.

"I've never delivered a dragonet on my own before," Harrison called out after him as he started to run, too. "But I'm sure it will be fine. I mean, I've delivered all kinds of clutches before, so how different could this be?"

Filled with dread, Sebastian ran faster.

29

PERRY

Present Day

Sebastian sprinted down the hall and straight to their hoard room, following the same path Perry had once taken to usher an addled Ignatius and an injured Harrison to safety during a Topaz attack. The lush greenery of the atrium gave way to familiar walls and doorways, and while Perry knew he should be glad that he'd be safe throughout his labor, his heart was heavy. Unlike last time, when only Steve had been forgotten during their escape, they'd left family behind.

"Leave me," Perry groaned as Sebastian pushed the secret button on the planter, collapsing the wall that hid the secret hallway leading to their hoard. "You must go back and make sure no harm befalls your brothers."

"You mean Everard," Sebastian grumbled as he hurried Harrison inside and ducked through the small opening. The wall closed behind them, plunging them in darkness, which Sebastian remedied with a flip of the nearby light switch. "Bertram is no brother of mine. Not anymore."

"You mustn't say that."

"I will say whatever I wish, especially when it's the truth." He carried Perry down the hall to the reinforced metal door. It was quite a long way, but Sebastian's long legs made quick work of the journey. Harrison practically had to jog to keep up. "Bertram has betrayed us. It matters not that he did not shoot—he has stolen proper medical attention from you. He is no brother of mine."

"Sebastian," Perry groaned. "You mustn't... there has to be a reason."

"I care not for any reason that comes from his treacherous mouth. Bertram is dead to me. Should he ever set foot in our lair again, I will rend him in twain." With some difficulty, Sebastian pressed his hand onto the biometric scanner beside the door. As a consequence, Perry's side and shoulder pushed against the wall, and while the pressure was slight, pain exploded inside of him. He hissed and squeezed his eyes shut. The fall must have done more than send him into early labor—there was something wrong.

"Perry?" Sebastian asked, panicked. He pulled away immediately, alleviating the pressure. The pain went with it, and Perry, at least for a moment, was able to relax. "What's wrong?"

"I don't know."

"He might have broken a rib," Harrison suggested. "When Ev gets here, he can fix it. I'm not sure I'm skilled enough. How much longer do we need to wait until the door opens?"

The same biometric scanner that had read Sebastian's fingerprints now scanned his retina. After a thoughtful moment, it beeped, and a metal panel on the wall slid back to reveal a keypad into which Sebastian punched a six-digit code. At long last, there came a click and the door opened.

"Wow," Harrison remarked as they stepped through the door. "I don't remember your door ever having done that."

He was right. The hoard room's defenses had been increased, and had Sebastian not been there to disengage them, Perry never would have riddled his way inside. How frustrated he would have been had he come all this way only to have to turn around and find Sebastian in order to get inside. Further investigations of their new security system, however, would have to wait, because at that moment a contraction so terrible tore through Perry that he was sure he was being ripped apart.

There was no holding the pain back this time.

He screamed.

"My love," Sebastian uttered, and rushed to the bed, where he laid Perry on the sheets. "You must be brave. You must be strong. You have come so far, and there is only a short way to go. You will get through this, I swear it. I will do whatever it takes to make sure you and the babe are safe."

The pain didn't abate for a long time. Perry gripped Sebastian's hand and squeezed with all his might, but it did nothing to help. Barely any time had passed at all, and he was already drenched in sweat and ready for this to be over.

It was nothing like laying a clutch.

Perry would rather lay a dozen eggs than go through an hour of this.

"I wish I had something to give you that could numb the pain," Harrison said in a quiet, worried way when Perry's contraction ended. "I figured Ev was coming here for a checkup, and since I'm not supposed to be in on the secret, I didn't bring anything. If I'd have known, I would have brought supplies. I'm sorry, Perry."

"Focus not on the if, but the now," Sebastian boomed. "What can you do to help with what you have on hand?"

"Well…" Harrison approached the bedside and looked down upon Perry. "I have been working on something that might help. You're going to feel a slight pressure on your abdomen, and maybe a tingling sensation. I need you to stay as still and as calm as you can, okay?"

Perry nodded, because he was sure that if he opened his mouth, he would scream.

"Okay. Here goes nothing." Harrison pushed a noisy breath through his nose and laid a hand on Perry's abdomen, close enough to his groin that Sebastian growled in warning. But rather than cower, Harrison, ever unflappable, smiled brilliantly at the dragon threatening his life. "You know, most herps are nonvocal, but you in particular love to growl and snarl and make all kinds of nonhuman noises. I'd love to study how dragons communicate sometime, but right now I need to concentrate. Would it be okay if you kept those noises for later? Maybe when I have a voice recorder around? If you need help distracting yourself, you can always play with Steve."

Steve, the iguana on Harrison's shoulder, lifted his head to look at Sebastian. He was dressed in a small striped tank top, like one might wear to the beach, and was wearing a pair of sunglasses on top of his head somewhat like a hat.

Sebastian stood still for a long moment, then reached out and collected the lizard from Harrison's shoulder, holding him in his arms like he had the children when they'd been smaller and scalier.

It was almost enough to melt Perry's heart.

Almost.

But then the next contraction hit, and not even Sebastian could distract him from his all-consuming pain.

"Another contraction," Harrison said helpfully. "Okay, we're in business. Let me see what I can do..."

It took a second, but a gentle wave of heat washed through Perry like a wave breaking on a shore, and the pain very nearly disappeared.

"How is that?" Harrison asked. "Did it work?"

The heat continued to spread. It wasn't hot enough to burn, but when it reached Perry's ribs, it heated up enough to become uncomfortable. Perry winced, but nodded. "I feel much better."

"I'm so glad! Now let's see what else I can do."

The heat persisted, but didn't worsen, and bit by bit the pain inside Perry eased. All the while, Harrison kept his lips pinched and his brow furrowed. It was the most quiet he'd ever been.

While he worked, Perry turned his gaze on Sebastian, who had Steve cradled in one arm and was petting his head with a single finger. Steve was not known to show emotion, but Perry got the feeling he was quite content indeed.

"Okay, I think I'm done," Harrison said, sounding rather exhausted. "You're having another contraction right now, so I'm not going to stop just yet, but your injuries have been healed, at least. We'll have to have Everard check and make sure I did it okay —I'm still pretty new to magic, and it's easy to make a mistake when you can't see the wounds you're stitching back together. I've heard that if you do it wrong, you can end up causing more harm than good."

"You heard right," Perry admitted with a heavy heart. "Magic is a tricky thing, and the human body is trickier yet. But you've done excellent work, Harrison. I feel much improved. I am in your debt."

"You're welcome." Harrison smiled, then set his sights on Sebastian. "Do you need help to heal, Sebastian? You're bleeding from your head wound. It looks pretty awful."

"My body will regenerate on its own. 'Tis but a scratch."

"I doubt that, but okay. If you're sure you're fine, I'll focus on Perry." Harrison sat on the bedside next to Perry. "You know," he said after some time, "if you're going to deliver this baby, you'll need to disrobe at some point. Your bump is getting awfully low, and, well, I think it's better safe than sorry. We should prepare for what's still to come."

Sebastian growled and took a menacing step forward, but stopped when Steve scampered up onto his shoulder and gummed his earlobe with his tiny lizard mouth. Like an evil robot foiled by a well-timed toss of a bucket of water, Sebastian twitched and shuddered, then stopped.

"Oh, excellent work, Steve!" Harrison beamed with pride. "I knew you'd find a way to calm Sebastian down. Now, Perry, are you ready?"

Perry nodded and began to undress as daintily as he could, given the situation, while trying very hard not to think of what was going on in the atrium, or why it was that Everard was taking so long to arrive.

Harrison pronounced Perry fully dilated not even half an hour after their arrival in the hoard room, and not long after it came time to push. Perry thought himself prepared for what was to come, having laid two respectably sized clutches, but he was wrong. Eggs were ovular, smooth, and pliant, but babies? They weren't uniformly shaped, and their bony shoulders posed far more of a challenge to pass than any clutch he'd laid before.

"Push!" Harrison insisted.

Which was ridiculous, since it was all Perry had been doing.

He clenched his teeth and strained, bearing down until it felt like he'd birth all of his insides and not just his child. The pain, while stemmed by Harrison's emerging magic, was dulled, but as he pushed it worked itself into a fevered frenzy that escaped Perry as a scream. Sebastian, who'd gone back to cradling Steve, took his hand, which Perry squeezed so tightly, he thought his fingers might break.

"Push!" Harrison repeated, a little more enthusiastically this time.

In a moment of pain-fueled weakness, Perry thought the only way he'd be able to push more was if he pushed everyone in the room out a window.

"You're so close," Harrison said. "I can see the baby's head. Just a little more, Perry. You're doing great. Just—*oh.*"

Perry gasped. The pain and pressure eased all at once, and a moment later a small, shrill cry filled the hoard room. A baby's cry. The second he heard it, he silently began to cry, too.

The baby was alive.

It seemed impossible, yet his ears did not deceive him. There was no treachery here, no deceit, no sugar-coated lies. The truth was, behind his hope, trauma centuries in the making had prickled at the back of his mind this entire time and whispered terrible things—that this pregnancy would end like the others and his heart would break again for another baby he so desperately wanted, but couldn't have. After all, he'd suffered close to a hundred losses. The probability that this time it would be different was so small, it might as well have not existed.

But here she was.

Her cry filled the space where there had once been silence and stitched together the broken pieces of his heart.

Their daughter.

Their baby.

Their miracle.

Harrison cooed and fussed over her while Perry wept. Sebastian, meanwhile, set Steve down, ripped off his shirt, and strode to where Harrison was tying their daughter's umbilical cord. He presented the tatters to Harrison, who took them, quickly wiped the baby off, wrapped her up, and gathered her in his arms.

Perry blinked away his tears. For the first time, he was able to see his daughter's face.

It was small and pink and wrinkled. Her eyes were closed and her tiny mouth was open as she continued to cry. There was a swirl of black hair atop her head and a very Drake-like countenance to her face. She'd grow up to look like her father, Perry was sure. He could only hope that she turned out every bit as fierce and brave.

"Is she well?" he asked breathlessly, urgently, as tears streamed down his cheeks. "Tell me she's well. I cannot lose her. I can't."

Sebastian, who'd been zeroed in on the baby until that very moment, stepped away from Harrison and came quickly to the bedside, where he sat and wrapped Perry up in his arms. Perry cuddled up to him and laid his head on the side of Sebastian's bare chest, safe in his dragon's embrace.

"Oh," Harrison said. He looked at the babe in his arms and smiled. "I wouldn't worry. She's as healthy as can be, just a little small from having been born prematurely. We'll have Everard look her over when he gets here, but as far as I can tell, she's perfect. Congratulations, Perry and Sebastian. You're fathers. Again. How exciting!"

Perry sucked in a breath that turned into a laugh, then dissolved into an overjoyed sob.

The baby was healthy.

She would live.

Upon hearing the news, a sound rumbled in Sebastian's chest somewhat like a purr. With utmost care, he dragged Perry onto his lap and kissed the top of his head, then again, and again, until Perry had well and truly melted from his affections.

"You've done it," Sebastian whispered against the shell of his ear. "My brave, strong, resilient mate. Look what you have given us. Look at the life you've made."

Harrison brought the baby to them and laid her in Perry's arms. She quieted, then stopped crying altogether. Perry was quick to take her place. He held her close and sobbed loudly while Sebastian kissed each of his curls, one after the other, until there wasn't a part of Perry within his reach he hadn't loved on.

"She sure is cute," said Harrison. He'd come to sit at the foot of the bed, Steve in his arms. "And her birthday is only a month after Joy's. I bet they'll be best friends. Do you know what you're going to name her?"

Perry sniffled but, thanks to his good breeding, did manage to pull himself together. "I'm not sure," he admitted, and stroked the swirl of hair on her head. "We've never gotten this far before. Both of us have suffered too much heartbreak to have considered it, for fear it might all go wrong."

"It must be very exciting for you."

"You have no idea," Perry said with a wobbly smile, looking down at his daughter. "I told you the story of my youth, Harrison, and the truth behind what happened my very first heat, when Sebastian swore to keep me despite my failings, but as is the case with any story, there will always be parts we can't capture, or that get left unsaid for one reason or another."

Sebastian, his arms still tight around Perry, stroked their daughter's cheek with a single curled finger.

What a wonderful father he would be to her, Perry thought, and began to silently cry again.

"The part of my story," Perry added, voice quivering with the onset of a sob, "that I could never tell, no matter how long I spent or how much I tried, is the hurt that lives inside of you after losing a child you so desperately want. It cuts in a way I hope you'll never get to know. And the more you suffer from it, the harder it is to believe that you will ever feel true happiness, because wounds like that fester in a way not even magic can fix." Perry sniffled, but he collected himself and continued. After centuries of carrying this pain, it was important he finish what he had to say. "I will not trick you into believing that I am better, because I am not. I will carry my heartbreak with me as long as I shall live. Even were Sebastian and I to have a thousand children, it would remain. I only wish"—he drew a stabilizing breath through his lips and held it in his lungs to ward off an unwelcome sob—"I could go back in time and tell myself that there are brighter days ahead. That I will accomplish all of the impossible things the Pedigree said I couldn't, rise above it all, and become stronger for my weakness. And I suppose, were I to truly have my druthers, that I would wrap my younger self up in a hug and tell him that, as impossible as it seems, one day, everything will be well." Perry leaned against Sebastian and closed his eyes. "Because despite all the loss and heartbreak, it will be."

30

PEREGRINE

1509

It seemed an impossible thing, but Peregrine's heat did not return, and three months later, in the middle of the night, a cramp overcame him so crippling that he woke from a dead sleep screaming. Sebastian, who slumbered beside him, shot upright immediately. *"Perry?"*

"It hurts," Peregrine hissed through clenched teeth, curling up on himself protectively. "I need it out. I need it to stop. I cannot do this again—I cannot lose another child."

"Is there blood?"

There was something slick between his legs, but Peregrine couldn't be sure of exactly what it was. He was about to say as much when another cramp tore through him, and he screamed.

Sebastian was out of bed in an instant, and in a flurry of activity, the sheets were torn back from the bed and candlelight flooded the room. Sebastian looked upon their bedding, then leaned in and breathed in deeply, his nostrils flaring. "It does not smell of rot. I will send for Everard."

"Ev—" Peregrine was cut off abruptly by another contraction,

278

this one so painful, he thrashed. Like the cramps before it, it ended, but it left an urgent feeling inside of Peregrine that screamed at him to push.

Everard would not make it in time.

Whatever was to happen would not wait.

Peregrine rolled onto his back and tented his knees. The pain was slightly less when he sat, so he scrambled to assemble their pillows and propped himself up as best he could while Sebastian looked on in shock.

"I cannot stop," Peregrine admitted through tears. It was another failure, he was sure—another pregnancy that would end in blood and heartache. It was what his body had decided, and there was to be no reasoning with it. This was what he got for daring to dream that a Disgrace might find happiness with a dragon. "Sebastian, I cannot stop it. I must push. I *must.*"

"You must not." Sebastian sounded as close to panicked as Peregrine had ever heard him. "You must resist. I will send for Everard. He will make this right. You are strong, Perry. You can fight it."

"*I can't,*" Peregrine sobbed.

Another cramp tore through him, and he gave in to it.

He pushed.

"Stop," Sebastian demanded, but not out of anger—out of fear. "Perry, you mustn't. One hour. All I ask is one hour. I will—"

Peregrine screamed. The cramps followed one after another rapidly, and when this one hit, it woke instincts in him he couldn't ignore. With all the force he had, Peregrine bore down.

There was something inside of him, and he needed to get it out.

"*Safiya,*" Sebastian bellowed, calling for the Attendant with whom Peregrine had bonded the most closely. "Come at once. Peregrine is—"

Safiya was not near the bedroom at this hour of the night and wouldn't have heard his cries, but Sebastian stopped himself short regardless. Simultaneously, a large something slid out of Peregrine and onto the bed, occupying the space between his legs.

Sebastian's eyes went very wide.

"I'm sorry," Peregrine sobbed. "I couldn't stop it. It was too much. My body would not listen. I have failed you again, I know, but please, *please* do not send me away. I will do better next time. I will be stronger. I will be able to listen."

But no matter what he said, Sebastian would not stop staring.

"Sebastian?" Peregrine sniffled. "Sebastian, what is—"

Another cramp tore through him, worse than the ones before, causing Peregrine to scream and bear down all at once. He'd thought he'd pushed out the thing inside of him, but he'd been wrong—there was more. It lurched and shifted in uncomfortable ways, then slid out of him, knocking into whatever was already there.

How could it be that losing this baby felt so different from losing the first? It was nothing like it had been before. Peregrine dared not look, because he was sure his heart would break, and judging by Sebastian's shock, it was a gruesome sight indeed.

"Perry," Sebastian uttered, and came to sit very delicately on the edge of the bed. All the while he kept his eyes on the mess between Peregrine's legs. "You haven't failed. Not in the least."

"But it is too soon," Peregrine sniffled. "It's happening all over again. I'm losing the baby and I can't stop it."

"You're doing no such thing." Sebastian took him by the wrist and guided his hand between his legs, into the mess. Peregrine squeezed his eyes shut and braced himself for whatever awful things he'd find there, but rather than tissue, his fingertips brushed something smooth and leathery.

"You are not losing a baby," Sebastian told him, more excited than Peregrine had ever heard him before. "You are laying our clutch."

"An egg," Peregrine gasped. "Our egg."

He sat up as straight as he could to look between his legs,

where two large eggs glistened in the candlelight. It was impossible to tell their exact color when it was still so dark, but Peregrine saw that they were rich and deep—Amethyst through and through. One was a hair lighter than the other, but by all other accounts, they were identical. Utterly perfect. *His.*

"Babies," he whispered, stroking one, then the other, as love pooled inside of him that ran so deep, he could sink into it forever and still never find the bottom. After glancing apprehensively at Sebastian, he collected each into his arms and carefully lay back down so he was on his side and the eggs were wrapped up safe in his embrace. "I will love you forever. I promise."

"Are there no more?" Sebastian asked.

Peregrine closed his eyes and, in total bliss, snuggled closer to the clutch. "I do not know."

"Is there no more pain?"

Peregrine considered it, then shook his head slowly. "It persists, although not as much as before. There are still some yet to be laid, I think, but I don't know how to go about laying them."

"Push," Sebastian urged, but it seemed a silly thing to do when his body wasn't trying to rip itself in two. "You must continue to push. There are eggs inside you yet—you know it as well as I. Follow your instincts and push until they are all here with us. Until the clutch is complete."

Peregrine ran his fingertips lovingly over the two eggs he'd already laid. While he would rather do anything than be parted from them, the thought that he might soon have more to cherish prompted him into action. He whispered a sweet something to each of them, then carefully rolled onto his back and propped himself up. There were more precious eggs inside of him, and he would not stop until he'd laid every last one.

Peregrine's labor lasted for another half hour, during which he laid five eggs in total. Five beautiful, perfect eggs. They were all approximately the same size and shape, and all of them gorgeous in their own right. What varied between them was their color. Two of the eggs—the first two to be born—were shades of midnight and so deeply purple, they nearly looked black. The other three eggs were medium shades, neither too dark nor too light, and Peregrine spent a great many sleepless hours dreaming of what they'd look like in the sunlight. If only he'd laid during the day. It was a special kind of torture to be able to see something so precious, but not know what it looked like.

Throughout those sleepless hours, Sebastian came and went. At times he lay behind Peregrine and held him close, whispering affirmations of love and protection into his hair, and at others he ventured into parts unknown and came back each time with fistfuls of treasure, each more stunning than the last. There were gold coins and necklaces with fat jewels, gilded sculptures, and earrings. Bracelets and bangles and rings. He laid the bulkier items around the eggs, surrounding them in riches, and draped all the finer jewelry over their shells, making them even more beautiful.

When there was no space left to fill, and no egg left to decorate, Sebastian set his sights on Peregrine, stacking gold coins on the curve of his hip and affixing pretty golden pins in his hair.

"There will be more treasure soon," Sebastian promised as dawn approached and the bedroom began to lighten. "When we return to England I will bring you to my hoard and I will shower you in riches the likes of which you have never seen. I will decorate you, Perry, and you will be the most precious treasure of all. You and the clutch both. I swear it."

A few coins slid down Peregrine's stomach, landing with a *clink!* on the gold surrounding the clutch. "It would not be befitting of a Disgrace," he admitted rather shyly. "I think your father might be upset were he to find out."

"It matters not what Father thinks, for you are no Disgrace. You are, and forever will be, my mate. My wytad. The father of my eggs." Sebastian nosed into Peregrine's curls and kissed the back of his head. "I will fight for you forever, and I will always keep you safe."

Such love flowed through Peregrine then that it was impossible it was all his own. It was the bond, he realized. The invisible connection between him and Sebastian that would keep them tethered for life. In it, their love resonated like a golden note plucked from a string. It was beautiful. And the more Peregrine focused on it, the more he realized it did not stand alone.

There were other strings.

Five of them.

They were far more quiet and uncertain, but the more he listened, the more he could make out each one. They vibrated with excitement and were tuned to joy and love. One day, he was sure, they would sing... but for now, they contented themselves with quiet discovery.

Their innocence and honesty was so pure, it brought tears to Peregrine's eyes.

"I know you will," he told Sebastian as he blinked the tears away. Lovingly, he placed a hand on the nearest egg and stroked its smooth shell. "I can feel the love you have for me, but I can feel them as well—the eggs. It's the bond, isn't it? I had no idea that this is the way it would feel. We were never taught these things in the Pedigree; I suppose because no one expected us to ever be a dragon's true mate."

Peregrine felt Sebastian smile. "What does it feel like, love?"

"It feels like joy. It's faint and barely there, but when I concentrate, I can feel it."

"That will change in time." One of Sebastian's hands trailed from Peregrine's hip to his stomach, which he stroked slowly and affectionately, as though he was already in love with the children they'd yet to conceive. "The clutch is barely developed. As they grow, the bond will strengthen. I've heard it said that our bond will strengthen, too, but I have no way to prove it."

"It will," Peregrine said, surprising even himself with his certainty. "I know it."

"How?"

"I do not know."

Sebastian laughed quietly and kissed the back of Peregrine's head a second time. "I suppose we shall see."

All was quiet for some time after that. The sun rose and bright light filled the room. The eggs were as Peregrine imagined—more stunning than the jewels surrounding them, and each of them distinct. The two darkest ones were cool toned. Their dark purple shells leaned heavily toward blue, although one much more than the other. The three other eggs were a medium purple, closer to true amethyst. The five of them were the prettiest things he'd ever seen.

"What do you think they'll be like, Sebastian?" he asked as he stroked each of the eggs in turn. "What kind of dragons do you imagine they'll grow up to be?"

Sebastian grunted and tightened his grip around Peregrine, dragging him into a hug. "I know not," he admitted. "If they're lucky, they will inherit your good looks."

Peregrine laughed. "I think not. I'd much rather they look like you."

Sebastian was silent after that, but Peregrine's mind didn't idle. It dreamed of a future where five black-haired children would clamber through the halls of the palace, laughing as they went.

But as sweet as the thought was, it was tinged with sadness.

There would be one child who would never get to play with his brothers. One child he'd never known, but who he loved all the same.

"I hope," he said after some time, "that no matter what they look like, that they are happy, and that they grow up knowing they are loved."

"Of that, I have no doubt."

"Do you claim to know the future then, too, my lord dragon?" Peregrine asked with a small smile, rolling in Sebastian's arms so they were chest to chest. "How can you be so sure?"

"One does not need a crystal ball to know the whelps will be loved, Perry," Sebastian said with a kiss to the top of his head. "For they have us to raise them, and despite the hardships we've yet to face and the quarrels still to come, we will love them. Deeply. From the bottoms of our hearts. As we will all our children. Every one of them. Be they human, or dragon, or somewhere in between."

EPILOGUE

PERRY

Present Day

Eight heads of jet-black hair bounded down the corridors of the palace, arms flying, feet pounding, and—in one instance—a scaly pair of wings flapping wildly. The boys shrieked with laughter as they ran, as boys are wont to do, each doing his best to be faster than his brothers. It wasn't long before they reached the end of the corridor, where they slid on socked feet around the corner.

Perry didn't follow.

It had been a long time since there had been children in the palace, and it would do the place wonders to see some chaos. The children's abundance of energy would help shake out the cobwebs of the past.

But there was one child who did not join in on the fun.

She was cradled in Perry's arms, garbed in a fetching purple dress with lacy white ruffles, and was far more interested in staring up at him than anything her brothers were getting up to in the eastern wing.

Mira Clementine Drake was all of three months old, but she was already curious about life, and could spend hours watching as

286

the world went on around her. She was a quiet baby. Well-behaved and never fussy. Not one to pitch a fit or cry. Stoic, like her father.

And Perry couldn't begin to express how happy she had made him.

"Once upon a time," he told her as he carried her toward the nursery, "there was a young dragon who lived here who did not know he was a dragon at all. It was a different time back then, you see. A time when we didn't know all of the things we know today.

"The young dragon," Perry said as he continued up the stairs, leaving the distant laughter of children behind him, "had young dragons of his own, but he wanted a child with all his heart... only it never quite worked out, and the young dragon became very sad for such a very long time."

At the top of the stairs, Perry went left, past rooms in which lived memories. Curious whelps perched in windows, looking over the grounds below. Midnight trysts with Sebastian. Conversations long forgotten, and faces of Attendants long since passed. It was painful to remember, but sweet at the same time. Nostalgic. But essential.

Who he was today had been shaped by those moments, so as difficult as they were on his heart, he welcomed them back all the same.

"Eventually," Perry continued, "the young dragon became so sad that his heart broke, and even the young dragons he cared for and loved with all his heart and soul were not enough to fix it. So the handsome dragon he loved took him and their little family from the palace to another home, where the young dragon wouldn't feel so sad anymore. For a time, at least.

"They moved many times over the next few hundred years to many beautiful places, each grander than the last. But no matter where they went, the young dragon never managed to have a baby, and he wept, and wept, and wept."

The door to the nursery came into sight. It was at the end of the corridor, near a staircase leading to the Attendants' quarters, so the nursemaids could better care for the human children they'd have.

Only there had been none, and the room had stayed empty.

And for each new loss, Perry's heart had fractured until he couldn't stand the sight of the room at all.

"But you see," he said as he forged onward, Mira in his arms, "there was so much love in the young dragon's heart that he never gave up hope, even when he was broken. And one day, that hope paid off. He and the handsome dragon had another clutch of dragon babies, and for a while he was able to forget all of his sadness... but the truth is, sadness never really goes away. It sits and waits for you to remember it's there. And when the young dragon next discovered he was pregnant, it all came rushing back. What should have been a happy time was overshadowed by fear, because the young dragon had never managed to have a baby before, and he was afraid this time would be just like all the others, and another piece of his heart would break."

Perry came to a stop outside the nursery door and looked down at Mira, who gazed up at him with love in her eyes. There was no magical bond between them through which he could channel love back, so Perry let his emotions play across his face. And as impossible as it seemed, he could have sworn Mira perked up as though she felt it.

"But you see, something magical happened," Perry explained. "Despite his fear and all the dangerous obstacles in the way, the young dragon was able to keep the baby, and a princess was born. The most beautiful princess in all the land. And while it was not her job to stitch back together her father's heart, she helped get the job started."

Perry pressed a kiss to Mira's forehead, and she made a breathy noise of delight that warmed him through and through. He kissed her again, overjoyed by her company, and continued on with the story. "With her help, the young dragon found the courage to confront the pain he kept inside so he could start to heal. And do you know what he did?"

Perry paused for dramatic effect.

"He brought the princess to the palace he'd loved all those years ago. The one he and the handsome dragon had to leave, because it hurt too much to stay. He brought her into the halls where no baby had ever been and laid her down for a nap in the nursery that went hundreds of years unused."

Perry opened the nursery door, fully intending to lay Mira in her bassinet, but didn't make it more than a few steps from the doorway. The room wasn't empty like it should have been. It was filled with familiar faces.

There were the older boys, now tall and grown, all five of them grinning like they were young again and had just gotten away with a particularly devious prank. Alistair and Ignatius were there, although their boys were missing—but judging by the loud crash from downstairs, they were elsewhere in the palace. Everard and Harrison were there as well, and Geoffrey and his mates. Reynard and Misha stood near them, a smirk on Misha's face like he'd just uncovered a scintillating secret. Hugh and Finch stood near the bassinet, Finch with their son, Theodore, in his arms. Even Grimbold and Walter were there, Walter's gaze shyly averted to Pake, who he was petting like a dog. Pake was soaking up the attention. The Drakes must have banded together in order to carry him up the stairs.

But Perry's thoughts didn't linger long on how they'd transported his tortoise, because at the front and center of the group stood a dragon whose very presence made Perry's heart skip a beat.

Sebastian.

He was dressed in a fine suit, his posture impeccable, and his expression as unreadable as ever. But when he saw Perry, he smiled. "Welcome home, my love."

Tears fell down Perry's cheeks before he could stop them. He blinked wildly, trying to chase them away, but couldn't. "What is this? What's going on? Why are you all here?"

Harrison looked left and right, then took a small step forward and smiled in his friendly way at Perry. "When everyone found out what had happened, and that your family would be leaving the country for a bit while Bertram handles things back home, all of us decided that since you couldn't come to visit us, we'd come to visit you."

"The security leaves much to be desired, but I suppose it will do." Misha winked. "Wait until I tell you about what I've discovered about our troublesome *friend*. As it turns out, you and I have more in common than you'd think."

"Can you stop orally vaguebooking?" Ignatius poked his head around Alistair to narrow his eyes at Misha. "You've been dropping all these little hints, but they're never enough for any of us to figure out what you're talking about, and it's driving me batty. Either spill the beans or can them. This in-between bullshit is killing me."

"Iggy," Harrison said, "are you okay? Misha doesn't have any beans."

Ignatius sighed.

Misha snickered. "So testy. All will be revealed. You must simply give me time. And vodka. Drinks are in order. We have a new life to celebrate."

"She is quite lovely," said Hugh, who appeared quite enamored by Mira already. "What is her name?"

"Mira," Perry said, but it was all he could muster before words failed him. How was this possible? It was hard enough to gather the entire family for a birthday, and now here they were half a world away. All of them. The only one missing was Bertram, but for good reason—despite Sebastian's violent opposition, he'd taken the villainous omega into his custody and resolved to put an end to his crimes once and for all.

But with or without Bertram, the sentiment was the same.

They'd come for him.

All of them.

They'd dropped what they were doing, left their lives behind, obtained clearance to travel through other clans' territories, and sneaked into the palace to assemble here.

To surprise him.

To welcome Mira into their lives with open arms.

Perry's tears came on more quickly, streaming down his cheeks without end. "You came for us?" he asked at last. "To celebrate? To meet the baby?"

"And to spend time with you," Harrison added cheerfully. "We all missed you. You're the glue that holds us together. Not that we think you're sticky."

"I think what Harry is trying to say is that you've always been there for us," Ignatius explained, stepping forward to stand beside his best friend. "So it's about time we were there for you."

It was unbecoming, but a warbling sob escaped Perry all the same. He had not expected this.

"Why are you crying?" Harrison asked. He came to stand at Perry's side and wrapped a comforting arm around him. "We're here to celebrate with you. We missed you, Perry. But if you need some time alone, we can go somewhere else for a while. I know you must be tired. Traveling so far is exhausting under regular circumstances, but with eight eight-year-olds and a newborn? Whew. I'm surprised you're still standing."

Perry laughed and spun so he and Harrison were face to face. Careful not to endanger Mira, he rested his head on Harrison's shoulder and continued to cry. What he wished to say, but couldn't, was that they were happy tears. Once upon a time he'd been told that no dragon would want a Disgrace like him, and now here he was, surrounded by family who loved him, and who'd do whatever it took to make him happy.

Ignatius crossed the room and laid a hand on Perry's back before hugging him from behind, and one by one, the others in the room followed his lead, until Perry was at the center of a group hug.

How he'd missed this.

How he'd missed them all.

Perry wept until he had no more tears left to cry. Bit by bit, the group fragmented, until only Sebastian remained next to Perry. He wrapped Perry and Mira in his powerful arms and kissed the top of Perry's head, his nose bumping Perry's curls. "I love you," he uttered in a low voice only meant for Perry's ears. "I know the last few months have been hard on you, and that you've been through more than anyone should. There is no way a single act can make up for what has happened, but I hope that this helps heal your heart, my love. I care for you, and there is no length to which I wouldn't go to make you happy."

It had been five hundred years and Sebastian still loved him, now perhaps more than ever. Perry sniffled and nodded. Had he not been holding Mira, he would have latched on to Sebastian and never let go.

"You are everything to me," he whispered in reply. "I love you now, and I will love you forever, Sebastian Drake. You have made me so uncommonly happy."

Sebastian smiled into his hair. "And you have done the same for me."

"What was that about drinks?" asked Matthieu. "We should go find them and begin the celebrations in full."

There came a crash from downstairs, this one much louder than before, accompanied by the triumphant shouts of a large group of children. Ignatius's back went rigid. "Chaucer," he breathed, then rushed out of the room, Alistair hot on his heels.

Their exit prompted an exodus, and the rest of the family streamed out in search of naughty children, alcohol, or in one case, exotic lizards. Soon enough, only Perry and Sebastian remained.

"Will you come down with us?" Sebastian asked. "It seems there will be a party."

"I will. I just need to tend to Mira first." Perry kissed Sebastian's cheek. "Why don't you go and supervise, love? The boys have no doubt discovered their cousins are here, and you know that must spell trouble."

Sebastian nodded gravely, but before he left to wrangle the children, he kissed Perry sweetly and channeled his love through their bond until Perry was so full of it, he was lightheaded.

"You have given me everything, Perry," he said when the kiss broke. "And I vow, even should it take the rest of my life, to give you everything, too."

"You already have, darling." Perry smiled prettily at him. "You've given me the world, and I can never thank you enough for it. Now, off with you. I have a princess to put down for a nap and a story to finish telling. Do see to it that the children have not come to harm. Chaucer is quite charismatic, and I fear what that might mean for our brood's well-being. I do so like when their bones are in one piece."

Sebastian smirked and off he went.

He was a good man, an excellent dragon, and an even better father.

When Perry was alone, he brought Mira to the bassinet. Pake had come to sun himself beside it, and as Perry approached, he lifted his ancient head and blinked, then laid it down again. Perry smiled at him, then turned his attention onto his daughter.

The story wasn't done yet.

Not quite.

"Inside the nursery," Perry said as he laid Mira down, "the young dragon was surprised to find his beloved family. He hadn't expected to see them, but there they were. They'd come to see him, to show their love, and to welcome the little princess into the world. And even though the young dragon's heart was broken in so

293

many ways, with them in his life, it was full. Their love helped him remember that while he was sad, he was not alone, and he would not have to face the memories of this place on his own. It was not their job to heal him, and in fact, very few of them knew he was broken to begin with, but they would help him heal all the same."

Perry kissed Mira's forehead.

"Family," he told her, "is everything, little princess. And it is fine to mourn the family you've lost, but equally as important to celebrate the family by your side, whether they are bound to you by blood, or made family through the powers of love or friendship.

"And so the young dragon celebrated," Perry said, his smile wobbling beneath the weight of his emotions. "Because for all he'd lost, he'd found so much, and in time, he had a feeling he'd find more. And the thing about the young dragon, princess?" Perry's smile strengthened. "He was very often right."

STAY IN TOUCH

Can't get enough omegaverse?
Join Piper Scott's mailing list and get your FREE copy of the oh,
so sexy Yes, Professor
https://www.subscribepage.com/pipersnewletter

Or join Piper's Patreon to read what she's working on as she
writes it!
https://www.patreon.com/piperandemma

Need more men with filthy, snarky mouths?
Subscribe to Lynn Van Dorn's mailing list and stay up to date on
the most addicting new releases you'll ever read
https://lynnvandorncom.wordpress.com/newsletter/

Find Piper Scott on Facebook:
https://www.facebook.com/groups/PiperScott

Find Virginia Kelly, writing as Lynn Van Dorn, on Facebook:
https://www.facebook.com/groups/LynnVanDorn

ALSO BY PIPER SCOTT

Rutledge Brothers Series

His Command Series

Single Dad Support Group Series

Waking the Dragon Series
(with Susi Hawke)

Rent-a-Dom Series
(with Susi Hawke)

Redneck Unicorns Series
(with Susi Hawke)

Forbidden Desires (and Spin-Off) Series
(with Lynn Van Dorn writing as Virginia Kelly)

He's Out of This World Series
(with Renee Fox)

WRITING AS EMMA ALCOTT

Small Town Hearts Series

Masters of Romance Series

ALSO BY VIRGINIA KELLY

Valleywood
In the Pink

Forbidden Desires (with Piper Scott):
Clutch
Bond
Mate

Forbidden Desires Spin-Off (with Piper Scott):
Swallow
Magpie
Finch
Peregrine
Raven: Part One
Raven: Part Two

As Lynn Van Dorn:

North Shore Stories:
Be My Mistake

Damage Control
Daddy Issues
Out of Control

The Oleander Chronicles:
Reunion
Rebound

Stand Alone Stories:
Rule Forty-Seven
Now You See Me
Wild By Nature
Royally Screwed
Misconduct
Straight to the Heart

Made in the USA
Columbia, SC
24 August 2024

24bd88ae-9f9f-465e-a7d7-8400593572d2R01